"Lizzie, don't tempt me like this."

She gazed into his eyes and he seemed lost, searching. She feared he would reject her. But his hand tightened in her hair. He lifted her face ever closer, then bent his head. He inhaled a sharp breath as his lips bore down on her mouth.

Kissing him this way seemed natural. It seemed right. Instincts took over and her body surrendered to Chance. She would give him anything he asked.

His lips moved along her shoulders, moistening her bare skin. Pleasure shot clear through her. "Oh…Chance," she whispered, her throat barely working. "Don't stop. *Please.*"

He froze. He appeared to have come out of a daze. He stepped back quickly, as if she'd lit him on fire.

"Chance?"

There was the slightest shake of his head, a quick dismissal. Lips that had greedily taken hers tightened to thin lines.

"It was my first kiss," she said quietly.

"It was just a kiss, Lizzie. Consider it one more lesson I've taught you on the trail."

* * *

A Cowboy Worth Claiming
Harlequin® Historical #1083—April 2012

Dear Reader,

Welcome to Red Ridge!

It's been a blast creating the Worth brothers for my Harlequin Desire series. You may have already met Taggart Worth in the *USA TODAY* bestselling romance *Carrying the Rancher's Heir.* Taggart is a loner, a man hell-bent on never falling in love again, much less falling for the enemy's daughter.

Then there's Clayton Worth in *The Cowboy's Pride.* He's a one-time country music superstar who has returned to Red Ridge to honor a deathbed vow he'd made to his father. Trouble is, his soon-to-be ex-wife has something to say about that, and the adorable baby she brings to the ranch only complicates Clay's life even more. Poor guy. He should have stayed on the road!

Jackson Worth's story is still cooking and you'll meet him this October in *Worth the Risk,* the final contribution to the Worth family romance!

But if you've read my Westerns you know I love history and I love true cowboys, too, so I thought it fitting and proper to let you in on how Worth Ranch got its start. We'll travel back in time to the 1880s to Red Ridge, Arizona, where you'll meet bad boy Chance Worth, the man who started it all, and the feisty young woman who might just soften his hardened heart. Oh yeah, as an added bonus, you'll learn the legend of the ruby necklace and a few other surprises.

I hope you love "beginnings"!

Stories WORTH reading from yours truly,

Charlene Sands

CHARLENE SANDS

A COWBOY
WORTH CLAIMING

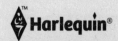

TORONTO NEW YORK LONDON
AMSTERDAM PARIS SYDNEY HAMBURG
STOCKHOLM ATHENS TOKYO MILAN MADRID
PRAGUE WARSAW BUDAPEST AUCKLAND

Recycling programs
for this product may
not exist in your area.

ISBN-13: 978-0-373-29683-5

A COWBOY WORTH CLAIMING

www.Harlequin.com

Printed in U.S.A.

Titles by this author are also available in ebook format.

Dedicated to my dear sweet friend Geraldine Sparks.
You are truly a "Friend Worth Claiming"
and a joy in my life.
With love,
Charlene

CHARLENE SANDS

Award-winning author Charlene Sands writes bold, passionate, heart-stopping heroes and always…really good men! She's a lover of all things romantic, having married her high school sweetheart, Don. She is the proud recipient of a Readers' Choice Award and double recipient of a Booksellers' Best Award, having written more than twenty-five romances to date, both contemporary and historical Western. Charlene is a member of Romance Writers of America and belongs to the Orange County and Los Angeles chapters of RWA, where she volunteers as the Published Authors' Liaison.

When not writing, she loves movie dates with her hubby, playing cards with her children, reading romance, great coffee, Pacific beaches, country music and anything chocolate. She also loves to hear from her readers. You can reach Charlene at www.charlenesands.com or P.O. Box 4883, West Hills, CA 91308. You can find her on the Harlequin Desire Authors Blog, and on Facebook, too!

Chapter One

Red Ridge
Arizona
1884

Chance Worth bent down on both knees and leaned over, splashing lake water onto his face. Refreshing drops sprayed his bare shoulders and chest as two-day-old dust melted away. The cleansing felt damn good.

He'd been careful treading through the foothills looking out onto the Red Ridge Mountains. He'd left Channing, Arizona, in a hurry, making sure he wasn't being followed. Only thing that ever could trail him was trouble and *it* seemed to follow him everywhere he went.

Narrowing his eyes, he searched the perimeter of the lake, taking in every detail, every bush, shrub and tree in the distance. Nothing stirred but his horse, Joyful. The mare was feeding on tall grass by a copse of trees.

Glistening waters tempted him like a whore's beckoning smile. "What the hell." He unfastened his gun belt and folded it into his shirt. His boots were next. Then he tucked it all in a hollowed-out patch under a boulder. Without further thought, he dove into the lake and pure heaven, cool and inviting, burst against his skin, soaking him through and through and washing away the remainder of his grime. Holding his breath, he swam underneath the smooth surface until his lungs burned.

He shot up out of the water gulping air and grinning like a kid who'd found a five-dollar gold piece. He remembered river runs with his friends at the orphanage. Taking turns jumping off mesquite branches into the rushing river and living to speak about it afterwards.

Lifting his face to the sun, he shook his hair out, splattering water in his wake. The heat seared his skin and for a moment, he enjoyed the warming from where he stood in the lake.

A noise broke his respite and instincts took hold. He reached for his gun then groaned. A quick glance at his clothes sitting on the bank, thirty feet away and housing his Peacemaker brought a curse to his lips. He lowered down, water up to his neck, and listened closely.

A female's scream pierced his ears and he focused his gaze in that direction, but the bend in the lake obstructed his view. He dove in and swam toward the source of the sound.

When he came up from the water he spotted a girl flailing her arms in a sinking rowboat. The straw hat she used to scoop out water wasn't emptying nearly fast enough. It was clear as day her efforts were useless as the boat made a slow descent under the water. But she continued to scream and scoop, scream and scoop until the boat's top lip met with the water's edge. "Just jump in and get it over with," he muttered.

The girl went under. He waited for her head to bob up. When she didn't surface immediately, he squeezed his eyes shut and swore. He had a bad feeling about this. His next glance found no ripples in the water. The lake had swallowed her up.

Hell, he wasn't anybody's hero. But drowning wasn't a pretty way to die.

He dove back under and swam with sure strokes, gliding across the lake quickly and reaching the area where the boat went down. He found the girl sinking down fast, her arms and legs tangling with her petticoats. She'd been under for less than a minute, he figured, but surely enough time to scare the life and breath out of someone who couldn't swim.

He grabbed on to her and hauled her up against him, his arm draped around her chest. Her boots met with his shins in a frantic attempt to save herself. "Ouch, dammit!" He held on and swam backward, pulling her head above the water's surface. Her arms and legs still flailed. "Hold on," he ordered. "Don't fight me."

"Let me go!" she shrieked in a panicked voice.

He held her firm. "Stay calm and breathe slow."

"No, let me go! Let me go!"

He'd never seen someone so intent on drowning. He spoke through gritted teeth. "Quiet down."

His muscles burning, he dragged her to shore. She wasn't but a little wisp of a girl yet her weight doubled from her dreary, soaked-to-the-bone clothes.

Once he got her to safety, he slid out from under her body and rolled away. His breaths came heavy and he took a few seconds to steady them, before he came up to kneel beside her.

Her eyes were closed and she'd gone real quiet. "Miss, are you alright?"

It was eerie how her eyes snapped open. They were sky-blue and a little hazy now, but it didn't take him long to figure out they were the prettiest thing about her.

"My...dolls." Her plea scratched through her throat.

"Did you say, dolls? Miss, if they were in that boat, they're gone. Probably at the bottom of the lake by now."

She turned away, a look of pain on her face. She fought tears, and he thought it the darnedest thing, seeing as she might have lost her life just a minute ago. Seemed all she cared about was her dolls.

"You're gonna be just fine," he told her.

She shook her head, her lips trembling.

"What's your name?"

She didn't answer.

He repeated, "What's your name?"

"Elizabeth."

"Okay, Elizabeth. You just hold on and wait here. I'll be right back."

The girl didn't respond.

He took off at a run along the lake bank, swearing an oath every time his bare feet hit a rock or a spiky twig.

I ain't anybody's hero, he kept repeating in his head. Didn't do a damn bit of good, thinking it, though. His daddy would say, "Thinking it ain't doing it, son." It was one of only a few memories he had left of his father.

He found his clothes and dressed quickly. Swinging his legs into the saddle, he rode Joyful hard along the lakeshore, retracing his steps until he reached the girl again. To his relief, she'd sat herself up though she appeared white as a sheet. Her clothes were stuck to her skin, looking like they'd need a good peeling to get them off her.

Not that he would suggest that. She'd have to be satisfied with the wool blanket he'd untied from his bedroll to keep her warm. Lucky the sun still shone bright in the sky.

He squatted beside her and wrapped the blanket around her shoulders. She didn't look at him. Her gaze, directed at the lake, was filled with yearning.

"This should warm you up."

She let the blanket hang from her body.

"You're trembling. Gonna catch a chill. Lake water's pretty cold."

Finally, she looked at him, her voice quiet and quivering, "They're ruined now. All of them. You shouldn't have stopped me."

His brows furrowed. "You got yourself a death wish?"

Her eyes dimmed with disappointment.

He sat down next to her. Bracing an arm on his bent knee, he gave her a moment of peace and absorbed the quiet of the lake, the heat of the sun.

After a few moments, he turned to her. "I'm no expert or anything, but that boat didn't look all too sturdy. Went down pretty fast. And clearly, you can't swim."

She snapped her eyes at him. "I can swim… I just got tangled up in my skirts."

"Yeah? That's not how I saw it." He plucked a thin blade of grass from a small patch growing nearby. The girl was acting as if he'd done her a disservice by saving her life.

"I wish you hadn't come along. I needed those dolls. I would have found them."

What in tarnation? The ungrateful girl didn't appreciate what he'd done for her. She'd interrupted his peaceful time at the lake with her screams and she didn't have the good grace to utter a thank-you when he came to her rescue.

"You would've drowned looking for them, your swimming abilities being such as they are."

She sent a look of dire misery toward the water. Then she spun her head his way. Fire snapped in her eyes. "I was coming up for air, then going back down again. I didn't need your help. Now, my dolls are gone! And we're going to lose the ranch…" Elizabeth's voice trailed off in despair.

Things with her must be mighty grim, he thought. She'd risked her life for those damn dolls. He didn't quite understand how her dolls would save a ranch. His knowledge of ranching was obviously lacking. Then it hit him. Elizabeth…could she be Lizzie? The same Lizzie that Edward Mitchell had written to him about?

He dug into his shirt pocket and unfolded the square parchment, reading the letter his older friend had written.

I'm asking a favor of you, boy. I wouldn't ask if I had any other choice. Need some help pretty quick. It's not for me, but for my granddaughter, Lizzie. Come to Red Ridge if you can and I'll explain.
Edward Mitchell

He stared at her. "You're Lizzie Mitchell?"

She whipped her head toward him. "How'd you know that?"

He pursed his lips, amused at the coincidence. "I'm Chance Worth. Your grandfather sent for me."

She jumped up with more vigor than he thought she could muster, being that she'd just nearly drowned, regardless of her claims otherwise. Her dark curly hair was plastered to her head, her face dull as his old scratchy blanket, her body covered throat to ankles with stuck-on wet clothes. Only things that glistened, bright as the lake that almost took her life, were her startled blue eyes. "You're Chance Worth?"

"Yeah, Lizzie, you heard me right."

She folded her arms across her middle, jutted out her chin and hoisted her head like Queen Elizabeth of England. "Well, I won't do it. Grandpa's got no right sending for you! I refuse to marry you. And that's final!"

"I told you I could walk home." Lizzie kept her chin high and her body stiff. She sat upon this sorrel named Joyful, sharing the saddle with the stranger. His arm was wrapped around her middle and she tried not to think about how if she leaned back ever so, she'd be flush against his big body.

"I should make you," he said. "Serve you right for taking that good-for-nothing boat across the lake."

For all her bold talk, Lizzie probably would drop of exhaustion if the cowboy did make her walk back home. The spill in the lake robbed her energy and losing her dolls had destroyed her spirit. She was bone tired, but wouldn't give the cowboy the satisfaction of that bit of knowledge. "You could leave me here right now and turn around. Tend to your business."

"I'm tending to my business. Told you that once already, Lizzie."

"It's Elizabeth." Her spine stiffened at the childlike name that everyone including her grandfather insisted upon calling her. Grandpa was forgetful lately, so she couldn't fault him, but that didn't explain why everyone else in Red Ridge saw fit to address her in that manner.

Chance Worth may have pulled her out of the water today but that didn't give him the right to insult her. After she'd jumped up, declaring she'd not marry him, he'd given her a long narrow-eyed look, then burst out laughing. He might've busted a gut with all the cheer he'd spread over the quiet lake at the very notion.

It *was* the reason Grandpa sent him that letter. Had to be. Her gramps had told her the tale of the orphan boy whose life he saved and how the boy had clung on, fighting for his life, refusing to give up the one thing he had left of value. The robbers would have beaten him to death if her grandfather hadn't been riding the back roads in Channing and heard the confrontation. Chance Worth owed her grandpa his life.

Good Lord, she thought, squeezing her eyes closed. Had that been the trade-off, he'd repay his debt by marrying her?

For the past year, her grandfather had been matchmaking, inviting every eligible young man in the territory to the ranch. Not that she'd gotten a single proposal. And that's how it would stay. Still, she smarted from the stranger's outright amusement when she'd refused to marry him.

Your grandfather's got more sense than that. The

man's declaration after his laughter had died down made her stomach knot.

Lizzie wasn't a beauty. She wasn't graceful or poised like the other females in town. She wasn't buxom or curvy. She looked younger than her eighteen years. She knew that she'd rightly die a spinster one day, but that didn't give the stranger call to rub her nose in it. Embarrass and offend her.

Hurt her.

She had a mind to retaliate with harsh words, but she'd gotten an eyeful of the cowboy, stripped naked from the waist up, after he'd pulled her out of the lake. She couldn't say that his jaw was chiseled a little too deep. Or his shoulders were spread a little too broad. Or the muscles that bulged on his arms were too darn big. If Lizzie was one thing, she was honest. Her rescuer with deep brown eyes and golden skin was about as perfect as one man had a right to be.

And thinking him perfect after the insult he'd bestowed upon her just made her angry.

"How is Edward?" he asked, his voice soft against her ear.

A tingle trailed down her neck. She willed it to stop and concentrated on the question. Her body's response to this man annoyed her. "He's struggling some, but we'll make do. We always do."

"Struggling?" he asked.

"Some."

"You care to elaborate."

"Isn't your business, is it, Mr. Worth?"

"Hmm, if I had to guess, I'd say having a stubborn, sass-mouthed granddaughter would make just about any man struggle."

She spun around so fast, her damp hair whipped at her cheekbones. "That's not fair! You don't know what we've been through. Cattle rustlers, drought that starved our herd two years ago, disease that came later. We've worked hard to keep the ranch from drying up, to keep food on the table and clothes on our backs. My grandpa would throw you off his property, hearing you speak that way to me."

His lips twitched. "That so?"

She glared into mud-brown eyes lit with amusement. He wasn't really perfect after all, she decided.

"Turn around, before you fall off." His voice firm, he scolded her like a child. He wasn't that much older than her. Couldn't be more than ten years that separated them.

"I'm not going to fall off. I've been riding since before I could walk. I could outride any of the boys in town. And I—"

He clucked his tongue and the sorrel took off in a fast trot. Lizzie bounced up and her world tilted to the left. She began falling at an angle, her body hinged sideways. She was on a collision course with a prickly blade of saguaro cactus before a big hand pulled her upright to safety. Chance set both hands firm on her shoulders and turned her to face forward on the saddle.

"You did that on purpose." She bristled.

He slowed Joyful to an easy gait. "You got a vivid imagination, Lizzie."

"Elizabeth."

"I think I liked you better in the lake."

"When you thought I was drowning?"

"When you were quiet."

"You're the one asking questions."

"And you've given such ladylike answers."

She whipped around again, showing him the point of her chin.

"For pity's sake, turn around and stay put." His voice held no patience. "You're tiring yourself out."

Leather creaked as she took her time twisting back in the saddle.

And just like that, he pulled her closer, his hand splaying over her stomach, his fingers teasing the underside of her breasts. She'd never had a man hold her so tight, in such a way. She held her breath. A warm thrill coursed down past her waist. Her breasts, small as they were, tingled. "W-what are you doing?"

He didn't answer. His iron grip said it all.

Lizzie sighed. She'd made a mess of things for certain. She'd been a fool, though she wouldn't admit it to the man whose knees cradled her. She'd been so eager to deliver her dolls and collect the money owed her, that she'd taken the shortcut, across the lake, rather than walking the extra two miles to town. She should've been more careful with her dolls, more cautious about that rickety ole boat. Now, she had nothing to show for one month's solid work. They had little cash left and were overextended on loans from the feed store and the mercantile. Her grandfather hadn't said as much, Edward Mitchell being a proud man and all, but he'd been relying on that cash to buy supplies in town.

Elizabeth's folly let him down.

Tears she'd held back, threatened again. She wouldn't let the stranger see her cry. She squared her shoulders and took a deep breath.

"You're tensing up again. Just lean against me and be still, Lizzie."

It was fruitless fighting him. And he was right. She was fatigued. More than she'd thought. And now he offered her his chest to lean back against. No harm in that, she thought, as the relentless sun spilled down. The heat burning through her wet clothes warmed her chilled body and soothed her sour mood.

A majestic view of crimson hills jutting up against a blue sky gave Chance pause as he neared the Mitchell spread. Rocky peak formations appearing close enough to touch created instant patterns in his mind. The one directly in front of him seemed to spread out like a soaring eagle in flight, the formation to his left was shaped like a tall bowler hat, the kind a gentleman from the East would wear, and the crest of another mountaintop off in the distance looked like a tipped coffeepot. The sun played with the deep earth hues of those mountain peaks, illuminating Mother Nature's most fascinating ornaments in blazing light.

In a clearing not far away sat the sorely neglected Mitchell Ranch, its rundown appearance a direct contrast to the majesty of the Red Ridge Mountains. Chance pressed Joyful on, taking in broken fences along the border, barn walls in disrepair and the house itself, which was no more than a small wood cabin.

The girl had fallen asleep against him. Her head was tucked under his chin, her lithe body cradled in his arms with her skirts draped down the mare's sides. She was a little thing, to be sure, but feisty as hell.

Chance grinned thinking about her mighty tirade. Marry her? Edward Mitchell could find a dozen better suitors for his granddaughter than him. Chance wasn't anybody's ideal and he certainly wasn't the settling-down kind. Edward knew Chance had no dreams of a wife and family. Life had knocked Chance down too many times for thinking like that. No, that wasn't why Edward Mitchell had summoned him.

He spoke in Lizzie's ear. "Wake up, Princess. You're home." Lizzie jerked back when she heard his voice. The back of her head met with his chin. "Ow!"

Nobody'd call her graceful.

She straightened and gazed at her home with trepidation.

He dismounted first and reached up for her. In less than an hour, he'd had more contact with this gal than any other female in a month of Sundays. He'd had lifelong practice keeping away from Marissa Dunston, the young daughter of Alistair's new wife. Marissa had been a troublemaker from the time she'd come to live at the Circle D Ranch. Chance wasn't about to get stupid now. Not with Edward Mitchell's granddaughter, that's for damn sure.

She peered down at him with tentative blue eyes, her brown hair still a messy bird's nest of curls. She didn't want to face her grandpa. That much he could read from her expression. He softened his voice. "C'mon, Lizzie."

She leaned down and he lifted her from the saddle, her hands steady on his shoulders as her boots hit the ground. She stood facing him, all her life's misery written on her face. Chance knew that look too well. But he hadn't survived all this time by being mollycoddled. If things were as bad as he thought on the Mitchell spread, she'd have to toughen up to endure hardship.

He stepped back and gestured to the house with a nod of his head. "Go tell your grandpa I'm here."

She chewed on her lower lip and closed her eyes.

When she opened them again, her expression had transformed and a downright determined look settled on her features. Chance watched her pick up her soggy skirts and march right into the house. Then he led Joyful to the barn to unsaddle her.

He hadn't seen Edward Mitchell since the day he'd stepped in and saved his life. Chance had been twelve, fighting for what was his against three ruffians. They'd cornered him behind a cropping of trees outside of town. If Edward hadn't taken that little-known side road to town, Chance would have been beaten to death for certain. Edward had intervened just in time, entering the fray and tossing off his attackers one at a time, taking several hard blows himself to save the bedraggled orphan boy.

Chance remembered little else after that. When he woke up, he found himself in the care of the town doctor with Edward Mitchell by his side making sure Chance had proper medical treatment. Edward stayed until Chance had recovered enough to be adopted by the town's wealthiest citizen, Alistair Dunston. The only thing Edward asked of Chance was to write to him in Red Ridge once a year.

Chance never broke that promise. Fifteen letters over fifteen years. And Chance kept every one of Edward's return posts. He'd read those long insightful letters over and over and taken Edward Mitchell's words to heart. In a way, Edward was more a father to him than Alistair Dunston had ever been.

"Well, look at you, boy." Edward Mitchell stood under the patched overhang in front of his door as Chance approached. Age had not done him any favors, Chance noted. His shoulders were rounded from a slight natural curve of his back. He looked like he hadn't seen a hearty meal in a decade; his arms and legs were stick thin. Yet, he wore a true smile, his brilliant blue eyes remarkable in a weary face that obviously had known suffering. "You've grown up."

"Tends to happen over the years." Chance grinned and strode the distance to shake Edward's hand. He was instantly struck by the frailty in the older man's grip. This was hardly the same man who'd gone up against three younger men to save Chance's life years ago. "How are you, Edward?"

"Thankful that you honored an old man's request, that's how I am." He patted Chance's back several times as he ushered him inside. "Come in. Come in. Lizzie went to change outta her wet clothes. Poor gal, she's beside herself with worry about her dolls."

Edward gestured for him to sit down on a settee upholstered with flowery material. Chance removed his hat and took a seat. Edward slumped in a blue-velvet tufted parlor chair. Chance took a moment to glance around the rest of the room. The furniture seemed far too grand and out of place for a small ranch house. There were two doors beyond the kitchen area that he assumed were bedrooms, and all in all the interior of the home held more warmth and refinement than he thought possible, considering the neglect to the exterior.

"She told me what happened, boy," Edward said with a strain in his voice. "Thank you for bringing my Lizzie home. I've told her time and again not to use that boat. Good thing Lizzie's a swimmer or she might have drowned."

Not that good of a swimmer, Chance thought. She'd been a victim of her own foolishness using that unreliable rowboat to cross the lake. And then thinking she could retrieve her precious dolls from the lake's bottom. Dang things were probably ruined anyways.

Edward coughed from deep in his chest. Chance noticed the toll it took on his body. "She's been brave, that girl. Trying to keep the ranch going." He looked into Chance's eyes and lowered his voice. "I can't thank you enough for coming, boy. I wouldn't have asked if it weren't essential."

"Tell me." Chance glanced at the bedroom door. Lizzie was still busy in there and he knew Edward wanted to speak his mind while she wasn't in the room.

Edward leaned forward. "I should be offering you a bite to eat. Something to drink. Don't mind my bad manners. I haven't been right lately."

"I don't need anything."

"You're eyes are hard, boy. You've known more misery in your life, haven't you?"

Chance had always had a roof over his head. He'd always had food to eat. He'd made a little money over the years. Yet, no matter how hard he'd tried to fit in and become an upstanding citizen, there were always people who'd judged him unkindly. Who'd tested him and who'd set him up to fail. They'd never let him forget that he came from the orphanage. He was the boy nobody wanted. When Alistair Dunston came along Chance thought his life would be grand. After all, the man had a big ranch, land that spread out for hundreds of acres. He had a wife that couldn't bear children. Chance was to be their son. Only, Clara Dunston died unexpectedly, and Alistair began treating him more like a hired hand than his kin. Soon everybody else got that notion, too.

"I'm not complaining, Edward."

The man smiled sadly. As if to say, there's much more in life. Chance wouldn't know about that. Edward rose from his seat and walked to a china cabinet displaying fancy blue and white dishes on the shelves. He opened a drawer from below and pulled out a small square box. He carried the box carefully as he shuffled over to him. "This is yours, Chance. It's about time I give it back to you."

Chance gazed down at the walnut box carved with the letter *W.*

"I had the box made when I arrived home from Channing." He shrugged a shoulder. "Times were better then."

Chance knew what was inside. Taking a deep breath, he opened the lid and there, resting on the white silk lining, was a thin gold chain with a pear-shaped ruby pendant. The sparkling deep crimson gem was the size of a plum pit. He stared at his mother's necklace—it was the only thing of value Chance Worth had ever owned. He was almost afraid to lift the chain, to touch the ruby. He remembered the day that he'd protected this necklace from three robbers who were intent on taking the one thing Chance valued above his own life. And after that beating, he realized he couldn't hold on to the necklace. One way or another, he'd never reach adulthood with it in his possession.

Take it, Mr. Mitchell. Take it and keep it for me.

Chance had pleaded with Edward to keep the only remembrance he had of his mother. Losing his parents to marauders and then struggling to survive in an orphanage, he'd learned early on there weren't too many people he could count on and trust. But Edward

Mitchell with his kind eyes and generous spirit had been one of them. In a sense, Chance's life had been whittled away to the sum total of that necklace and he entrusted Edward with its safekeeping.

I'll know it'll always be safe. With you.

Edward had agreed to keep the necklace until Chance could retrieve it. "Why are you giving this to me now, Edward?"

The older man glanced at the closed bedroom door and lowered his voice. Any minute now Lizzie would step out, and Chance noted his urgency to speak before she did.

"I'm dying, Chance. I had to be sure to give this back to you."

Chance inhaled sharply. He couldn't say he wasn't expecting this. The minute he laid eyes on him, he'd seen the weariness in the old man's body.

"I'm growing weaker every day. Lizzie knows, too, but we don't talk about it. It's easier for her to deny it."

"That's why you sent for me."

"It's one of the reasons. I'm trying to keep the ranch from failing. I need your help. If you're willing."

The necklace would have brought Edward Mitchell enough money to keep the ranch going for a time, yet he'd held on to it, saving it for Chance. Just like he promised. Chance's throat got heavy with emotion. He hated the thought of the older man dying. There weren't too many men on this earth of such honor and honesty. He took a moment to assemble his thoughts and conceal feelings he rarely showed anyone.

On a shaky breath he said, "I can't thank you enough for what you've done for me." He held up the jewelry box. "For keeping this safe. It's the only thing I have left of my life before my parents were murdered." Chance spoke with firm resolve. "You can count on me, Edward. I'll do whatever you need."

Chance thought about Lizzie's crazy notion that he was brought here to marry her. Now, it seemed possible that's what Edward had in mind.

"Thank you." Relief crossed Edward's features as he nodded. Chance could, at the very least, give him that much peace of mind. But then the old man's face turned beet-red and he began coughing. Chance rose to help him, but he quickly gestured for him to sit back down. When his coughing fit ended, he leaned back against his chair.

Once he'd caught his breath, he explained, "We're in a bad way financially. Got barely enough to make it through the month. It'll break Lizzie's heart, but this here furniture, her mama's furniture, is next to go. Won't get all that much for it, that's why I haven't brought it up to Lizzie yet. That girl is dang upset about her dolls. She had orders and was rushing off to collect the money in town. Took her more than a month to sew those dolls and the girl feels she's let me down." He stopped. Squeezed his eyes shut and pinched his nose. He was near tears. "Only, I'm the one letting her down. My granddaughter has calloused hands from working the ranch. She cooks our meals and at night, she fashions her dolls until she about collapses into bed."

"I have some cash saved up," Chance said, wanting to spare the old man any more pain. He'd give him everything he had.

Edward shook his head. "I'm a prideful man. It was hard enough asking you this favor, I won't take your money."

"Then what can I do for you?"

"My last ranch hand quit a month ago. Can't say as I blame him. Toby stuck around without pay for three weeks. Just as a favor to Lizzie and me. Fact is, I need to get my Longhorns to the railhead. We got thirty head that'll bring a good price. But I got no one to go with Lizzie on the drive."

"Lizzie? She drives cattle?"

Edward's eyes lit with pride. "She's been going on drives with me since she was a youngster. The railhead is in Prescott. Should only take five days to get there."

His cough took hold again and plagued him for the next half a minute. Chance rose up as he'd done before, wanting to help, to give the man some aid, but once again Edward gestured for him to sit down. Each cough took more life from him, as if an evil force counted down the breaths until he took his very last one.

"Grandpa?" Lizzie called from the other side of the door.

Edward sat up and caught his breath quickly, hiding his true condition from his granddaughter. "I'm fine, Lizzie. Don't fret."

Chance questioned him. "She know what you got planned?"

He shook his head. "Nope. But we haven't got much choice. She won't put up much fuss once I explain."

Chance had doubts about that. He'd seen some of Lizzie's fussing. "Why not sell the steers to a neighbor? Have them drive the cattle."

"I thought of that. They'd take too big a cut of the profits. Wouldn't leave us enough to live."

Chance didn't like the idea of driving cattle with a female, but Edward wouldn't have asked if he didn't think it necessary. And it wasn't much of a drive. Hell, they'd be back in a week. "Then it's settled. I'll go."

Edward leaned back in his seat and rested his head on the chair's carved wooden backing, closing his eyes. His voice became a mere whisper. "Thank you, but there's more. And this…this is going to be a mite more difficult."

Chance braced himself. "You want me to shoot someone dead?"

The old man smiled. "Of course not."

"Then how bad could it be?"

He opened his eyes and Chance was hit with the impact of the old man's determined gaze. "I want you to find Lizzie a husband."

Chapter Two

After she'd dried off and changed into a brown dress, Lizzie pushed through her bedroom door, keeping her misery close to heart. It wouldn't do to have Grandpa knowing how desperate she was. She found him and Chance Worth sitting in the front room, head down, whispering, in obvious cahoots about something. The second they spotted her they clamped their mouths shut. What in heaven's name were they up to? And why did her Grandpa see fit to summon him here in the first place?

"Lizzie, dear girl, come sit with us for a spell."

"I will for just a little while." She smiled at her grandpa and plopped down on the sofa as far away from the stranger as possible. She wasn't afraid of him, no sir, but she'd been close enough to feel his warm breath on her throat, to feel his arms tug her close while riding his mare. Why, she'd practically seen him naked at the lake and didn't like for one minute the warm sensations he'd stirred in her.

"That's my girl." Her grandpa leaned back in his seat and drew a deep breath. His cough was getting worse every day and it scared her to see him look so pale. She cooked hearty meals to keep meat on his bones, but even still, his shirts hung loose from his shoulders. Didn't matter how much bread she added to the stew, or how much jam she spread across his biscuits, she couldn't seem to build his strength and fatten him up. "You look nice and dry, Lizzie. Feeling better now?"

She couldn't feel better. She'd lost their only means of income and just thinking about those dolls soaked at the bottom of the lake made her stomach clench. She looked down at her brown skirt and nodded. "Yes, a little bit."

"It's a lucky thing Chance coming along when he did, bringing you home. Course it's been a while but I recall how cold that lake is. Would have been a mighty uncomfortable walk with you dripping wet. Did you thank him, Lizzie?"

She darted Chance a glance and found him watching her, his gaze flowing over the hair she didn't bother to untangle, curling every which way now and tied back with a thin strip of ribbon. When their eyes met she found his filled with amusement. "I, uh—"

"She thanked me, Edward."

She shot him a quick look and he arched his right brow. He'd done a good thing, covering for her, but somehow she still felt pinpricked. If he hadn't come along, she might've had a chance at rescuing her dolls. Now, all was lost and she didn't know what else to do but to try to replace them with new ones made from the scraps of material she had left in her sewing basket.

Her grandpa coughed again, and the pain she noted

on his face made her turn away. Every day she witnessed how much strength his coughing sapped from his body. The doctor from Red Ridge had come out to check on him and gave him an elixir, which she prayed would help, but nothing seemed to do a lick of good.

"Edward, I'll get you some water," Chance said, rising from his seat.

"I'll get it." She bounded up quickly and rushed to the kitchen area.

"Get…some…for our guest." Her grandfather struggled to get the words out between coughs.

She poured two glasses of water from a pitcher but by the time she returned, thankfully, his coughing spell was over. She handed the water to her grandfather. "Please, Grandpa, you need to drink more. The doctor says it'll help."

"All right, Lizzie." She stood over him until he took a long sip. Then she turned to Chance and offered up the other glass.

"Don't mind if I do." His hand came out to accept the drink and when their fingers brushed, she was startled by the jolt and nearly jumped out of her skin.

Something powerful happened whenever he touched her. The stirrings were unexpected and…and downright confusing. Thankfully, Chance didn't seem to notice her distress. She figured it'd be a good idea to keep her distance. Hopefully, he wouldn't be on the ranch too long. "I'd best start supper."

"It's early yet," her grandfather said. "Sit down, girl. Take a rest."

Lizzie did as she was told. Everyone seemed content to just sit there, comfortably, without uttering a word. She didn't begrudge her grandfather the rest or her company, but when he leaned his head back and closed his eyes, Lizzie couldn't help but steal another look at Chance. His throat worked as he finished off the water in his glass. Why did she find watching him swallow so darn fascinating?

"Chance is here to help." Her grandfather spoke quietly, keeping his head back against the chair. "In case you were wondering, Lizzie. And I owed him something."

She noticed the square walnut box sitting next to Chance on the sofa. She'd grown up seeing that box—it was as if it belonged here on the ranch. For as long as she could remember, that box had sat in the bottom drawer of her mama's china cabinet.

When she was a young fanciful girl, she'd sneak into that drawer when no one was looking and ever so carefully open the box to stare at the blood-red ruby. Her imagination would run wild, thinking it a rare stolen treasure, a gem that was more beautiful than any she could ever fathom. Had it belonged to a princess from a faraway land, a pirate queen or a stately woman of wealth?

Lizzie never touched the ruby for fear her dirt-smudged fingers would mar the perfection of the stunning pear-shaped stone. Eventually, she came to learn the story about the ruby and how it had fallen into her grandfather's possession.

The ruby she'd once secretly coveted belonged to Chance Worth. And her grandfather had summoned him here to return it. "I know now that you sent for him," she said, "to return the ruby."

Grandpa leaned forward and spoke with resolution. "And to *help* us, Lizzie," he reminded her.

Lord knew, they needed help, but so far all the stranger had managed to do was to prevent her from rescuing her dolls and make things worse. She didn't have a good feeling about this. She lowered her voice to a whisper. "How can he help?"

Her grandfather's face brightened and it was a joy to see, so rarely did he smile anymore. "Now, Lizzie. I want you to think before reacting, okay?"

She nodded, wary. Usually when Grandpa said that, she didn't like what came next.

"Chance has agreed to drive our herd to the railhead in Prescott with you."

Alarmed, she shook her head. "But, Grandpa, you and I will drive the herd, once you're feeling better."

A flicker of sadness stole over his face and her heart dropped. There was something so resolute in that look, so final. "I'm not getting better, Lizzie. I'm weak and getting weaker every day." The bleak reality struck her as he reached for her with cold, fragile hands. "I wish it weren't so for your sake, dear girl. I wish I could go with you on the drive, the way we used to."

"Grandpa, we could do it again. We could. The winter was harsh this year and I know that's what made you sick, but it's spring now. You'll gain your strength back."

Her grandfather peered at Chance and the two locked glances. "Chance knows cattle drives. He'll make the trip without any difficulty and the two of you will be back shortly."

Her body tensed. The emotions she'd kept at bay all these months were too much for her. Tears welled in her eyes. She rose and shook her head, lowering her voice, unable to hide the pain. "I don't want to go without you."

Her grandfather squeezed his eyes shut briefly then met her gaze. "We have no choice, Lizzie."

She shot a glare at Chance and then marched out of the room so the stranger wouldn't see the tears spill from her eyes.

Lizzie boiled up strips of beef in a big pot, added beans and potatoes to the mix for son-of-a-gun stew. It was a recipe she'd learned from the cookie, years ago, when she'd gone on cattle drives with her father and the crew. She'd been without a care in the world then—the ranch was thriving and those drives were an adventure for a young girl. But now, she had enough worries to fill the cookie's chuck wagon and then some.

She'd had a good cry out by the barn minutes ago, trying to justify leaving grandpa all alone. She didn't want to go on that drive. Not without him. And she surely didn't want to drive cattle with Chance Worth. Why, he'd most likely mock her every step of the way and she'd hate every minute of it.

She stirred the stew and sniffled.

"Need some help?"

She whirled around to find Chance leaning against the wall, arms crossed, watching her. "How long have you been there?"

He moved into the room, ignoring her question. "Your grandpa's taking a nap."

He did that, napped several times during the day. She'd find him looking fatigued and the next thing she knew, he'd be on the sofa, head at an awkward angle against the back cushion, sleeping. "He needs rest."

"Can't argue with that."

"Well, mercy. I think you and I agree on something."

She rubbed her nose and sniffled again. She didn't want Chance in the kitchen, hovering. He was too big. And he made her nerves stand on end. "Why don't you get settled at the bunkhouse? There's a few beds in there that aren't—"

"I want to talk to you about the drive."

She blinked. Then turned her attention to stirring the stew. "What about it?"

"We'll go day after tomorrow."

She nodded, lowering her voice. "I suppose if we have to," she said, though she couldn't bear the thought of Grandpa being alone for more than a week.

"And you're gonna listen to me every step of the way. No tantrums, no arguments. We do things my way, Lizzie." His eyes were hard, his voice gruff. "We need to make good time and I don't want a female slowing us down."

She dropped the wooden spoon in the stew and braced her hands on her hips. "My name's not Lizzie, not to you. It's Elizabeth. I don't have tantrums and I won't slow anybody down. I know more about drives than any other woman in the territory."

He cocked half a smile, satisfied. "Good. Then you and me shouldn't have a problem, so long as you realize I'm the trail boss."

"It's *our* herd and *our* lives at stake. Not yours. If I disagree with you, I'm gonna tell you."

"You took a broken-down boat out in the lake and nearly got yourself killed. Hardly testimony to your clear thinking and good judgment. And don't deny it. God knows you're denying enough about your life."

She stiffened at his curious remark. "What's that supposed to mean?"

He walked toward her, the rowels of his spurs jangling as his boots scraped against the wood floor. He stopped inches from her, his gaze dark and direct. "You want to help your grandfather? Then you go on this drive without any fuss. Don't make him feel bad. Give him some peace of mind."

Peace of mind? What was he talking about? She'd done everything she could to help her grandfather. She'd worked all day and into the night to keep the ranch going, earning extra cash whenever she could. Could she help it that she'd rather go on the trail drive with her kin, than with a stranger whose uncouth ways were bound to rile her?

But what if he wasn't speaking about that? What if he had something else in mind? Her mind reeling, she spoke softly now, suddenly unsure. "What do you mean 'peace of mind'?"

Chance reached for her face, taking her chin in his large hand and forcing her eyes up to his. A moment ticked by as he studied her, unblinking, his nearness, the intensity of his gaze stirring her senses. They stood that way, facing each other, his grip tight yet gentle and when she thought he'd say what was on his mind, he seemed to think better of it. He released her and backed up. "I think you know, Lizzie."

She put her head down, refusing to look in his eyes and whispered, "I don't. I swear I don't know what you mean at all."

He sighed and walked away from her. After a time, his footsteps faded and the door squeaked closed behind him. Marching to the window, she pulled aside the curtains and watched him stride into the barn, readying to settle on the ranch and barge into her life.

She wished Grandpa had never sent for him.

It was one of a long list of wishes that Lizzie hadn't seen come true this year.

Chance strode into the barn to check on Joyful and retrieve his saddlebags. The sorry sorrel he'd noticed earlier snorted quietly as he walked by. The slight effort seemed laborious for the animal that looked weary and old enough to have seen war days. Wasn't a wonder why Lizzie chose to walk into town today—the mare wouldn't have hastened her trip at all.

It was hard to believe that Edward had kept the ranch running this long. Chance was damn glad he showed up when he did, though he wasn't looking forward to having Lizzie along on the cattle drive. Without a crew and a string of horses to switch out, she'd have to put in long hours and eat her share of dust on the trail. Good thing they only had a hundred miles to travel to the railhead.

Chance wouldn't let Edward down.

Leastways not with the short trail drive.

Finding Lizzie a husband was another matter.

He approached his mare, muttering, "The old man's worried over his granddaughter and I've got to find her a man."

Joyful turned to the sound of his voice, her brown eyes on him. Chance stroked her mane, running his hands along the length of the coarse hairs and then gave her a pat as thoughts of Edward's quickly laid-out plan came to mind. Chance wasn't too sure it would work. His old friend explained the situation—so far Lizzie had pretty much shooed away any of the would-be suitors that Edward had brought out to the ranch.

Can't say as he blamed the men from turning tail and running. As much as he'd seen of her, Lizzie lacked female wiles and didn't have enough charm to entice a stray pup to Sunday supper, much less a would-be husband.

Chance grabbed his saddlebags and bedroll and entered the bunkhouse. Cobwebs crisscrossed the ceiling above his head and a layer of red dust kicked up as he moved into the space, yet the place wouldn't be the worst he'd lived in. He scanned the six bunks across the far wall deciding one was no better than the other, worn blankets and all, but they were sturdy enough for a man his size. He tossed his gear on the floor, took off his gun belt and sat down on the nearest bunk testing the thin mattress. It was a far cry better than hard ground. He laid his head back, setting his hat low to cover his eyes, and adjusted his body on the bunk, hanging his boots off the edge.

He'd barely had a few minutes of respite before he sensed a presence hovering over him. On instinct, he reached for his six-shooter and cocked it, hinging his body up so fast his hat went flying from his head.

"Oh!" Startled, Lizzie backed up, her eyes trained on the gun.

He glared at her. "What are you doing sneaking up on me?"

Her usual bravado gone, she lowered her voice. "I… wasn't."

He set the gun down on the bed. "You weren't? Funny, but I didn't hear you knock."

"The door was open. I came looking for you. Supper's ready."

He rubbed the back of his neck and nodded. "Fine. I'll be there in a minute."

When he thought she'd go, she continued to stand there, carefully studying him. "You got something else to say?"

"What are you afraid of, anyway?" she asked, her brows furrowing together. "You grabbed your gun so fast, I thought I was going to meet my maker years before my time."

"Scared you, did I?"

She paused, her expression tightening. She didn't like to give in, that much he'd already found out about the Mitchell girl. She raised her chin and nodded. "Maybe."

"It's good if I did and a valuable lesson to learn, Lizzie. You've not seen the world the way I have. You got to be on your guard every second of the day. Being alert has kept me alive and you'd best learn early that you can't trust everyone."

"Does that include you?"

He caught her stare and thought for a moment before giving her an answer. "Your grandfather trusts me."

"Can't imagine why."

Now she was being just plain argumentative. Her chin lifted another inch and he noticed the feminine lines of her jaw, the slender length of her throat. "You don't have to trust me, Lizzie. In fact, it'd be better if you didn't."

She blinked as his words sank in. Then with a sharper tone, she continued, "You didn't answer my first question. Why are you sleeping with your gun?"

"Stupid question."

"Stupid or not, I'd like an answer. Is someone after you?"

Nobody double-crossed Alistair Dunston and got away with it. Chance had left the man riled about him leaving the Circle D Ranch but it wasn't as if he'd committed a crime or anything. Yet, he was in rare company defying the powerful man's wishes, so Chance figured to keep his guard up. It never hurt a man to be smart. "Nope. A lot of men sleep with their guns. Keep that in mind and don't go stealing into rooms unless you're tired of breathing."

"And you might try not shooting my head off when I announce supper," she snapped.

He glanced at her pinched-tight lips and thought Lizzie needed lessons in manners. "You have a sass mouth."

"You've told me that already. I doubt that's going to change."

"It's gotta change, Lizzie. Just remember what I said about the trail drive and we'll get along just fine." He rose from the bunk and, towering above her, stared into her eyes. "You're no match for me."

Her expression faltered for a second, then filled with dawning realization. His attempt to instill fear in her hadn't worked as planned. Lizzie set her chin stubbornly and met his gaze head-on. "I just might surprise you, Chance Worth."

With that, she lifted her ugly skirt, whirled around and hastily exited the bunkhouse.

A wayward thought popped into his head and he hoped to high heaven that the surprise Lizzie had in mind for him wouldn't be arsenic in his beef stew tonight.

Chapter Three

"Wasn't too awful," Lizzie muttered, closing her bedroom door and heaving a big sigh in the privacy of her room. After an uneventful dinner listening to her grandfather and Chance talk quietly about cattle prices and the upcoming trip, she'd made fast work of cleaning the kitchen and excusing herself. She had nothing to say to the stranger. He'd said all there was to say in the bunkhouse and Lizzie had no choice but to make the trail drive with him and hope the time on the road would pass quickly.

In her room, she sorted through her sewing basket hoping to find enough leftover material to make at least one doll. That doll would go to Sarah Swenson, the sickly little girl who hadn't been strong enough to attend church lately. Sarah's parents had asked Lizzie to make it bright, with flowery material and pretty yellow yarn hair to cheer their daughter up. But all Lizzie could find were scraps of dull colors, browns and blues that she'd intended to stitch onto the feet for the doll's shoes.

Lizzie had made a promise to deliver the doll today and the circumstances preventing her from keeping that promise knotted her stomach and made her feel miserable. After the trail drive, she'd have money enough to buy new materials and honor her orders, but Lizzie couldn't forget Sarah's eager face, her sweet smile when the promise was made. Lizzie knew something about disappointment and how a little girl's dreams could shatter in an instant. Lord above, she'd felt that way more than a time or two in her own life.

Lizzie sank down on her bed and glanced at the doll with brown button eyes and a white lace pinafore, pigtails of yellow yarn hair and a small stitched smile sitting atop her pillow. She'd taken extra special care of the cloth doll her father had given her right after her mama passed away. Together, they'd named the doll Sally Ann, in remembrance of her mother, Annette.

A few years ago, she began copying the doll with her own sewing technique and creating fashions that compared to no other. What set her dolls apart was her attention to detail, the intricate patterns of dress, the lacy sleeves and tiny buttons down the back, the pinafores with delicate ribbons and shoes that laced. The doll's creation warranted great time and effort on her part as each one had their own unique personality, their own style of dress. How many hours had Lizzie spent creating new fashions or enhancing those she'd seen in Harper's Bazaar?

Lizzie put her materials back in the basket, knowing it was fruitless to try to sew a doll for Sarah out of her remainders. Plain and simple, she didn't have what she needed. But she did have another idea and though it would pain her, she knew she could do at least that much for Sarah Swenson.

After undressing down to her chemise, Lizzie slipped into bed, fatigued and anguished from a day that had brought many unexpected surprises. She glanced at Sally Ann one last time before closing her eyes to tears, and prayed that tomorrow would be a better day.

When morning dawned, an early glow of gold peeking up from the horizon gave Lizzie hope and a newfound rejuvenation. She'd always found faith in the new day and thought that all things were possible in that moment. She rose from bed and washed from a blue porcelain basin on her dresser. The rose-scented water refreshed her. She combed her unruly hair, a chore that took time and great effort. She wasn't one for fixing up, so once her hair was free from snarls, she tied it back with a strip of leather then dressed in a light blouse and gray skirt.

She moved quietly through the house, peering into her grandfather's room. He was still asleep. It seemed each week their breakfast came later and later as she waited for him to rise. She entered the kitchen and slipped her head into an apron, tying it into a bow at the back. After setting the coffee to brew, she walked outside and headed toward the chicken coop to collect today's batch of eggs. Spring sunshine warmed the morning air and heated her insides just right.

As she rounded the bend behind the barn, she came upon Chance Worth with his back to her, washing his face over the water barrel. Rays of sunshine caressed his bare shoulders and streamed over thick cords of muscle—the beckoning dawn revealing his beautiful upper body to be as strong and sturdy as the Red

Ridge Mountains themselves. Without knowledge of her watching, he scrubbed his face and shook the water from his dark hair. Droplets landed on his back and forged down his spine to tuck inside the waistband of his pants.

Lizzie forgot to breathe. Unnerved at the sight of him half dressed, the skin on her arms prickled and a slow burning heat built in her stomach. She backed up a step, ready to turn away and ignore the gripping sensations. But she talked herself out of running. Tomorrow, she and Chance would set out on a journey where they'd spend days upon days together. Alone. It was better to face this confusion now. Clearly, she couldn't stand the man, so what she was feeling had to be something aside from complete awe. She'd never come upon a man who'd created such unfamiliar and unwanted yearnings in her.

She'd only known boys. Many of whom she'd bested in school and some she'd rejected outright when they'd come calling. The only boy she tolerated at all was her best friend, Hayden Finch, who wasn't living in Red Ridge presently.

But no boy ever made her belly so queasy or got her heart pumping so fast.

Lizzie inhaled deeply and said, "Mornin'."

Chance took his sweet time turning around, and Lizzie caught a glimpse of pure naked flesh ridged with muscles as he moved to face her. She forced her gaze from his chest, praying to the Almighty that he hadn't seen her ogling him. A lazy smile graced his face. "Well, mornin' to you, Lizzie."

"I'm going to the henhouse," she said, annoyed at the

flurries in her belly. "Didn't want to get shot collecting eggs."

He wiped himself down with a towel and then shrugged his arms into a blue shirt, eyeing her carefully. "No chance of that. I knew you were there."

"You did not."

His lips twitched and he began buttoning his shirt. "Sure I did. Heard you coming. Sort of wondered when you were gonna announce yourself."

He couldn't have known she was there, not with his head down, splashing water on his face. "I shouldn't have to announce myself. This is my ranch."

"But you did. Shows you're learning."

Lizzie prayed for patience. She walked past him and just before she entered the henhouse, she stopped and turned. "I'll be going into town with you today. Just so you know. I have something I have to do."

"I'm leaving directly after breakfast."

She nodded. "I'll be ready."

"Don't suppose you got a wagon anywhere on the ranch?"

She peered at the two wagon wheels leaning against the barn wall, one with broken spokes and the other growing wildflowers from its base. "That's what's left of it. The winter was hard. We used the wood to keep warm."

He tucked his shirt into his pants and adjusted his gun belt. His Colt .45 sat low on his hip, cradled in the holster. "Shouldn't be a problem packing our horses with supplies. We don't need that much."

She nodded and paused, contemplating. This trip wasn't going to be like any trail drive she'd ever taken.

She continued to stare at him until his deep voice broke into her thoughts.

"Breakfast is going to be late if you don't get to those eggs." He turned and just like that, dismissed her, as if he was the schoolmaster and she, the pupil.

She marched into the chicken coop, her blood boiling. She didn't look her eighteen years, but Chance Worth would soon find out that Lizzie Mitchell wasn't a child but a woman with smarts and enough grit to match him stride for stride.

"We could have taken Juniper. She's stronger than she looks." Lizzie didn't really believe so. Their one remaining mare was comfortable on the ranch, but wasn't fit for carrying a rider packed down with supplies. Now, she sat on Joyful's saddle in front of Chance, his arm slung around her waist and wished the trip into town would hurry up.

Smug, he asked, "Then why didn't you take Ole June into town yesterday?"

"I left her for Grandpa. He was planning to ride out and check on the herd." Chance thought he'd won his point, but he didn't know everything.

"He do that much anymore?" he asked.

Lizzie replied with honesty. "Not too much."

Every day her grandfather had intentions of working the ranch the way he used to, but ultimately, he tired too quickly and she would take up the slack. This spring alone, she'd managed to pull half a dozen calves by herself, a task she'd learned from her father but one better left to someone a mite stronger. Yet, she was proud of her accomplishments and determined to rebuild the Mitchell Ranch doing whatever she had to do to gain that end. Even if it meant riding double on the saddle with Chance—even if it meant dealing with his all-too-sure ways and her queasy stomach.

"Good thing it's a small herd," he said.

"If it were bigger, we wouldn't be in such a dilemma."

"You think so?" he asked.

"I *do* think so." For half a dozen reasons, but mostly because they'd have sold off more cattle and earned enough cash to see them through hard times.

"I guess you're right."

It was the first time Chance admitted she was right about anything and she took a measure of satisfaction in that.

With him being so near, Lizzie had trouble thinking at all and every time his breath tickled her neck, she squirmed in the saddle. So much so, that Chance didn't hold back his complaints, so she willed herself to settle down.

He's just a man.

Nothing to squirm over, she thought. The scenery's more interesting than him. To prove it to herself she glanced around, taking in the view from atop Joyful, as the mare ambled down the road leading to Red Ridge. Winter rains had left tall grass and trees that flourished with greenery. The contrast in hues on this land always made her glory in the day; red earth, blue sky and vegetation that stole from a rainbow of colors. She loved living at Red Ridge, loved ranching, but she didn't love the hardships that had befallen them lately. She hoped to earn money enough on the drive to get her grandfather the true doctoring he needed. Maybe take him to an infirmary where he could be properly treated.

He'd put up a fuss about it and refuse to go, stubborn as he could be at times, so Lizzie had never revealed her secret hopes to him.

They reached the edge of town half an hour later, coming upon the Swenson homestead. "Please stop here," she said as she gazed at the small cheerful house surrounded by a whitewashed picket fence.

"Here?"

She nodded, turning part way toward him. "Yes, there's something I need to do."

"That something have to do with what's in the package you tied behind the saddle?"

"Yes," she said and as she turned back around, she saw Greta Swenson outside sweeping dust from her front porch.

The woman noticed her and set her broom aside to give them both a wave of welcome. She had the kindest eyes and Lizzie wondered if her mama would've looked upon her visitors with the same sort of friendly invitation.

"Hello, Mrs. Swenson," she called out.

"Mornin', Lizzie. It's good to see you today."

Chance reined in Joyful in front of the house. He dismounted with his usual grace and ground tethered his mare. He stood close and peered into her eyes, waiting with arms outstretched to help her down. Grudgingly, and knowing Mrs. Swenson was watching, Lizzie accepted his gallantry, shaking off another bout of jittery nerves as he held her close and lowered her from the saddle. Once her boots hit solid earth, he released her and she averted her gaze, afraid of what her eyes might reveal. She moved away from him and made quick work of releasing the ties that held the package in place.

With the package tucked under her arm, she turned to Chance. "I'll be a few minutes."

But instead of staying put by his horse, Chance surprised her by falling in step beside her as she walked up the path to the house.

"Well, now, we expected you yesterday, but I'm happy to see you today." The woman with dark blond hair, graying at the temples, wore a gracious smile. "And who is this you brought with you?"

Chance tipped his hat cordially, then removed it. "Chance Worth, ma'am. I'm working at the Mitchell spread now."

"Well it's nice to meet you, Mr. Worth. We're always pleased to have newcomers in Red Ridge. I'm Greta Swenson."

"He's with the ranch temporarily," Lizzie explained.

"Well, I'm sure he'll be a big help to you and Edward." The woman opened her front door. "Please come in. I'll get you both a glass of cider."

"That'd be nice," Chance said, waiting for the women to enter, before following behind.

They were ushered into her parlor and stood there for only a second before she rushed her explanation. "I came to visit Sarah, but I'm afraid I don't have the doll you ordered. It's a long story and I apologize for not honoring my word. If you'd kindly get Sarah, I'd like to explain it to both of you."

"Of course, Lizzie." Mrs. Swenson showed no disappointment. She was too nice to make anyone feel badly about anything, but Lizzie was certain she felt bad enough for all of three of them. "My daughter is resting, but I'm sure she'd love to see you. Please, have a seat in here and make yourselves comfortable. I'll get your refreshments."

They took their seats, one on either end of the soft, melt-into-the-cushion sofa and waited, Lizzie refusing to meet Chance's steady gaze. Mrs. Swenson came back into the room with two cranberry tumblers, handing one to each of them cordially before excusing herself to dress her daughter for company.

They sat in silence, Lizzie sipping her drink slowly, letting the spicy liquid soothe her parched throat and refresh her while Chance gulped his down quickly.

A few moments later, Sarah walked in holding her mother's hand. She wore a pretty dress the color of bright sunflowers with matching ribbons in her hair. Lizzie's heart ached seeing Sarah's weak, ashen body in those vibrant clothes. The contrast made the child appear more frail and sickly than if she wore plain unadorned garments.

Sarah gave the tall man sitting on her mama's sofa a cautious look. But as she refocused her attention on Lizzie, her eyes brightened and a sweet smile spread across her face.

"Lizzie is here to see you," her mother said. "And this young man is Mr. Worth."

The shy six-year-old glanced his way and whispered, "Nice to meet you."

Chance smiled a friendly smile, which seemed to convince the little girl he was not to be feared. "Hello, Sarah."

She looked at her mother, then at Lizzie. "Go on, sit down next to Lizzie, honey."

Sarah did so, taking up the space directly next to her.

Though the child's gaze kept shifting to the package on Lizzie's lap, she remained silent, waiting with eager anticipation for Lizzie to say something.

Lizzie plunged right in. She hated her circumstances. And hated that she would have to disappoint the little girl, yet she owed her an explanation. "I'm sorry, Sarah. But I don't have your very special doll today. I... There was an accident and—"

"You don't?"

"No, I'm very sorry, Sarah."

Sarah put her head down and Lizzie looked up just in time to see Chance's eyes soften on the child.

Lizzie sighed and continued, speaking slowly to Sarah, while at the same time darting glances at Mrs. Swenson, her explanation meant for both of them. She didn't elaborate about how she'd gone down in the water, fishing for dolls near the lake bottom until her lungs burned. No, she didn't want to see the look on Chance's face if she admitted that, but she did tell them about how the rickety old boat had failed her and how quickly the lake had swallowed up all the dolls.

"I'm sorry to say your doll and five others are sitting on the bottom of the lake out by my house."

Sarah nodded, her head still down.

"Lizzie, I know how hard you worked on those dolls," Mrs. Swenson said. "It must have been horrible to see all that work destroyed." She lowered down on a flowery material-backed armchair adjacent to her.

"Yes, ma'am. It was."

"Lizzie is mighty lucky she came away with her life," Chance added, unnecessarily. He ignored her glare, speaking directly to Sarah's mother. "The lake was about ready to swallow her up, too."

She sent him a brittle smile, then shifted her attention to convince Sarah's mother. "It wasn't truly dangerous."

Greta Swenson's eyes widened with surprise and horror as she laid her hand over her heart. "Oh, Lizzie. Those dolls aren't worth your life. I'm glad you got out of the lake safe and sound."

"Thank you," Lizzie said, giving up trying to convince anyone about anything. She was more concerned with Sarah. The little girl was crestfallen and still hadn't looked up. She softened her tone. "Sarah, I know this isn't what you were hoping for, but I have something for you. It's something very special to me and I want you to do me a favor."

Finally, Sarah lifted her face and cast her a round-eyed look as desolate as Arizona's drought land. Lizzie prayed this would be enough to remove the disappointment from Sarah's face. "A favor?"

"Uh-huh," Lizzie said. "I have to go away for a little while. And, well, I thought that maybe you'd like to watch Sally Ann for me."

She unfolded the package carefully, undoing the edges one corner at a time, until Sally Ann's smiling face came into view. "She was a gift from my father."

Sarah gasped, her body stirring with vitality. "She's pretty."

Not nearly as pretty as the doll Lizzie had fashioned for Sarah. But from the child's expression of awe, she didn't seem to notice the discolored clothes and slight tears in the fabric. "And old. I never let her out of my sight after...well, when I was a little girl. She went everywhere with me. I sure did love her. And now, since I'm going on a trail drive and won't be able to replace your very special doll for a while, I'm hoping you can keep an eye on Sally Ann for me."

Sarah began nodding eagerly, her eyes bright.

"I think you could do that, don't you, Sarah?" Mrs. Swenson asked.

"Yes, Mama. I can."

"Do you want to hold her?" When Sarah's head bobbed up and down, Lizzie lifted the doll from her lap and handed her over. "Here you go."

Sarah wrapped her arms around the doll and squeezed it tenderly as though it was the answer to all her prayers. She brought the doll's body against her face. "She's soft."

"I know. All that stuffing," Lizzie said, grinning.

Sarah chuckled.

"Will you take good care of her for me?" Lizzie asked.

The little girl's voice was sweet to Lizzie's ears and full of eager excitement. "Yes, I promise. I'll sleep with her and everything."

Lizzie fingered the doll's braided brown yarn hair and whispered past the lump in her throat, "I was hoping you would."

Sarah beamed with joy and a bit of youthful color tinged her sallow cheeks to a pink glow.

"When I get back from driving cattle, I'll be sure to sew you a doll all your own. But for now, I sure do appreciate you doing me this favor."

Lizzie glanced at Sarah's mother and choked up all over again at the woman's grateful expression. Mrs. Swenson's voice softened as she managed the words. "She'll take excellent care of her for you, Lizzie."

"I know she will."

Mrs. Swenson leaned over and brought her into a close embrace, whispering near her ear, "Thank you."

Too overwrought with emotion to reply, Lizzie simply nodded.

After they waved goodbye to mother and daughter on the porch, Chance helped her up onto the saddle and then took hold of the reins, leading Joyful on foot. "You're walking the rest of the way?" she asked.

"Can't take all that fidgeting you do."

"I do not fidget."

"You do. And you're good at it."

"Well, at least you think I'm good at something."

Chance glanced over his shoulder to gaze at her from under the brim of his hat. "You're good at more than one thing."

Her mouth dropped open and she was about to ask what he meant until his gaze shifted and she followed it back to the Swenson house. Sarah was still there, waving to them with one hand, while holding onto Sally Ann in a tight grip with the other and wearing a big smile on her face.

"Was a real nice thing you did just now, Lizzie."

With that, he turned around and picked up the pace, walking at a steady beat toward town.

Lizzie remained in the saddle, speechless. Chance had paid her a compliment, and it felt better than a warm steamy soak in a bathtub. In truth, it annoyed her how much his flattering remark pleased her.

And if she wasn't terribly careful, she might wind up actually liking him.

Lord, have mercy.

* * *

People gawked from the storefronts and sidewalks as Chance guided Joyful through Red Ridge with Lizzie atop the mare. He was used to being a stranger, to being watched, and he didn't fault the town for being cautious. He'd been the outcast enough in his time to know when stares meant simple curiosity or when they meant trouble. Today, curiosity was in favor, so Chance met with their eyes with a nod of his head and a smile. As he took in the town, he made note of the wide sidewalks and pristine shops, the clean streets and orderly manner in which the town was laid out.

So unlike the booming cow towns he'd known where indecency and despair seemed the way of life. Where saloons outnumbered churches by five to one and where crime and debauchery were not only tolerated, but expected by the few fine citizens whose roots were so ingrained that leaving wasn't a consideration, no matter how rowdy the town had become.

"Peter Roberson owns the livery," Lizzie said, as the double wide barnlike establishment came into view. "His sons work there. You'll find Earl an expert horseman and Warren as honest as a preacher at Sunday services."

"Good to know," Chance said.

When he reached the entrance to the livery, he turned to help Lizzie down from the saddle. She was light as a feather, a mere wisp of a girl, so it took no effort at all to bring her to steady ground. She had pretty eyes though and when leveled on him with a blue-as-sky stare, like she was doing right now, Chance got a little lost in them.

A boy approached who appeared a bit older than Lizzie and a foot taller, but just as slender.

"Mornin', folks." He shot a quick glance at Chance with furrowed brows and then laid eyes on Lizzie and kept them there.

"Good morning, Warren."

"Lizzie, it's real nice to see you."

Lizzie didn't return the warm sentiment, but got right to business. "This is Chance Worth. He's gonna rent us some cow horses for the cattle drive."

They shook hands.

"Your grandpa and you going on the drive?" Warren asked, cheerful as the day was long. "Same as usual?"

The girl couldn't hide emotion very well. She sent Chance a sour look. "No, Grandpa isn't…he isn't going, is all."

"I'll be driving the herd this time around," Chance said, tipping his hat back.

Warren looked at Lizzie, blinking a few times. "You two plan on going together?"

"Yep," Chance said, watching envy enter into Warren's eyes. It was clear the boy was smitten, and Lizzie, true to form, wasn't obliging Warren's eager looks. The horseman could be the answer to Edward's other request, an easy solution to Chance's problem of finding Lizzie a suitor, if only Lizzie was willing. But she'd have to smile more and actually give the poor boy a little encouragement for that to happen. Wouldn't be like Lizzie to make life easy for him, though. She was determined to be a pain in the ass, whether she was aware of it or not. "I'm helping Edward Mitchell at the ranch."

Lizzie folded her arms across her middle. "No need

going into detail. We need some horses, Warren. You rent horses. That's why we're here."

The boy snapped to attention at Lizzie's churlish manner. "Sure," he said, his brown eyes dimming. "We got some real strong horses."

After twenty minutes and a few arguments with Lizzie about which cow horses would suit her best, Chance rode out on Joyful, while Lizzie rode a gelding that was strong, sturdy and small enough to do the job and keep her safe.

The gal had a tongue on her and used it every chance she got. No matter what Warren offered, or what Chance said, Lizzie had a contrary response. Made a man want to scratch his head and paddle her bottom at the same time. But Chance was the boss on the drive and wasn't shy about reminding her. He wasn't about to let her dictate any terms, and they wound up with four horses overall that would serve their purpose well.

They entered the general store to buy supplies for the trail—coffee, flour, dry tack and cans of beans, among other items. Chance added a bit of his own money for some extra luxuries along the way. He had a sweet tooth and knew that after a long day of eating dust and pounding earth, something tasty and sugary helped soothe a weary cowboy.

Lizzie was still smarting from not getting her way at the livery when they'd walked out, loaded down with supplies. It took a bit of doing, but they packed two of the horses down, tying everything securely. Chance noticed that when set to task, Lizzie didn't disappoint. She worked hard without complaint, and he hoped to high heaven that that would hold true during the week they'd be on the road together.

"You could've been nicer to Warren," he said, plucking a licorice stick out from a nest of them in a brown sack. He waved it at her.

Her jaw set stubbornly. "I was nice enough to Warren."

"Nice? You call that nice?" He dug his teeth into the licorice and it stretched easily as he pulled off a chunk. He began to chew, enjoying the strong sweet flavor as he contemplated. "A female's got to be as sweet as this here licorice stick. You know, soft and delicate and definitely worth the wait."

"The wait?" Lizzie's brows furrowed as she watched him jaw a few more bites. "What on earth?"

"I haven't had any licorice in a long time."

"That's evident." Lizzie eyed the candy and shook her head. "You're devouring it like your last meal."

"A man needs some sweetness in his life." He caught her befuddled stare. "Uh, from time to time."

"I think the sugar's gone to your head."

Chance grinned. "Might be."

He enjoyed teasing Lizzie, but he couldn't forget who she was. An innocent. And here he was, making reference to things she surely had no knowledge about. His lack of sexual pleasure the past few months wasn't ever going to be a topic of discussion with Edward's granddaughter.

"Here," he said, offering her some candy. "Might sweeten you up a bit."

"I don't need sweetening up, Chance Worth."

"Fine, if you don't want any." He took back his offer but before he could close the sack, Lizzie put her hand in there, pulling out a piece.

She chomped down on the black confection, biting

off a big piece. She chewed it like it was her last meal. Silently amused, Chance decided not to comment.

"I have one more stop to make. Over at Mrs. Finch's Millinery."

"You buying yourself a hat?" Chance glanced at her hair, pretty in curls down her back. Once she'd cleaned up from that rat's nest yesterday and smoothed out the tangles, Lizzie's long strands hung as rich and glossy as black ink. Chance imagined how fine it would feel free of the braid and flowing through his fingers.

She gave him a long suffering look. "Might just buy me two hats. No, make that a dozen."

"A dozen?" A chuckle rose up from his throat and she greeted his amusement with a tilt of her chin. She huffed away, marching toward the millinery shop.

He followed with the horses in tow, watching Lizzie make her way down the sidewalk, the feminine sway of her hips catching his eye. She wasn't without some female qualities. With a little coaching, a bit more manners and a sweeter disposition, Lizzie would be a desirable woman. His brows rose as he imagined her dressed in something less bleak, a gown of color with dainty lace around her small bosom and hugging her slender curves, making a man wish he had a right to draw her close and kiss her.

Chance tore his gaze from her backside and shook those thoughts free.

He came upon the decorated shop and looked at the storefront window displaying hats of every size, color and shape with feathers, leather, silver and plumes decorating the brims. How many social events did a town like Red Ridge entertain to warrant the womenfolk wearing such fancy hats?

His gaze traveled beyond those bonnets to Lizzie speaking with apology on her expression to the woman behind the counter. When the conversation was over, the woman gently embraced Lizzie. She came out of the shop, her lips downturned and a sour pout on her face.

If she would smile once in a while, a man might actually think her pretty. But Lizzie wasn't happy right now and she walked past him and the horses, heading in the direction of the ranch.

Chance mounted Joyful, tying the other horses to the saddle horn, and headed in the same direction.

Lizzie kept up a brisk pace.

"You gonna walk all the way back home?"

Her shoulder lifted in a shrug and she kept walking.

"That woman upset you?"

Her head shook slightly.

"Lizzie?"

"I don't want to talk about it."

Chance understood that. There was many a time when his life just wasn't worth talking about. Lizzie had it rough lately, he'd give her that, and if she needed a little peace right now, Chance would grant her silence.

Without her sass mouth doing any arguing, it would be two of the most pleasant miles he'd travel with her.

Lizzie's feet ached and her stomach growled as they rounded the bend by the lake. She'd walked half the distance home so far, her feet moving beneath her rapidly as if they had a mind of their own. At times, Lizzie needed to walk off her remorse and her sorrow, but it wasn't working out too well at the moment. She wasn't alone and that was part of the problem. Chance was there, beside her, every step of the way. He'd been quiet on the way home from Red Ridge. Too quiet. It unnerved her and allowed her mind to fill with distressing thoughts.

Just when she was ready to make a comment about his silence, he began whistling a tune, *out* of tune. His carefree attitude grated on her even more. He had no cares in the world, it seemed, yet Lizzie had too much to care about. Too many troubles fogged up her brain and strong as she was, sometimes it all seemed overly much for her to take.

She stopped walking and turned to him. "What's that awful sound?"

Chance pulled up on the reins and looked around. "I didn't hear anything."

She rolled her eyes. "You know I'm talking about your whistling. Sounds more like two starving hawks fighting over a carcass."

"Lizzie, you're not hearing straight. Got something in your ears?"

"No, but cotton would be good about now."

Chance grinned.

It infuriated her that he looked upon her time and again with amusement, as if to say, she wasn't a woman to be taken seriously. She refrained from stomping her feet and marching off. Planting her hands on her hips, she stood her ground. "What's that smile for?"

He shrugged and leaned over the saddle which made it easier to meet his piercing eyes. "Well, uh, Lizzie. You looked a little sad for some reason and I thought that my whistling might just brighten your day."

Lizzie didn't believe that for a second. "You're not that kind."

Chance glanced away, guilty, as if he'd been caught

stealing from the church box. "You take pleasure in insulting me."

Indignant, her voice elevated a bit. "I didn't insult you."

"Didn't you? You don't like my whistling and you don't think I'm kind."

She *had* said that, hadn't she? "Well, I just meant that you could follow a tune more closely."

"Uh-huh." He tipped his hat back and she received the full force of his amused stare. "And the other?"

"You expect me to believe you wanted to cheer me up with your whistling?"

He heaved a sigh. "Maybe not exactly. I was gettin' kind of bored with all the quiet."

"So you thought to annoy me?" she asked.

"Did I?" He appeared hopeful.

"No. Yes. Like I said you can't carry a tune and it's a bit irritating."

"Got you out of your doldrums, didn't it?"

"I'm not having doldrums."

Chance dipped his head low and shot her a serious look.

"Well, maybe I was. Not that it's any of your concern."

Chance granted her that much with a quick nod. At least he respected her privacy.

"Get up on the horse, Lizzie," he said. "You're starting to tire. You need to be in good form tomorrow for the drive."

Lizzie opened her mouth to argue the point—Chance could be so bossy—but clamped it down just as fast. She was tired and Chance was right. She needed to be well-rested for their journey.

Chance didn't budge a muscle to help her mount the dappled gray mare he'd saddled, so she fumbled with the stirrup and saddle horn and found her way up. Settling her derriere and adjusting her body, she took the reins and slid him a glance. He cast an approving nod her way and they took off down the road.

Within a minute, Chance began whistling again, this time the sound perfectly in tune, the song a harmonious blending of chords that rose deep from his throat. She peered at him and gasped from the perfect pitch and tone.

And then it dawned on her.

He had been kind.

In his own way.

He'd taken her out of her melancholy by sparking her indignation and annoying her. He'd gotten her mind off her troubles.

And just like that, the words started tumbling out and it felt good, oh so good, to relieve herself of the burden. "I hated disappointing Mrs. Finch today. She was kind enough to take orders for my dolls and she had customers waiting for them. She offered me the money I would have earned delivering those dolls. She tried to put cash into my hands and shoo me away. But I couldn't take it, Chance. I couldn't. And then she told me about Hayden coming home to Red Ridge soon. I should be happy, since he's my very best friend in the whole wide world. Why, he's like a brother to me. We've always been thick as thieves. But Hayden's told me a dozen times that when he returned from his schooling, he'd be getting married. And then I'll lose him. I'll lose my best friend." She swallowed hard and felt like a silly fool for rambling on to Chance like this, but she couldn't seem to stop her heart from pouring out. "It just seems too much sometimes."

Chance was quiet, and when she glanced at him, he didn't look at her. He stared straight ahead at the open pastures that were Mitchell land. His words came slow and easy, but filled with intent. "Pride's a good thing, Lizzie. Most times. I probably would have done the same with Mrs. Finch. As for your friend, if he really is one, you won't lose him, no matter what."

She stared at him as his words sank into her soul. Something strange happened in her head and her belly when she took his advice as gospel. Pitying herself wasn't a virtue and certainly disappointing people she cared about wasn't, either. But the terrible distress that plagued her these past few days eased up a bit.

She felt better.

How could Chance make her see things clearly, when everything seemed so muddled in her own head? Before she could comment, though she hadn't a clue what words would tumble out, Chance nudged Joyful and took off at a trot, the string of horses he'd rented following closely behind.

She closed her eyes to the sunshine, grateful that her heavy load was lifted this afternoon and another odd thing happened—the melodious sound of Chance's perfect whistling filled her mind and she smiled.

Chapter Four

"I can't tell you how much this means to me, son," Edward said, leaning his body against the barn wall.

Chance hammered a wooden board over the gash in the wall until it was sufficiently covered. The board wasn't fresh lumber, but wood he'd removed and hauled to the house from an old shed he'd noticed on the property. With a little ingenuity, he'd have the barn looking like a barn instead of an overhang with broken down walls.

He moved on to the next area needing his attention, a gaping hole that left a window-size opening toward the east pasture. "Making repairs doesn't compare to saving a life."

Chance positioned another board and hammered away. When he was done, he stole a glance at Edward, who looked a little better this afternoon. Leastways, the Arizona sun had burnished his skin to show a bit of color.

"Wasn't just talking about the repairs. You're a godsend to me, Chance. You know, with Lizzie and all. We both know I'd never have survived the trail drive."

Edward hacked out several coughs, and the lifeless pallor returned to his complexion. It was like that with Edward, one minute he looked fine, the next, he appeared to be knocking on death's door.

When he was done coughing, he handed Chance another board and followed him around the corner of the barn. "I don't know any such thing. Lizzie seems to think some doctoring is all you need."

"Lizzie isn't rational when it comes to my health. She's turning a blind eye. But I expect more understanding from you."

Chance set the board down and met with Edward's old wise eyes. He heaved a sigh. He couldn't let the man know how much his demise would hurt him, too. He'd looked upon Edward as a father of sorts. Even though miles and time had separated them, Chance took solace knowing the older man lived and thrived in Red Ridge. His letters and words of advice had gotten him through some bad times and Chance had honest affection for him.

Finally and without qualm, Chance sent the man an understanding nod. "You got it, Edward. My understanding. But, you don't have to thank me. I wouldn't be standing here, able to help you, if you were a less honorable man."

"A man shouldn't be thanked for doing what was right."

"You stuck your neck out for me. That's more than anyone's done since my folks passed."

"And now you're sticking your neck out for me."

Chance snapped his eyes up to find the old man's

face lit in a smile, his eyes gleaming like never before. Some thought had obviously amused him. "How so?"

"You agreed to find Lizzie a husband."

Chance twisted his lips recalling how unpleasant Lizzie had been to young Warren at the livery stables. He wasn't forgetting the challenge Lizzie posed or the promise he'd made to Edward. "You think it's funny, do you?"

"No, just the opposite," he answered, with mirth in his voice. "Only wish I could be around to see how you manage it. It'd be a sight to behold. Lord knows, my attempts have failed."

"I'll manage it all right. You can trust me on that," Chance said with a measure of confidence. Someway, somehow, Lizzie would be wed before he left Red Ridge. "She mentioned her friend Hayden today."

"Did she now?" Edward nodded with approval. "Well, I heard he'll be home soon. That's good. Hayden's a fine boy."

Their eyes met in a long stare before Edward's throat constricted and another bout of incessant coughing marred the quiet of the afternoon.

Lizzie walked up holding a glass of water, her eyes wide and filled with concern. She was forever doting on Edward, almost as though he were the child and she the adult. "Here, Grandpa. Drink up." She handed him the drink and watched while he emptied it. "Let me get you inside. You need to rest." She moved closer to wrap her arm around his shoulder.

"I'll be resting soon enough," Edward said, sending her a kind smile. "I appreciate the drink, darling girl, but I'm fine. It's a glorious day."

Lizzie dropped her arm to her side and spoke with

determination. "But, Grandpa, your coughing's getting worse and you need—"

Before Edward acquiesced, Chance intervened, noting the distress on Edward's face. "He needs fresh air and sunshine."

It was clear the man wanted to enjoy his last days on his ranch out in the open but was too weak to argue the point with his granddaughter.

Lizzie shot Chance a surly glare that could freeze melting butter. "You got no say in this, Chance."

"He's been helping me with the barn."

"He can't do—"

Chance stood firm and leaned close enough to see indignant sparks flare in her eyes. "He can."

Not one to back down, she stepped closer and faced him with an upward tilt of her chin, meeting him almost nose to nose. "You don't know what you're talking about. You show up here and think you know everything, but you don't know a hill of—"

"Stop arguing!" Edward's rough, authoritative voice stopped them cold. Both Chance and Lizzie turned to see fire in Edward's eyes and strength in a body that had appeared weak and frail just moments ago. "I won't have it. You two have to work together and get along. Lizzie," he said, softening his voice, "I'm old and with age comes wisdom. I know when I've pushed my limits. When I tire, I rest. Right now, I want to spend time outside. I appreciate your worry and I love you dearly, but I asked Chance here to help out. The last thing I want is to see you two arguing all the time."

Lizzie buttoned her lips.

Chance pursed his.

They stared at each other.

No one said a word.

Edward muttered to himself and Chance thought he caught a few blasphemous words spew out.

"Fine," Lizzie said in a tone that wasn't fine at all. "I'll go start our supper."

Edward nodded. "That's an excellent idea. I'll be in shortly." Chance went back to his repairs with Edward alongside him.

The meal that night was overly quiet but delicious. Lizzie fixed a hearty supper of beef steaks, potatoes and creamed corn. She brought warm oatmeal cookies from the oven afterward and they ate them while drinking coffee as Edward went over details about the drive with the two of them.

Lizzie's eyes never strayed from watching every movement her grandpa made. Worry lines creased her young face and if Chance could read her thoughts, they were of regret at having to leave him here alone for a week to tend to himself. There was no way around it, though. Chance had stopped by the closest neighbor's homestead before supper and had been reassured that Benjamin Avery, the oldest child of the family, would look in on Edward from time to time. Sharing that news with Lizzie didn't put a smile on her face, but she'd seemed a bit relieved after that.

A little later, Chance walked his dish to the washstand where Lizzie was busy scrubbing a pot. She slid him a glance and returned to her work as if he wasn't there. Chance leaned in, speaking near her ear, making sure he wouldn't be ignored. "We'll head out at dawn. Get an early start. I'm fixing to turn in early. Leave you to spend time alone with your grandpa."

Lizzie looked out the window. The sun all but setting

cast pinkish-purple hues along the descending horizon. If she'd been merely stubborn, Chance would've walked out right then without a glance back. But he noticed her body sag, just an inch, enough that her shoulders slumped to an uncharacteristic posture. Then he noticed her mouth trembling, her bottom lip straining to stay still without any success. Her face flushed, Lizzie looked like she would break down any moment.

"Lizzie?"

She slammed her eyes shut.

"Lizzie, look at me," he demanded.

She faced him now, eyes open, but with dire agony in her expression, trying so damn hard to be brave.

"What are you afraid of?"

A tear dripped from her eye and she didn't bother wiping it away. Instead, she stared at him, searching for an answer. "Tell me he's going to be okay."

Chance drew a deep breath. He knew what it meant to lose the only kin you had. He knew the toll it took on a person. But he couldn't guarantee her anything. It wouldn't be fair to give her that much hope. Edward was only yards away, resting on the sofa. Chance set a comforting hand on her shoulder and spoke quietly. "I can't do that, Lizzie. But he wants it this way. You going on the drive with me. Bringing back cash enough to sustain you through the year. Keep that thought in your head. You're doing his bidding. Always remember that."

She turned away from him and took up her task again, scrubbing the pot without offering a word. Chance grabbed his hat from the peg beside the door and right before he walked out he heard her say, "I'll try."

* * *

Lizzie woke before dawn and lay in her bed, dreading the day to come. She'd barely slept at all and that wouldn't bode well for the amount of work she'd do while on the trail. But last night, she couldn't shake the feeling that her world was about to change. With a queasy stomach and nerves about to jump from her skin, sleep hadn't been her friend but a mere acquaintance that bounded in and out of the night.

If circumstances were different, she'd be the first one up and ready for the trail drive. The first one at breakfast, the first one to pack the supplies, the first one to ride off with glee in her heart, eager to start on a journey that would take her off the ranch.

But today wasn't such a day. Today, her heart was heavy, burdened with leaving Grandpa and all the worry that would follow. Lizzie wasn't looking forward to this drive at all.

She had said her prayers last night, and this morning as she hugged her pillow and nestled down in the comfort of her bed one last time, she squeezed her eyes tight and reminded God again.

When she heard her grandfather up, shuffling around outside her door, Lizzie dressed quickly in her trail clothes—a long-sleeve shirt tucked into a pair of tan trousers. Her brown boots had belonged to her mother—she'd always loved the fancy curlicue stitching that decorated the sides. It made Lizzie feel more womanly and a bit closer to her mother's memory. Though the boots were weathered some and the heels worn down, they were sturdy enough to protect her legs from prickly bushes and horsehair.

Once dressed, she glanced in her cheval mirror,

noting her bleak expression. She set her hand to her stomach, tamping down a sickly feeling and prayed one last time for strength today. That odd feeling she'd had this morning wouldn't relent, yet it wouldn't do to let her grandpa see her distress. She couldn't let on that leaving him, even for this short period of time, pained her so.

She found him sitting with Chance in the kitchen. He'd already brewed a pot of coffee and both were sipping from their mugs. "Morning, dear girl."

"Mornin'," Chance said.

She pasted on a smile for her grandpa's sake and darted them a glance. "Morning."

"Weather's good today, Lizzie. A fine day to start on the drive."

Grandpa always pretended good cheer in the morning. While she'd lain awake in bed last night, she'd heard him struggle for breath, the horrible hacks stealing precious life from his body. She'd held herself back from marching into his room to lend him comfort.

Now, she gritted her teeth and pretended along with him. "Yes. We should make good time today. Nothing to slow us down."

Chance took a big swallow of his coffee and nodded. "I'll warm biscuits and get us some eggs."

Grandpa pointed to the bowl sitting on the counter. "No need. Chance brought eggs in a while ago."

"Thank you," she bit out through clenched teeth. She couldn't figure why thanking Chance for anything rubbed her raw. Wasn't much sense in it, yet she'd rather spend time disparaging his nature than liking him.

Lizzie made fast work of cooking up the eggs, adding

bits of bacon and grease into a scramble and setting them along with the biscuits in front of the men.

Her Grandpa took note of how she wasn't touching her own food. "You're not eating?"

"Don't much feel like it this morning." She pushed her plate away gently.

Chance's head came up from finishing off his meal. "We won't be stopping for hours, once we get going."

"You should eat something, Lizzie," her grandpa said softly.

Two against one. Those weren't fair odds. She sighed and picked up a biscuit.

She'd force down a meal to make her grandfather happy. After managing the biscuit, she ate some eggs and it was worth it to see the satisfied look on her grandpa's face when he smiled at her.

She'd deal with her stomach's rebellion privately. It was almost time to say goodbye. She cleaned up the kitchen in a hurry, forcing tears away, and found Grandpa waiting for her outside, standing on the porch with his face arching to the rising sun. "You'll do fine, Lizzie."

She sidled up next to him. "I know, Grandpa."

"I expect you and Chance to get along on this trip."

"We…will." She didn't sound all too convincing, but it was the best she could do.

"He's a good man. You and him have more in common than you think. He's known loss and hurt in his life, too."

"I don't deny him that. It's just that he's—"

"Heed his words," Grandpa said with warning in his voice. "He'll keep you safe."

She choked back a sob. Who would keep Grandpa

safe? Who would watch out for him now? She knew it took great effort for him to stand tall, his shoulders straight and voice strong. He was doing it for her. He was holding back his weakness until she was well on the road. He was pretending again.

She took a deep swallow. "I will."

He turned to her then and pulled her into his arms. "Promise me, Lizzie? Promise me so I can know some peace," he whispered in her ear.

She nodded, willing to promise him anything to give him the solace and rest he sorely needed. "I promise, Grandpa. I do."

He pulled back a little and looked into her eyes. "That's my girl. I love you, Elizabeth."

"Oh, Grandpa!" She hugged him none too gently, her head pressed into his chest. She held on to his frail shoulders, feeling his strength fade, feeling the weakness overtake him. Tears spilled from her eyes and she wiped them away with a swipe of her shirt. She had to be strong. She had to be brave. She'd done it all her life and today was no different. She whispered, "I love you, too."

Taking a steady breath, she pulled away in time to see him reach into his pocket.

"Take this." He handed her his freshly cleaned neckerchief. "It's always served me well."

Lizzie's spirit rose and the ache in her heart subsided some. The neckerchief was Grandpa's favorite, the one he wore to start off all the drives. Having this with her while on the trail each day would give her a measure of hope. She felt it flow through her, a feeling that maybe she was wrong about her life changing. Maybe once she returned, her life, the only life she'd known, would be waiting for her again.

Eagerly and holding back a fresh round of tears, she fastened the fabric around her neck, noting the bright red color had faded to brick from wear on the trail. "Thank you, Grandpa. I'll use it every day."

His eyes warm and loving, he smiled. "Now go. Chance is waiting. I'll be here when you return."

She wanted to make him promise. She wanted a guarantee but instead, she nodded and banked on his words, holding them close to her heart as she plopped a hat on her head, brushed a soft kiss to his cheek and bid him farewell.

Lizzie didn't look back, though she was sorely tempted. She didn't have to turn around to know when the Red Ridge Mountains and the valley she'd called home disappeared from sight. She felt it in her belly. Even the air seemed different on the open range, the familiar scent of wildflowers and honeysuckle, of hundreds of grazing cattle, of apple pies coming out of ovens and fire pits cooking up the noon-day meals gave way to wide-open spaces with diluted subtle scents. The vastness of the land required it.

Surefoot, the chestnut gelding she rode, was strong and well-suited for the trail. He seemed to know his job, which made Lizzie's time riding flank and drag that much easier. The horse took commands well and she had to grudgingly give both Chance and Warren credit for choosing the right horse for her to ride, though she doubted either one of them would hear that praise fall from her lips.

Chance rode point, leading the herd on their journey,

and at times, he would double back to check on things, not saying much, just giving her a nod and eyeing the herd.

Checking up on her, most likely.

Lizzie ate some dust this morning, riding drag behind the herd first. Most times, the Mitchells gave the job of riding in back of the herd and catching the most dust to the greenhorn in the crew, the one with the least experience or the one who had hired on last. But Lizzie knew Chance had given her the easier morning shift of riding drag. They'd be shifting out after the noon meal where she and Chance would trade positions. She'd ride point and swing while Chance took the brunt of windstorms that kicked up a fuss in the afternoons.

She thought to argue with him, to let him know she could handle anything the trail offered up. She could do the job any of the crew could do without complaint and whining. She sought to make her point, but Chance cast her a stern, I'm-the-trail-boss look when he issued the order and then rode off on Joyful, just like that, without a look back.

One of Lizzie's jobs was to tally the herd, making sure they wound up with the same amount of cattle at the end of the trail as they started out with. They had exactly thirty-one heads and she'd already counted them three times, just because there wasn't much else to do but prod the lazier cattle at the back to keep them from slowing everything down.

Her stomach grumbled. And then it grumbled again. She was being punished, to be sure, for not eating a hearty meal this morning. Ten minutes later and none too soon by her accounts, Chance doubled back to take a place next to her. "We'll stop in half an hour for lunch."

Half an hour?

Lizzie's stomach protested noisily and she wondered if Chance heard the unholy sounds coming from her empty belly. If he did, he didn't say a word or make a gesture to indicate it.

Lifting his face to the sun, he squinted, leaning forward on the saddle to glance at the herd before him. "We're making good time today. The weather's holding."

"I suppose."

Her stomach rebelled as soon as she uttered the words, and Chance met her gaze.

"Anything wrong?"

"Uh…no. Nothing's wrong."

"Fine, then. Check for my signal to stop."

She sent him a quick nod. Chance tipped the brim of his hat lower on his forehead and right before he rode off, she could've sworn she'd seen a big ole smirk on his face.

The half hour moved at a snail's pace. With the herd settled, Lizzie and Chance found a mesquite tree nearby and rode the few yards there together. Chance dismounted his mare with usual grace and Lizzie slid down from Surefoot, hanging on to the saddle horn until her boots hit the ground. Riding a smaller horse made it much easier for her to mount and dismount and she was forever grateful that she didn't need Chance's assistance anymore.

Chance tossed a blanket on the ground and Lizzie helped him spread it out. She prayed her stomach would stop complaining. But there was just no controlling some things.

"How you holding up, Lizzie?" he asked as he brought over a sack of food.

Her stomach growled.

Chance grinned.

"I'm hungry, Chance."

"Oh, and here I thought you were serenading the herd earlier. Could barely hear my own thoughts with all the noise you were making."

She sent him a frown and plopped down onto the blanket. "You're not amusing." She pointed to the sack. "What's in there?"

"In here?" he asked with the innocence of a young boy.

He stood by the blanket. She squinted to see his face. "Yes, in there."

Chance lifted both arms overhead, the sack still in his hand. He joined them together and pulled both arms back behind his head in a slow easy stretch, keeping the sack of food out of her reach. If Lizzie wasn't so darn hungry, she might have enjoyed watching him move like that. She might have fastened her gaze on the muscles that worked in his forearms and reveled in his sheer strength and power. He was all man, and Lizzie didn't like that she'd been noticing, more and more. Because he annoyed her, just for the sake of doing so—there was no arguing that point.

She watched the sack sway to and fro as his body moved, still stretching, like time wasn't important, like they were picnicking on a lazy Sunday afternoon and like he didn't know she was starving. When her face flamed and her patience was about to quit, Chance slid a glance her way, smiled and then finally sat down beside her.

He dug into the burlap bag and brought out a small loaf of bread. He broke it in two. "Here you go, princess."

She grabbed for the bread and took a bite. She chewed thoughtfully, letting the thick tasty dough slide down her throat. "If I'm such a princess, why am I taking orders from you?"

His lips curled up. "You may be the princess, but I'm the boss."

"Ha!" She took another big bite and closed her eyes, savoring the food filling her belly. She'd baked biscuits and bread yesterday for the drive and now she was glad she did. "What else is there?" she asked, still chewing.

He brought out a thick hunk of cheese and used a knife he kept close at hand to slice off a big chunk. She took the first piece and after a few bites, Lizzie's stomach settled enough for her to relax.

Chance downed his half of the bread and cheese and both were quiet for a time. Lizzie sat on the blanket, looking out at the herd, while Chance leaned up against the tree trunk, stretching out his long legs. She felt his eyes on her and the skin at the back of her neck prickled with awareness. Turning in his direction, she gathered her brows together and sent him her best glare. "Isn't polite to stare."

He ignored her pronouncement. "Why do you want to be called Elizabeth?"

"It's my given name. I like it. But no one else seems to. Everybody is silly happy calling me Lizzie."

"Lizzie suits you better," he said in matter-of-fact fashion.

With a shake of her head, she shrugged. "I don't understand why that is."

"Some things just…are, Lizzie."

"So you're saying Elizabeth is too refined a name for someone like me?"

Chance's face twisted in puzzlement. "How'd you come up with that conclusion?"

She looked away to the cattle grazing, trying to will herself to think of something else. She concentrated hard but the obstinate notions kept entering her head. If she knew one thing for certain, it was that Chance wasn't the person to have this conversation with.

Oh, sometimes she just missed Hayden to death. He'd been her friend practically since birth, and she thought of him as her protective older brother. And as someone who truly understood her.

She wasn't like most girls. She knew that. But that didn't mean that at times, she didn't want to be.

"Lizzie?" Chance's soft tone made her turn to him. Rarely had he spoken to her with tenderness. She'd thought he'd be asleep about now. Like most cowpokes that have a few minutes to rest, they rarely waste them talking. They devour their meal and get some shut-eye, before taking up their positions at the herd.

But Chance kept on looking at her, expecting an answer. Unable to draw her gaze away and with the possibility he might understand and not laugh at her, she blurted out what was on her mind. "Can't a girl want to be treated like a woman?"

Chance blinked. His expression changed and he pushed back so hard against the tree trunk, he bumped his head. "You think that'll make you feel womanly? Being called Elizabeth?"

He *didn't* understand. No one did. And he didn't even try to hide the twitching of his lips. "Never mind." She set her gaze on a speck of land far off in the distance and admonished herself for confiding in Chance. She vowed never to do so again.

Leaning forward, he bent one knee and braced his forearm there. "Now, don't get huffy, Lizzie."

"I'm not huffy."

"You always get huffy. And you're not making sense."

Her back stiffened. She slammed her eyes shut and prayed for patience. "I—I...you wouldn't understand."

"I'm sure I wouldn't," he muttered.

She snapped her eyes to him and found him staring at her again. "What?"

He brought his face close. Dark specks of gold gleamed in his brown eyes. His scent tingled through her nostrils—musk like God's earth and fresh, like the pastures he rode over. A tremble shook her insides as she met his gaze. He dropped his eyes down and perused the rest of her body from face to toes with achingly slow deliberation, and she sat there, unnerved, fascinated, and allowing his direct scrutiny.

His words were sharp when he spoke, as if she should know this already. "A name doesn't make the woman, Lizzie."

For an instant, she believed him. "What does?"

His gaze went to her mouth and Lizzie froze, wondering what it would be like to be kissed by such a man. Everything inside her went soft, like the cotton stuffing she used to make her dolls, only this softness was warm and getting warmer every second he continued to look at her with hooded eyes.

He was handsome and manly and lord knew, she'd been having queasy feelings about him for days now.

But it wasn't right that she should have these powerful sensations about a man who belittled her every chance he got. And yet the trembling she felt when he was near couldn't be explained any other way.

She wasn't all that certain she liked Chance Worth.

So why was she feeling all gooey inside over him?

Something flickered in his eyes, enough to change the mood. He set his fist to the bottom of her chin and chucked her gently. "You'll know when it happens, Lizzie."

"That's it? I'll know?"

He nodded and rose quickly from the blanket they shared, bounding to his feet.

"Seems you could come up with a better answer than that," she said. She refused to admit that her sudden bad mood was brought on by Chance not kissing her.

"Roll up the blanket, Lizzie. It's time we move on."

When he offered his hand to help her up, she refused it.

"Suit yourself," he said with a shrug, then stalked off to his horse, leaving Lizzie alone by the tree and fearing that Chance and just about everyone else in the world would never look upon her as a woman.

Chapter Five

Everything ached.

After just three days on the trail, Lizzie felt sore from the John B. setting atop her head right down to the swollen toes of her too-tight boots. It was surely surprising that her body reacted this way. She'd been on many a trail drive before. The difference was that this time, Lizzie had no chuck wagon to ride in when her legs cramped up and cried for relief. She had no cozy bunk inside that chuck wagon to curl up into a ball for a warm and pleasing night's sleep.

Her nights were spent under the stars on the cold unforgiving earth. To her dismal dismay, her exhaustion wasn't enough to keep her asleep all through the night as she'd hoped. When she'd thought to sleep for hours, she'd been roused by the sound of steers rustling around and a lone coyote howling in the distance. She would look up at the stars if she thought that would settle her, but knew it was futile. There'd be no more guessing the constellations, no more lessons from a father keen on astronomy. The stars no longer held her fascination.

Instead she would toss and turn on the hard-packed ground searching for a measure of comfort. A smidge of fear would enter her head, knowing she was sleeping alone in the camp and maybe that had something to do with her unease. Chance watched over the cattle during the night. At times, she would hear him come close by, checking on her again, before he walked over to the herd to continue his shift. He let her rest the longest, only waking her in those few hours before dawn to spell him. How he managed to drive the cattle all day and watch over them at night, getting only a few hours of sleep, was a wonder to her.

"We'll stop and make camp now," Chance called from his position at the flank of the herd.

Hallelujah! Chance's declaration was joyous to her ears. Each day she'd prayed to hear those words. And because Lizzie was obstinate enough for five women and refused to show him her discomfort, he'd taken advantage and pressed the drive an extra hour each day. That last hour on the trail was the worst. Grueling and so painful to her rear end. She was sure she had calluses on her rump now. There was most likely a whole batch of blisters and bruises that colored her cheeks purple back there. The ache of sitting on the saddle, rubbing her skin against leather all day, every day, put her in a foul disposition. And a small part of her suspected that Chance might be torturing her on purpose.

She gathered her brows when he approached, pulling up on the reins when he got near. "Clouds are coming in. We might get rain."

She grimaced and peered up at the sky. Darn if he

wasn't right. The air around her grew cooler and the clouds coming from the north were moving fast. If she was prone to swearing, vile curses would slip from her lips now. The one thing that they'd had on this drive that brought a little ease was sunshine and warm weather. Now, even that was about to change.

"Great," she said with a sour puss.

Chance glanced up, assessing the sky after taking note of her ill humor. "It won't be storming, Lizzie. Just a little rain. We'll be fine."

Chance left her with a list of chores to do and then rode off to gather whatever he could find to make a fire, cow dung being the most readily available material on the trail.

As she slithered down from Surefoot, her body screamed its rebellion. Her legs hit solid ground and she gasped from the burn that shot up from her toes clear to her rubbed-raw thighs. The chaps she wore only protected so much and they didn't provide any help for the muscles that she'd abused.

Lizzie ignored the pain the best she could, though the ache fought mightily for attention. As Chance had directed, she gathered the horses together and led them to a small stream where they could drink their fill.

Maybe she'd been too harsh in her thinking about Chance and his need to torture her. He did know the land. She was learning that he made wise choices. He'd found sites to settle for the night close to shelter and water and Lizzie would be foolish not to recognize that.

She filled four canteens and gazed longingly at the water, wishing for a hot bath. Nothing was better to soothe wary muscles. She imagined sinking down into a luxurious tub of lilac-scented water and letting the warmth seep into her bones. Taking the soreness away. Refreshing her. Oh, what she wouldn't give for that right now.

The yearning stayed with her as she walked the horses back to a stand of trees near where they'd set up camp. She'd tied each horse in the string to a long rope that she'd looped around two thin trees. Once the horses were secure, she removed her saddle and combed down her mare. It wasn't so much sweat as it was dust that layered her coat, and Lizzie worked for several minutes getting her to shine clean again. Then she dragged the saddle to the clearing using much of the remaining strength she had left. Her father always joked that the rig was heavier than she was and in truth, he might have been right.

Clearing a small patch with her gloved hands, she patted the ground down. She searched for twigs and leaves, anything that would burn and keep them warm through the night.

Chance returned minutes later with firewood bundled on the back of his horse. "I got lucky. Found some dry wood." He dismounted quickly and took note of her work. "Horses watered down?"

She nodded and trembled from the cool breezes coming from the north. "They're satisfied. And I filled our canteens."

"Good, I'll start the fire. We'll make coffee. And maybe heat some beans."

Yesterday, they'd finished up the biscuits and cheese they'd packed, and all that was left to fill their bellies was strips of dried meat and beans. Those provisions wouldn't do for a real outfit on a big cattle drive, but without a cookie and chuck wagon, it would have to make do. They'd had to travel light. Luckily, Lizzie didn't need much to satisfy her appetite. Chance, on the other hand, could be eating more being as large a man as he was, but Lizzie figured he was used to going without. He could make do, with whatever God saw fit to give him.

As the clouds displaced the sun, the air chilled quickly and a shiver rode up and down her body. Everything still ached, only now the cold had set in. Lizzie grabbed her coat and put it on. She was dirty, cold, tired and hungry. From a distance she watched Chance squat down to build a fire using leaves and cow dung. Once the fire sparked to life, he added the dry branches he'd found.

"Come here," Chance said, looking over his shoulder at her.

"Why?"

"Don't argue. Just come."

Lizzie didn't like him being so bossy and at times, she argued with him, just to let him know she had a point of view, too. But today, Lizzie was too tired to argue. She moved closer just as he gestured to a place directly next to him where he'd arranged a blanket. "Sit. Stay downwind of the smoke and get warm."

She plopped down on the blanket and decided that if she couldn't have a hot bath, sitting by a blazing fire was the next best thing. "I didn't need you to tell me that."

Chance sighed and sent her a hard look. "Sometimes, I think you're contrary just to hear yourself talk."

She closed her eyes and muttered, "I'm not contrary," but she couldn't muster much enthusiasm for her defense.

"I was going to pay you a compliment, until you sassed me."

She snapped her eyes open, wondering what kind of compliment Chance might have for her. To the best of her recollection he hadn't said a kind word to her in days. Oh, he hadn't been harsh, but he'd been something short of cordial. Not that she could blame him with the amount of sleep he was getting. He put in a long day's work as well but darn it, he never looked tired. The only indication that he was on the trail and working day and night at all was the beard that shadowed his handsome face. That stubble looked mighty sinister on him. He reminded her of an outlaw she'd once seen being held in the Red Ridge jail. The man had been sentenced to ten years for robbery and assault and had been taken to prison. Lizzie had stolen a long look at him when the sheriff had transferred him into a prison wagon. "I didn't sass you."

"Oh, no?" His brows arched and a skeptical look crossed his features.

She wrapped her arms around her middle, curious as to the compliment. Staring into the fire, she didn't know why it mattered so much what Chance said or thought about her, but it did. "I—I didn't mean to. I'm a little tired, is all."

"Makes you grumpy?"

"I'm not…"

She halted midsentence and peered at Chance. His lips twitched. He had a habit of doing that around her. Like he wanted to burst out laughing, but held back, enjoying the private amusement all too much.

But the fact was, Lizzie was grumpy. And she wouldn't debate the issue, not if she wanted to hear what kind thing Chance had to say about her. "Just tired, Chance."

She lifted her chin to meet his gaze. They stared at each other, eyes locked for the span of three heartbeats. Then his gaze dropped lower to her mouth. Lizzie froze, just as she had the other day when he'd given her that very same look. Butterflies invaded her stomach and fluttered around in frenzied turmoil. The unanswered feeling confused her.

Chance opened his mouth to say something and she waited. Patiently. But then his face twisted up and he turned away.

"What were you going to say?" she asked, her curiosity and those swimming flutters making her bold.

"Nothing."

"You had a compliment for me. What, now you don't think I deserve it?"

He slid a sideways glance her way and squinted as if in pain. "Hell, Lizzie. You are a handful."

"I may be wrong, but that doesn't sound like a compliment."

He chuckled but refused to look at her.

She laughed, too, the conversation and her fatigue making her giddy.

"All right, you wore me down," Chance said. "I'll tell you."

Her breath whooshed out in a whisper. "What's the compliment?"

He scrubbed his jaw as if hating to relinquish this bit of information. "You're working hard. And not giving me any real trouble. I see the toll this drive is taking on you and you haven't complained once." He shrugged and while Lizzie should have been overjoyed to hear him commend her for a job well done, her heart sagged just a little. What had she been expecting? She wasn't quite sure.

"I thought you should know you have my admiration. You're taking it like a real…cowboy."

Lizzie hid her disappointment well, kept her shoulders straight and her breath steady. She even managed a smile for Chance that took every ounce of her will to muster. But at that very instant, Lizzie realized what she'd wanted Chance to say.

And it was something more unattainable than a tub filled with steamy lilac water waiting for her just around the next bend.

Chance peered at the sky overhead and the mounting threat of rain. He'd hoped he'd been right, that a storm wasn't brewing. But the air had grown unbelievably cold for this time of year and off in the distance, he heard the faintest booming of thunder. They were out on the open range, with no protection or shelter. Only a few scattered trees covered the ground within eyesight and offered no real defense against what Mother Nature might be conjuring up.

He filled his belly with beans and meat as he sat with Lizzie by the fire. She'd eaten a healthy amount, too and for all her bustle and bother, he was gratified that she wasn't acting like a wilting flower on the trail. He'd meant what he'd said to her a few minutes ago. She had true ranching in her spirit. She knew how to handle herself on the trail. Complaining wouldn't make anything easier and giving in to your body's complaints wouldn't serve any real purpose. Lizzie seemed to understand that, even though she loved sassing him. If that was all he had to contend with during this time with her, well, hell, he wouldn't kick up a fuss, except to sass her back.

He sipped coffee, warming his hands on the mug and watching the firelight dance over Lizzie's face and cast her in a pale glow. Her eyes, the brightest kind of blue, reflected in the blaze and each hue of those melding colors struck him like a punch to his gut.

She had the prettiest eyes he'd ever seen.

They were unique and expressive and the longer he stared, the more he wanted to keep on staring. It was the damnedest thing.

"Chance," she whispered and the yearning in her voice stunned him out of his trance.

Hell, he'd almost told her how pretty her eyes were. He'd almost paid her a compliment that this time wouldn't disappoint her, because while his last one had been honest, he'd known by her fake smile and bravado that it hadn't been the kind of compliment she'd wanted to hear.

Lizzie wasn't someone to dally with.

Edward was counting on him to do right by her, protect her and find her a husband. Not entertain thoughts that would sabotage all three objectives.

Luckily he'd smartened up before igniting a flame that would be hard putting out.

He downed his coffee in one huge gulp and it went a long way to keep him warm. He poured some into Lizzie's mug and handed it over, ignoring her pretty eyes that continued to stare at him. "Here, have another cup of coffee. It'll take the chill off."

"I'm beginning to think nothing will."

Chance snapped his eyes to hers and wondered what she'd meant by that, truly. He was grateful when she grabbed the cup from his hands, though she refused to look at him. He rose from his seat and put his gloves on, holding his hands above the fire to warm them. Then he grabbed two rain slickers and tossed one to Lizzie. "Put this on. I'll check on the horses and herd. You should try to get some sleep."

Thunder boomed, this time discernibly closer, and Chance saw lightning illuminate the sky a few seconds later.

Lizzie looked skyward with a shiver.

Chance had a bad feeling about this.

He walked away from her and strode to the roped area where the horses rested. Joyful was jumpy. She never liked thunder and it seemed all of the horses followed suit and were aware of bad weather approaching. Chance fed them each some sugar cubes and patted them down using reassuring words, but all of his efforts were wasted when another clash of thunder boomed overhead.

"Whoa, steady. Steady," he murmured. He stayed with the horses until they settled down, his eyes and ears open to the cattle just yards away the entire time.

If there was a stampede it would take days to retrieve them and they'd lose precious time. But they were a small herd and cattle were basically lazy animals that plodded along, so Chance had to put his faith in that. He found the herd unmindful of the weather at the moment, and that was a good sign.

The rain came an hour later. The drizzle he'd hoped for had turned into a real downpour. Chance was torn between watching the herd and checking on Lizzie. Ultimately, he knew what mattered the most, to Edward and to…him.

He left guarding the herd and found Lizzie leaning against a thin mesquite tree grabbing the smidgen of shelter it provided. Standing with a blanket over her head, she trembled uncontrollably.

Chance cursed and berated himself for not checking on her sooner. There was no shelter, no way to get warm. The fire had gone out and it would be hours before it was dry enough to start one again. He strode over to her, his boots sloshing over the prairie grass and mud. "Lizzie, you're freezing."

Her eyes were moist and he suspected it wasn't the rain dripping down her cheeks. "I'm s-so c-cold."

Quickly, he tossed a blanket over a few thin branches and tugged her body under the pathetic shelter he'd forged. It wasn't much, but it was better than nothing. He wrapped her tight in his embrace and cradled her head against his chest. She wasn't just cold, but frozen to the bone. Her teeth chattered. Chance wrapped them in a blanket, the cool wet wool the only barrier from the outside cold.

He rubbed her back and arms trying to bring some life into her blood, get it circulating enough to warm her a bit. "I'm sorry, Lizzie," he murmured into her ear. "I shouldn't have left you."

She shivered again and hugged him tighter.

Chance closed his eyes. Usually when he held a woman this close, it was for a much more entertaining reason. If there was any trembling involved, it was in anticipation of the things they would do to each other. But Chance kept those thoughts away, concentrating on pressing his hands to her back and massaging the stiffness and cold from her body to keep Lizzie from freezing to death.

When her knees buckled, he held her upright the best he could. "Hang on, darlin'. Hang on or we'll both go down."

"I'm t-trying."

"The storm's about to pass."

"H-how's the herd?"

He touched his lips to her forehead. "Still there, soaked and not happy about it, but they're there."

She nodded, her chin digging into his chest. "And the h-horses?"

"About the same, Lizzie. Don't go worrying over them. They'll be fine."

"They h-have to be-e."

She was determined to see this cattle drive through. He couldn't fault her concern. Everything she had—her life, her grandfather's life—was tied to that herd. If given a choice, she wouldn't hesitate to do this all over again, if need be, to ensure her future.

Chance took the brunt of the storm, letting it hit him fully. He made sure Lizzie was as protected as possible. The rain hit his hat and flowed onto the brim then streamed down to the ground like a waterfall. He made sure to angle his body in such a way that nothing wet touched Lizzie.

But him.

Problem was that with her lithe body plastered to him real tight, her small breasts crushed his chest and her hips dug into his legs. Chance wasn't a damn saint and Lizzie wasn't a child. No, sir. She wasn't. This cattle drive proved that better than any amount of frills and lace and female airs of coyness. And having her so close, nestled in his arms, her body pressed between his spread legs, it was difficult to remember who Lizzie was and why the hell he couldn't touch her.

For the most part, they didn't like each other, he reminded himself.

Finally, the rain stopped and Chance was never so grateful for weather to let up in his entire life.

He set Lizzie away from him and held her steady by the arms. Her eyes lifted to his and she glanced at his mouth as awareness flickered in her eyes. He hadn't fooled her. Hell, what did she expect? He'd been rubbing her body, feeling everything female about her and of course, he'd reacted. Rain didn't make a man less a man. But then, how would Lizzie know that?

Her long curls were soaked, coming free of the braid she wore. Her face was ashen; the exhaustion on her face earlier was nothing compared to how she looked right now. And still, she shivered.

Uncontrollably.

"Are you all right?"

She hugged herself around her middle, her teeth clanking against each other. "I w-will be. Soon as I get w-warm."

How was that going to happen? It was black as pitch, cold as ice and wet as a rushing river. Lizzie was bushed. And he didn't know how long he could go on holding her upright.

"Lizzie, take off your clothes."

She swallowed and looked at him like he was crazy. "What?"

"You have to get out of your wet clothes."

"No."

Chance sighed and instead of getting mad—Lizzie was forever trying his patience—he reasoned with her.

"Lizzie, listen to me. You're frozen solid. You're going to get deathly sick if you don't do as I say. I'm going to try to light a fire, but it probably won't work. We can either stand here all night or lie down and attempt to get some rest."

"But everything's w-wet. We'll be s-soaked."

"We're soaked now. I'll keep you warm and in the morning, we'll dry out our clothes and move on. But it's the middle of the night, Lizzie. And if you stay wet in those clothes…"

"But, you'll be w-wet, too." She shivered again.

He winced realizing he had to enlighten her as to how this would work. "I'll be taking my clothes off, too."

Lizzie's face was close and through the dimmest light he saw her flinch. She breathed out so quietly, he would barely hear her but for the silence surrounding them. "We'll be lying together. Naked."

The image slammed into his head and he recalled the soft small buds of Lizzie's breasts pressing through his clothes. The scoundrel in him remembered her hips grinding into his groin and how good it felt. Chance swore silently. Was he a fool to suggest this? It'd been months since he'd lain with a woman. "Not entirely. You decide what's…what's necessary to stay on. But Lizzie, I'm responsible for you. And I can't—"

A cold breeze blew by, evidence of the wicked wind to come, and it seemed enough to convince her. "I'll do it."

"Fine," he said, wishing there was some other way and thinking this wasn't fine at all.

Chance made an assessment of the land he could see in the darkness. The herd had settled and the horses were doing the best they could under the circumstances. He spotted an area away from the trees that would catch the first light of morning and laid the blanket down there. "Come on over here, Lizzie."

The clouds separated and moonlight filtered down, a slender streak of light that gave a measure of illumination.

Chance could see her better now. She wasn't moving at all, but staring at the blanket they would share. Biting her lips, she might have drawn blood from the intense look on her face. The wind howled and nearly blew her down as it whipped by, little as she was. She righted her footing and let out a curse. "Damnation!"

Chance held his tongue in check and watched as she lowered her body down into a crouch, protecting herself from another blast of air. She approached the blanket and when she reached him, a scowl covered her face. "Turn around."

He thought her modesty foolish. Soon they would be lying together, their bodies touching intimately, and they were going to feel everything they had to feel. But this one time, he did Lizzie's bidding. He turned his back and let her have her pride. "Let me know when you're ready."

He heard rustling and more oaths shed from her mouth as she fumbled with her clothes. She didn't have too much to remove, no fancy buttons to unfasten or layers of petticoats that needed to come off one at a time. All she wore tonight was a rain slicker over a jacket, and her riding clothes. What she wore underneath it all, though, was a mystery to him. But he had a feeling he was going to find out right now.

After a few more seconds, she said, "I'm under the b-blankets. And I'm s-still c-cold."

"I'll be right there," he said. He took off his gun belt and removed everything he wore down to his long johns. Those he unbuttoned, then removed his arms from the sleeves, allowing the wet half of them to dangle from his waist. The more skin-to-skin contact, the faster Lizzie would warm up.

Shortly, she'd see his wisdom and know some comfort. If only he could be that lucky.

Chapter Six

Lizzie couldn't get the idea of lying naked with Chance out of her mind. Waves of heat spread through her system like blazing fire. She welcomed the momentary warmth and grasped on to it for as long as it would last. Her heart in her mouth, she was now naked but for the thin chemise she wore tucked inside even thinner bloomers. Anticipation gnawed at her. Even her fear and humiliation weren't enough to warm her for long. The chill had come back but her dignity had not.

She'd never been this cold in her life. Why would she be? Not even the dunking in the lake at home had iced her blood like this.

She'd seen Chance bare chested the day he'd rescued her. She'd been only half-conscious but she recalled the magnificence of him. His shoulders had spread out as beautifully as an eagle's wings. His powerful arms, his big hands and sheer strength as he moved her to water's edge that day, tugged at her memory and only added to her agony now.

Lizzie brought the blanket up underneath her chin, waiting for Chance to join her. Her body a mass of trembles, she thanked heaven that Chance wouldn't know the true reason for her quaking.

She concentrated on the blanket under her and how wet and scratchy the wool had become. It tore at her skin some and itched like the dickens. The discomfort wasn't enough to distract her though when she heard Chance approach. She closed her eyes and stilled.

"I've gotta yank off your boots, Lizzie. If your feet are cold, the rest of you won't release the chill."

"Long as you don't yank anything else off me, I'll do fine."

She heard Chance chuckle and then she felt his hands circling her right boot. He gave a tug and off came her stockings, too. He took the other boot off and she flinched when he accidentally touched her legs. She felt the blanket lift as he tucked her feet under it.

"Soon as I get my boots off, I'm coming in."

Oh, mercy.

Seconds later, Chance lifted the blanket. Lizzie kept her eyes shut. It would be easier imagining him next to her, than actually seeing him buck naked beside her, though neither option garnered any sanity.

He climbed under the blanket and without any warning at all, covered her body with his. He closed himself around her like a thick coat of fur. "Put your hands on my chest. You'll warm up quicker if nothing is exposed."

Everything was exposed.

"You're sure this is going to work?" she asked, hesitantly putting her cold-as-ice hands on him. Through his cool damp chest came warmth that was as much a relief as it was a surprise.

He was warmer than she'd thought he'd be.

Hadn't he been out in the same rain and wind that she had? How could his body radiate so much more warmth?

"Chance, you didn't answer me?"

"It's working already," he said rather harshly and then added, "your teeth aren't chattering."

He was unbearably close. Their breaths mingled and she drew the scent of fresh rain, earth and coffee into her nostrils. His smell wasn't displeasing and Lizzie thought herself a silly fool for thinking of such a thing while he was lying atop her, trying to keep her warm.

Her palms pressed the skin of his chest and it reminded her of wildfire catching on a field of dry grass, those initial embers that started to flame slowly in the beginning before setting the entire prairie to blaze. That's how Chance felt to her as those embers began to thaw her out, one body part at a time.

"Are you warming up, too?" she asked. Her legs were cold, but she wouldn't complain that he hadn't wrapped his legs around hers. Some things a girl just knew not to say.

"Getting there, Lizzie."

"You feel warm to me."

"That's the point of it all."

She felt the scattered hairs beneath her fingertips and wondered how it would feel to move her hands through them and feel the corded muscles underneath her palms. Only in her imaginings would she ever actually do it, but, oh, what an ease to her burgeoning curiosity it would be to put her hands on a man that way and have freedom enough to explore. It was a wicked thought and one she'd probably never see come to life but if she ever had the opportunity she'd want it to be with someone like Chance.

"So this is what it's like," she whispered, once Chance settled down. He seemed at an odd angle, as if he was holding back, trying not to crush her.

"Getting warm?"

She corrected him with a whisper. "Lying with a man."

"Geesh, Lizzie. You're not lying with me. This isn't what it's like at all."

"Oh?" Her face was tucked into the hollow part of his neck, right where his throat met with his chest. Every time he spoke she felt the vibration as his throat worked to move the deep sound of his voice. "But isn't this how it feels? Being so close we only need to whisper to be heard."

"That part's true."

"And we're sharing a blanket?"

"True again."

"And we're—"

"We're *nothing,* Lizzie. Just keeping warm on a night you might have froze. That's all."

"I don't feel quite as frozen anymore. But, oh, this blanket is itchy underneath. Feels like a batch of spiders pricking at my skin." She shifted a little, wiggling her body to get more comfortable. The move brought her hips up to meet with his groin.

"Don't do that," he snapped, pulling away from her. His quick action yanked the blanket off both of them and a cold rush of air seeped in. She felt his absence immediately and the chill that sped up and down her body felt like ice flowing through her veins.

She stiffened and rested back against the wet woolen material. "Sorry, but I...the blanket is rough against my back." She shivered. "It's cold without you."

Chance muttered an oath and a few seconds ticked by before he hooked the blanket over his shoulders again. He resumed his position, setting her hands back on his chest. She felt his heat instantly as he covered her. A heavy sigh pulled from his lungs. "Seems to me, you can either be warm or comfortable. Can't have both. Not tonight."

She could barely make out his eyes, seeing just the dark outline from a glimmer of light overhead. "I'm not a child, Chance. I know the situation."

He grumbled.

"I wasn't complaining. Just thought I could get a mite more comfortable, is all. Why'd you get so riled?"

"You're more a child than I thought," he said quietly, "if you don't know the answer to that."

She'd never had a mama to speak to regarding these things, so as much as she'd like to sass Chance right now, she couldn't. No clever words came to mind and she wasn't sure what to make of that. She nibbled on her lower lip for a moment and then figured she might chew it off if she wasn't careful, her mouth was so darn numb.

She understood that a man got bothered when lying with a woman. But hadn't Chance just said, lying with a woman wasn't anything like this. He couldn't be right, because as she began to thaw, having him atop her, covering her with his big body, and breathing the same air from under the blanket, her insides felt as soft and sweet as strawberry jam.

Why, she could imagine touching him, doing that exploring she'd been wanting to do and, yes, kissing him. What would it be like to kiss a man like Chance? Would having his lips on hers steal all the breath from her lungs? Would the stubble on his face scratch her as much as the blanket beneath her? Would he taste like coffee and earth and air all mixed into one?

Lizzie sighed, the tiny sound escaping her mouth one of pure pleasure.

She heard Chance's intake of breath. "Lizzie, whatever you're thinking, *don't.*"

"Chance?"

"Don't, Lizzie," he warned again.

"But I was just going to ask if you're planning on sleeping this way all night? I mean, you can't possibly get any sleep in that position, half on, half off of me, sort of suspended the way you are." She could feel him holding back, keeping their most intimate parts from touching. How long could he go on holding himself that way?

"That's my problem."

"It'll be mine, if you land on me and crush me during the night. I don't think I'll sleep a wink in this position, not being able to move a muscle and all."

"If I land on you, you just shove me off. You got that?"

"Yes, I got that. But what if I move by acc—"

"Damn it, Lizzie," he growled. Then he flopped down and turned onto his side, grabbing her and curling her body into him like a curved spoon. She fit into the bend of his body perfectly and his heat this time came from behind as he locked his arm over her shoulder, tucking her in tight against his rigid body. His voice was raspy and low. "Not another word. Now, get some sleep. And whatever you do, don't tell a soul you laid with me like this."

She nodded and closed her eyes. She was nestled in his body heat and felt safe in his arms. She wouldn't have believed it possible, but she'd felt his heartbeats race under her palms just seconds ago. The beats matched the rhythm of her own hurried pulse and only one reason for that came to mind—she'd tempted Chance, as a woman, and nothing flamed her insides more than that realization.

Lizzie woke to heat, the sun's rays searing through her body and soothing the aches that had settled in her bones last night. Sunshine was heaven, she thought as her eyes fluttered opened. And there was plenty of that this morning. She squinted and lifted her face upward, relishing the warmth. No clouds marred the blue skies, the storm had passed and if it weren't for drying mud and dew moistening the prairie grass, she might not have guessed the night before had been cold, wet and dreadful.

Then she remembered how she'd spent the night, with Chance curled around her, selflessly keeping her warm and dry. He'd been kind again, in his own way, and there was no doubting that he's saved her from freezing to death. He wasn't under the blanket with her anymore. She'd sensed she was alone on their makeshift bedding even before she opened her eyes. Chance must have risen at dawn. Judging by the position of the sun now, it had to be well past time to move the herd.

She bent her body to an upright position and then gasped. She'd forgotten about the meager underclothes she wore. She tightened the blanket around her and peered out for some sign of Chance.

A fire blazed some yards away and her clothes were drying nearby. The horses looked like they'd weathered the storm just fine and thankfully the herd hadn't been spooked last night. She'd only seen a stampede once before and if she lived a hundred years she prayed she'd never witness another.

When she spotted Chance approaching, coming from beyond a thin cropping of trees off in the distance, her heart skipped. She rose quickly and with the blanket secured around her body, she walked past the fire and picked up her trousers and blouse. They were stiff and none too clean, but they were almost dry.

"Hurry up and get dressed," Chance barked as he came up behind her. "We're behind schedule."

"You should've woken me," she replied, hurt by his brash tone. Here she was about to thank him for last night and for letting her get extra sleep this morning.

"Clothes needed drying, anyway. But we should shove off, soon as you get something to eat."

"Fine." She gathered her clothes to her chest and began walking toward the trees.

"Where are you going?"

She stopped midstep and turned. "To get dressed."

"For Pete's sake, Lizzie. Just get dressed here, by the fire."

"But I, you…"

"You've wasted enough time." He gestured at the blanket that held her modesty intact. "Isn't as if I didn't just see what you've got on under there."

She tilted her chin and argued the point. "You didn't see me. It was dark."

"No, but I touched every part...hell, never mind." His lips twisted into a scowl.

He was grouchy this morning and looked fit to be tied.

But he was right. He had touched her. And she'd touched him. Her cheeks burned and she was grateful he turned toward the herd at that moment and didn't see her mortification. Mortified or not, she'd never forget how she felt last night safely secured in Chance's arms, having his breath tickle her neck and his body surrounding her with warmth.

I could sleep that way every night.

"Well?" His gaze shifted impatiently to her.

"Nature's calling and I can't take care of that by the fire." She'd had to contend with a good many things being alone with a man on a trail drive. One was that Chance demanded he know where she was at all times. "I'll be back as soon as I can."

He nodded and jammed his hat on his head. "Make it quick."

Lizzie knew it was wrong, but he was just so bossy at times, that she slowed her steps just to vex him. She smiled when she heard him let out a deep exasperated sigh.

They got on the trail immediately after Lizzie had gulped down her coffee and chewed on the flour cakes Chance had whipped up on a small fry pan. The cakes filled her belly but she was sure her boots had more flavor, and she was happy to let Chance know his cooking skills weren't up to snuff.

He barely looked at her, not even to defend himself against her accusation.

They stopped for lunch and it was a short affair, eating and watering the horses before heading out again. Chance pushed the herd hard riding point and only doubled back once to check on her, before resuming his position at the head. He was trying to make up for lost time, but something told her that his foul mood had to do with the way they spent last night, lying together.

They drove the herd along a long narrow river, a tributary of the mighty Colorado, the sun beaming overhead late in the afternoon. Chance surprised her when he pulled up on one of the rented mares beside her. "We'll stop here."

"So soon? We've got another hour of daylight." And wasn't he the one who'd been a big ole grouch this morning, making her feel like she'd been the reason they got off to a late start?

"We're making good enough time today. Setting up camp a little early won't hurt anything."

Lizzie looked at him, baffled. "You sure do change your mind a lot. And they say women are the ones who dither."

"There's fish jumping in that river and I'm hankering for a hot meal."

The idea of eating something besides dried beef and beans brought joy to her heart. She'd agree to just about anything to have a warm tasty meal on her plate and halting the drive before sunset wouldn't be a hardship at all. "You catch them and I'll cook them."

"That's what I intend to do." He smiled and tipped his hat before riding off.

"Well, if that isn't the darnedest thing," she said,

grateful to see something besides a scowl on his face. Why, he was like a boy playing hooky, going fishing and looking mighty eager about it.

They made camp twenty yards from the river and while Lizzie built a fire and watched over the herd nearby Chance gathered up what he needed and sat down on a boulder a few feet away. She watched him fashion a fishing pole out of a sturdy tree branch, a rope he meticulously unraveled to a fine string and a fish hook. "That's Grandpa's, isn't it?"

Chance spared her a glance. "He's a smart man, giving me this hook. I should've thought of it myself."

The thought of her grandfather put an ache in her heart. She couldn't wait to get back home with money enough to see him get proper medical care. There had to be treatments for consumption in city hospitals. She'd planned on convincing Grandpa to go, just as soon as she returned.

"He taught me how to fish," Lizzie said. "Sometimes just him and me would take the day and go fishing. I wasn't at all squeamish about hooking the worms." She grinned. "Most girls wouldn't go near them."

Chance sent her a nod, his head down concentrating on the task. "Never knew a woman who liked worms."

"I, uh, guess I'm not like most women." That much was true. She wasn't the sort of girl who could turn Chance Worth's head. She wasn't full of frills and lace. She didn't do her hair up pretty in fancy chignons. Most days she tied her unruly strands into a braid to keep them out of her way. Lizzie didn't dream up ways to act girly and delicate to impress a man. She'd grown up doing what was practical, what needed doing.

Chance met her gaze. "That's not such a bad thing."

But before she could respond to what she hoped was a compliment he stood and tested out his simple fishing pole, casting the line out and bringing it back. "Gotta hope this brings us a good meal. I'll be back shortly."

He walked away and she watched him until he reached the riverbed. With a sigh, she turned around and got out the supplies she needed to make coffee and heat some beans, praying dried beef was off the menu tonight.

Once all those chores were done, Lizzie took stock of the herd, counting heads as it was her job to do. It wasn't a hard task at all, being that the herd was small and they hadn't lost a single one. All thirty-one heads were accounted for. Next she checked on the string of horses, feeding each one a carrot. They'd been reliable horses and giving them a treat along the way was a welcome reward.

When she got back to the camp, she found Chance coming up from the river with three fish dangling from a string. "You caught some!"

He lifted them up and grinned. His mood had certainly changed from this morning. "Gonna have a feast tonight."

"They're a good size."

"You should've seen the one that got away. I had it hooked for a second and was pulling it in, but the dang thing flipped and flopped so hard it unhooked itself and dropped back into the water."

She laughed. "You've got enough for both of us and then some."

"I'm hungry enough to eat a bear."

He sat down cross-legged and Lizzie put a dish under

him and watched as he gutted the fish with his knife. "You eat fish heads?"

Her stomach clenched at the notion. She hooked the worms. She'd gutted her share of fish, but eating those heads was one thing that made her shudder. She'd never go near the eyeballs. They were enough to frighten the devil. "No. They're all yours."

"I don't like them, either." He tossed all three heads a far distance away and his eyes met hers in amusement.

She watched as he split the fish down the spine and spread them open. He filleted them with a steady hand and then gave them over to Lizzie. She put them in the fry pan and walked over to the fire.

As she cooked them up, Chance laid down against his saddle with his hands braced behind his head. His eyes closed and a look of sheer contentment crossed over his handsome face. "Smells like heaven on earth."

"Gonna taste like heaven, too."

"When we get to town, we'll have us a real fine meal—chicken and dumplings, or steak and sweet potatoes and cherry pie or apple strudel. The hotel's got a very fine dining room."

"Hotel? I don't think we should be spending so much cash on hotel meals. We're gonna need every cent."

"We won't. I will. And don't go worrying over it now."

She wouldn't worry. The idea of having a real meal in a hotel dining room with Chance set her nerves to jingling and her heart to pumping harder. Tonight, he was downright agreeable and that put her in a good mood, too.

"You're gonna take me for a fancy meal?"

His eyes opened halfway and he slid her a glance. "Long as you don't give me any trouble."

She opened her mouth to argue. She hadn't given him a lick of trouble while on this trip and he knew it but she didn't want to spoil his good humor. She quite simply announced, "I'm no trouble."

And Chance closed his eyes again, his smile never fading.

She finished frying the fish and cooking beans and dished up their portions on tin plates. They sat by the glow of the fire as the sunset colored the horizon with pink-orange hues.

"So good," she said, taking a bite of fish.

"Can't argue there."

He sat next to her, devouring the meal. She watched his throat work as he chewed. There was something so elemental and male about it. She'd spent a good deal of time close to him and she could honestly say there wasn't anything about his physical being she could find fault with. He was perfect in that respect and when his mood was light, she couldn't find any fault with him at all.

Now, *that* was enough to cause her concern.

Chance ate two fish and Lizzie could barely finish the one on her plate. "I'm so full." She gave her stomach a pat and sighed. "Don't think I can eat another bite."

Chance grinned. "You can't? Now, that's too bad. 'Cause I got some dessert and it's a darn shame you're too full of fish to have a bite."

"What dessert? What are you talking about?" Lizzie hoisted up from her lazy position against her saddle.

Chance rose and walked over to the supply bag. He

pushed his hand deep down to the bottom and pulled out a small sack. "Remember when we bought supplies?"

Lizzie blinked. She'd forgotten all about the candies he'd purchased the day he'd offered her a licorice stick. "You've had candies in there all this time?"

Chance grinned. "I thought the storm might have ruined them, but they were tucked inside snug and dry."

He walked over to the fire and sat down by his saddle. He dug into the bag, coming up with a handful of candied corn. He plopped one into his mouth and chewed, sighing, his face filled with contentment she'd only seen when he'd consumed something sugary. "It ain't cherry pie but my sweet tooth doesn't know the difference."

Lizzie looked longingly at the candies in his hand. "You had those and you haven't brought them out until now?"

"Uh-huh." He popped another into his mouth.

"Mercy me. Why not?"

"Always better to wait until the end of the drive. Gives me something to look forward to. Sort of like a reward."

"Well, that takes strength of will." Her mouth watered. She was sure there was room in her belly for a few of those confections.

"I must have that," he said, chewing still, "for putting up with—"

She glared at him. "Putting up with what?"

"—eating dust. Bad weather and all." He grinned and the amusement reached his eyes. He was teasing and Lizzie couldn't pretend to be mad at him. He was too darn happy with himself.

"I guess I could find room in my belly for a few of those if you'd be offering."

"You sure? I mean a little thing like you…"

But by that time, Chance had already extended his hand. She picked three out and tossed one in her mouth. She chewed slowly, savoring the flavor. The sweetness of the candy burst forth and made her lips pucker. Chance watched her carefully, studying her in the firelight.

After she finished the first candy, she stared toward the fire. "Thank you."

"Welcome."

"Not just for the candy, Chance. But for last night. For keeping me from freezing my toes off."

"You need your toes."

"You were kind."

She heard him shift around to face her. "That always surprises you, doesn't it?"

She shrugged, chewing on her second piece of candy. This time the sweetness went straight to her head. "Not so much anymore."

"Fine, then…. I'm not your enemy. We've established that fact."

"But I just wish you wouldn't see me as a little thing. I'm a woman, aren't I? I mean, I've got everything a woman is supposed to have and last night when you touched me…"

He spoke with quiet conviction. "It wasn't that kind of touching, Lizzie."

"But I felt…something."

Chance's face twisted and he shook his head. "You weren't supposed to feel anything but warmth. If you did, it's not by my doing."

"You're lying. You felt something, too. I was touching your chest and your heartbeats went a little crazy. I felt it."

He muttered a curse and then heaved a sigh. "Lord above, Lizzie. You've got to learn not to say those things to a man."

"You denying it?"

"Hell, yeah. I'm denying it. Look, it's just a natural occurrence when a man and woman share a blanket for him to get…for his body to get a little…"

"Excited?"

Chance went still and closed his eyes. He contemplated for a few seconds, before turning to face her. He brought his hand up to cup her chin and directed her gaze to meet with his deep brown eyes. They were so dark, so beautiful, she thought, as her eyes widened and they locked stares. He was close, just inches from her face. Her nerves jangled once again, her stomach fluttered uncontrollably, yet she was patient, waiting for him to say something.

He blinked, losing his focus for a moment as if he'd been mesmerized. Then the warmth and heat went out of his eyes. He spoke quietly, firmly, all softness gone. "I've got two things to do on this drive. And you know what they are. To bring the herd to the railhead and to keep you safe. That's it. That's my job and I aim to do just that. Last night was about keeping you safe."

"So you don't think of me as a woman? You don't think I have any pleasing attributes?"

Chance dropped his hand and leaned back. "You have the prettiest eyes I've ever seen in my life, Lizzie."

Joy spread through her body. "Really?"

Chance faced the dying fire and nodded. Picking up

a dried branch, he tossed it into the embers and watched the flame spark to life again. "But that doesn't mean anything."

"It means more than you know," she whispered, breathless. She'd never wanted a man's approval more than right now. She'd never cared about such things before. Her heart and soul had always been on the ranch and her love of fashioning dolls. She'd never entertained thoughts of being with a man, that's why Grandpa's attempts at matchmaking had never inspired even a kernel of interest. "To a girl like me, who's never been overly…female."

Chance turned from the fire to search her face. Then he dropped his gaze to her chest. She didn't have much there, but her breasts were round and firm and she wondered if they'd please him enough and bring him pleasure. The very notion caused her face to flame. An ache below her belly throbbed and it was uncanny how potent that feeling was. Chance's gaze flowed over her, flickering at the juncture of her thighs, right where she pulsed. Could he know? Could he sense her lusty thoughts?

"Look, Lizzie. You're female enough to hold a man. That'll happen one day. Maybe soon."

"But not you?"

He didn't hesitate to shake his head. "Could never be me."

A cold shot of pain coursed through her body, dashing out the flames that had warmed her seconds ago. "Why?"

Chance inhaled deep. "You're Edward's granddaughter."

As if that explained it all, Chance rose and set his

blanket a far distance from hers. "Get some sleep. I'll watch over the herd tonight."

And then he was gone.

Chapter Seven

Prescott, the territorial capitol of Arizona, was laid out in a square that Lizzie could see from a hill that overlooked the town. Streets were planned out in orderly fashion, almost the whole of the town looking like one neat box. She saw a whitewashed chapel's steeple bordering the town to the west, several ornate fountains decorating the central part of town and a big steel water tank on the eastern border.

Lizzie felt a sense of accomplishment that she'd made it this far. The pit of her stomach filled with hope. Coming to town meant the end of the trail drive. It meant a hot bath and the fancy meal Chance had promised her. Her belly grumbled at the thought, but more important than all that, Lizzie would earn the money she desperately needed.

As she made her way through tall grass and scattered Ponderosa pines riding flank to the herd, Chance rode up beside her.

Lizzie glanced at him. "Looks like a peaceful town."

The corners of Chance's mouth pulled down. "Can't be sure."

"Why?"

He squinted into the morning light and shook his head. "Can't ever be sure. Things aren't always what they seem. Best you remember that."

Lizzie was tired of getting a lecture from Chance every time she made a pleasant comment. Chance didn't hold much trust in things, she was learning. Maybe he had a right to his opinions, but Lizzie didn't see dark all the time. She didn't have such a suspicious nature.

They pushed the cattle forward, coming down from the rise in slight degrees and Lizzie was suddenly dumbstruck when a pink brick building caught her attention. Pink bricks? If that didn't beat all and make her case, that truly, sometimes things were as bright as they appeared. "I've never seen such a colorful structure in my life."

"That'd be the courthouse."

"A pink courthouse," Lizzie said with a sigh.

Chance stared at her, probably because he hadn't seen her so whimsical before. Then his face creased and they shared a sudden smile. A warm feeling spread through her body until Chance's smile faded and he shifted his focus toward town. She followed his gaze to the railroad tracks.

"The Arizona Central's new to Prescott. Been here six months. Good thing, too. Most of the mines in the area shut down."

"How do you know?"

"It's been awhile, but I've been here before. Dunston owned a silver mine or two. He sold out when the getting was good. Most folks abandoned the town, but the ones still living here turned to raising cattle. There's a stockyard about half a mile to the east of town. We'll sell the cattle to brokers there and be done with it."

Be done with it.

Meaning, he'd be done with her.

Chance had been somewhat surly ever since the night they spent together under the sheets. He'd forbidden any more talk about it, making her promise not to tell a soul. Since then he'd kept a good distance from her, making small conversation whenever she would start up, but he kept quiet most of the time otherwise.

Lizzie didn't mind the quiet overly much, except when her mind would wander. Out on the trail, there was nothing much else to do but let your mind drift off. And often her thoughts turned to Chance. She'd never been so close to a man before, she reminded herself. Her queasy feelings would eventually ebb. They had to. If Chance chose to move on when they got back home, Lizzie wouldn't miss him. She just plain wouldn't. Thank goodness, Hayden was coming home. At least, she'd have her friend back. With him, she didn't have to worry about queasy feelings.

When they reached the stockyard, she noted the place was nearly deserted. The majority of holding pens were empty. No cattlemen were milling about. She wondered if this was normal for Prescott. Chance said the railway had just been built here.

An uneasy feeling gnawed at her. She glanced at Chance, but as usual, he wasn't giving his feelings away one way or the other.

"Stay here," he said, then dismounted to close the cattle gate. He was met by a short burly man coming out of a small office. The man wore leather chaps that dragged on the ground and a tan hat on his head. Lizzie was grateful someone was around to greet them. The two men spoke for a time and she saw the man take stock of their Longhorns, count them and then give Chance the piece of parchment he'd written on. Chance headed toward her and mounted his gelding.

"I've gotta come back tomorrow," he said. "Ole Earl is the only one working here right now. It's a little late in the day. They weren't expecting anyone to show up. C'mon, let's find the hotel and get cleaned up."

"Are we going to leave the herd here?"

He nodded. "Yep."

"Did he say why the place is empty?"

"I reckon I'll find out tomorrow. Let's go."

It wasn't ten minutes before they reached the hotel. The Prescott Grand Hotel lived up to its name. The hotel was bigger and fancier than any establishment Lizzie had ever been in. She assumed its grandeur came about during the mining boom and to the proprietor's credit the place hadn't fallen to ruin since then.

As soon as Lizzie stepped over the threshold, she was hit by a sorry feeling of inadequacy. Two ladies dressed in silk gowns spared her a look of disdain before they turned their heads and walked by. Lizzie looked a mess with her rumpled dusty clothes and hair that hadn't had a good wash in days. Usually she didn't give two hoots what others thought about her, but today she couldn't get to her room fast enough to clean herself up.

She glanced at Chance, saddlebags over one shoulder, signing the register and getting the keys to their rooms. She wondered if he had anything to do with her sudden change of heart.

"Can we afford this?" she whispered as they climbed the stairs.

"I can. I'm paying."

His kindness brought queasiness upon her again.

She liked it better when Chance gave her sass. Then she had good reason to dislike him.

Chance put the key in the lock and with a shove opened the door to her hotel room.

"Oh, my." Her hand to her chest, the breath whooshed out of her. The room was everything she'd imagined for a hotel so fine. Yet, she didn't just see the fine draperies, the big bed covered with a plush quilt and the fancy furniture.... She saw comfort. Comfort like she'd not had in months, maybe years.

"Well, go on in," Chance said. She turned to look at him. "Go on," he encouraged her again with a nod of his head.

She stepped inside, still speechless.

"Don't that beat all," he announced, his lips curving upward. "All it takes to keep you quiet is a fancy room. Wish I'd have known that before this."

Lizzie snapped out of her daze to frown at him. "You're not amusing, Chance Worth." But she didn't put much stock in her reprimand. Not while tiny flutters of happiness skittered around her insides.

He grinned and those flutters turned to wide-winged butterflies. "I'll be right next door. They're bringing up water for our baths." He handed her a saddlebag. "I'll see you in an hour and we'll eat."

Before Chance closed the door, he said, "Don't go anywhere. Stay put until I come get you."

Lizzie couldn't muster an argument for his bossy tone. She nodded and then he was gone.

* * *

Lizzie peeled herself out of her clothes and walked to the alcove where a bathtub sat behind a tall screen. The sweet scent of lilac wafted in the air and beckoned her. She didn't need much encouraging. She'd been itching for this for days. She poked one foot into the water, then the other. Heavens, the initial sensation shot up her legs and coursed through her naked body.

A hot bath in a real tub.

She eased her body in slowly, relishing the rising steam that engulfed her. She savored every inch of heat searing through her skin as she sunk farther and farther down. It was heavenly to stretch out and let the water soothe her aches from days on the trail. She felt herself melting, and the relaxing of stiff limbs to nothingness was a sensation Lizzie would forever remember. Fully immersed now, she tossed her head back to wet her hair. The thick mass was usually difficult to scrub, but the soaps provided made her task all the more easy.

She stayed in the tub for the better part of the hour with eyes closed, allowing herself this special time to simply be. All worries left her mind. She gave in to the pure joy of the soak. Heat and steam. Relaxation and comfort.

She heard the hotel door creak open. "Who's there?" Bathwater sloshed out as she scrambled to a sitting position.

"It's me, Lizzie."

Chance? He'd let himself inside the room?

"Don't come in!" Panicked, she held her breath and prayed he'd heed her warning and not come any farther. She grabbed for a towel and listened. His footsteps quieted.

"You've got ten minutes," he said, from behind the screen. "Be ready or I'm eating without you."

"You could've knocked."

He didn't answer. She heard the door shut. Her mood soured. Not only had he given her a fright, he'd come for her early.

She muttered an unholy oath, lifted up from the water and stepped out of the tub. Using the thick towel, she dried off, breathing in the pleasing scent of lilac on her skin. She whipped her hair back and forth then up and down to hasten drying. Her hair was such a nuisance. How often she'd thought of chopping it off, but Grandpa loved her hair this long so Lizzie endured it.

As she walked past the screen to grab her clothes from the saddlebag, something on the edge of the bed caught her eye. Curious, she walked over to it and stared at the brown paper package tied up with twine. There wasn't a note. Not that Lizzie needed one. Chance had put it there.

"What on earth?" She wasted no time unraveling the twine and the wrapping immediately fell away, leaving her to gawk at a pretty cotton dress with lacy sleeves and neckline, the material patterned with tiny blue and white flowers. "Heavens."

She pulled the dress up to see its full length and examined the fine detail. Having made miniature clothing for her dolls, Lizzie regarded the perfectly sewn stitches and the form of the dress, which was just the right size for her slender frame. Choking back emotion, tears brimmed over her eyes. She felt moisture trickle down her cheeks and all ill feelings she held for Chance disappeared into the air. Closing her eyes, she hugged the dress to her chest and clung on dearly. This was a kindness she couldn't doubt or disparage. For all his grouchy ways, Lizzie couldn't fault Chance for anything at the moment. Warmth filled her heart and she pulled the dress away from her body to look at it once again.

Giddy with anticipation, she slipped on her undergarments and donned the dress over her head. Setting her arms into the sleeves, she smoothed the rest of the dress over her hips until the hem flowed to the floor. She whirled around to look at her reflection in the full-length mirror. The dress swished in waves before settling on her shape. It was a simple calico, made of spun cotton, yet Lizzie felt pretty wearing it. Well, as pretty as she could feel, being Lizzie Mitchell.

Her mama used to say a smile could brighten even the darkest of days. And far too often lately, Lizzie felt dark and desolate inside. She'd felt as if her life was slipping away with no hope in sight. The feelings overwhelmed her at times. The dress and the thought behind it gave her a smidgen of that hope back. Maybe circumstances would get better at the ranch. Maybe Grandpa would recover and life would get back to normal.

Her lips lifted. Then a full-fledged happy smile broke through and suddenly Lizzie felt light as a feather. She smiled and smiled and you'd think she would've drifted heavenward as weightless as she felt.

Coming back down to earth, she remembered the time and hurried the rest of her grooming. She combed fingers through her hair, threading the damp strands back and using twine left from the package to tie a bow. With no time to braid her hair, she left it loose and slipped her feet into boots she'd taken a moment to rub clean. She was grateful the dress had ample length to cover them.

This time when Chance knocked on the door Lizzie was ready for him. She opened the door, her face beaming, and her first thought was how handsome he looked. Clean shaven—she'd almost forgotten what he looked like without dark stubble on his face—and wearing a new red shirt, he stole the very breath from her lungs.

Chance looked her up and down for second or two, and then nodded. "Thought so."

Baffled, she stared at him. She hadn't expected claims to her beauty or his undying love, but this greeting wiped the smile from her lips. She angled her head. "Pardon?"

"The dress matches your eyes."

On the trail, he'd told her she had pretty eyes. Had he picked the dress to match her eyes? Her pulse raced at the thought of him being considerate.

"It's, uh…. It's a fine dress." Her throat could barely work now. "Thank you."

"Welcome."

"I'll find a way to repay you."

He spared her an impatient glance. "No need."

"It was a very kind gesture, Chance. I appreciate—"

"Don't go appreciating me too much," he said quietly. "Nothing in your saddlebag was fitting for the hotel's dining room. Besides, those dingy colors you wear all the time are downright depressing."

She struggled to keep her mouth from gaping open.

"You hungry?" he asked, taking her elbow and leading her out the doorway. He made sure her door was locked. "I'm starved. You won't be disappointed in the meal."

Her shoulders slumped and what was left of her good cheer melted away. That weightless feeling that lifted her up moments ago plummeted like an iron anchor tossed into the sea. "No, I, uh, I don't suppose I will be."

Her disappointment wouldn't have anything to do with the food tonight.

Chance had managed to dishearten her all on his own.

Chance tried his best to ignore Lizzie sitting across from him in the hotel dining room. He called himself ten times a fool for giving her that dress to wear. For putting a big, brilliant smile on her face and worse yet, putting hope into her heart. He didn't like the way she'd been looking at him when she opened the door. Lizzie wasn't a doe-eyed female with ulterior intentions like Marissa, Alistair's stepdaughter. That girl had been pursuing him since the minute she'd laid eyes on him, back at the Duncan spread. No, Lizzie wasn't manipulative in that way yet she could cause him just as much trouble with those blue-as-sky eyes and that soft look on her face.

Chance wasn't courting her. No, sir.

She was his job. His debt to pay a man for saving his life and he was glad to do it for Edward.

When they'd ridden into town today he'd caught sight of the dress shop and the impulse struck him to do something for Lizzie. Wasn't much at all. Just a dress. He'd seen the extent of her wardrobe, and none of the clothes were fitting for a fancy meal in a fine hotel. Hell, the girl was probably headed for a rough road ahead, with her only kin dying right before her eyes and her argumentative nature giving little hope for landing herself a husband.

The end of the trail always put fool ideas into his head. Like the time he'd bet Morey Dunphy that he could outlast him in a drinking contest. Or the time he'd kissed his week's pay goodbye on a horse race. Then there was the time he'd been dared to tame a wild stallion and nearly broke his neck doing it.

Yep, gifting Lizzie Mitchell a pretty blue dress that made her eyes look like two sapphire gems, well, that was probably the dumbest thing he'd ever done at the end of a trail drive.

She was quiet now, not saying much, pushing food around on her delicately patterned plate. Overhead, a twelve-candle chandelier flickered, casting the table in a soft glow. In truth, even with Chance in his just-bought red shirt and trousers and Lizzie in her calico dress, they were under-adorned for such surroundings. But he knew the food was top caliber and his stomach won out over any sense of decorum. Besides, Lizzie, for some odd reason, seemed to look just right in this place.

"The steak's pretty good," he said, annoyed by the silence.

"Hmm. Delicious."

"How would you know, you haven't taken a bite yet?"

"Surprised you noticed."

She had her head down with a pout on her lips.

"I notice things, Lizzie."

She refused to meet his eyes.

"You had two bites of the corn dumplings. And you buttered your bread."

She snapped her head up and he was struck again by the beauty of her eyes. He should be used to seeing those eyes landing on him by now, but the hue of the dress made them look an even brighter and deeper blue, like the depths of a rushing river. Chance flinched from the shock.

"Why'd you do it, Chance? Spend money on me and give me a new dress?"

Ah, hell. He should've been happy with her silence.

"I told you why," he answered with a shrug.

"Because you think I'm a poor excuse for a woman?"

"No. I told you." He held on to his patience. Lizzie needed her feathers soothed. "I saw the dress in the shop and thought you might find use for it tonight."

"Because you find my clothes sorely lacking?"

Yes. He deliberately didn't answer. He wouldn't let her goad him into a fight.

"You know I can't afford fine clothes, Chance," she said, color rising to her cheeks. Her anger only made her eyes appear more vivid. "If I could and things were better, I wouldn't be on the trail with the likes of you."

Her insult didn't do him injury. "Exactly my point. I thought you'd find good use for a new dress."

She didn't seem to hear him. Her voice was hot with accusation. "I don't rightly care that my clothes depress you."

Oh, for Pete's sake. This was a female trap. Chance recognized it from years of dealing with women. She said she didn't care, but everything else about her said she did. You'd have thought he'd tarred and feathered her instead of done something nice.

"You look pretty tonight, Lizzie. Is that what you want me to say? With your eyes so brilliant and your hair clean and curly, falling down your back, you're the prettiest thing in this fancy room. There's two men over there at the corner table looking at you and I swear, if they stare one more minute, I'm gonna have to get up from my seat and make them put their eyes back in their heads. There now, I said it. Satisfied?"

Chance blinked and mentally cursed himself for being a fool.

Lizzie blinked, too, stunned by his outburst. The crystal water glass she held froze in midair as she darted a glance at the two men in the corner. She noted them indeed watching her. She turned back to him in true astonishment. The strong pull of her eyes sucked him in and he got lost in them. They stared at each other for a long time.

Then a wide smile spread across her face. "Really? You'd do that?"

Chance frowned, unhappy that he'd spoken the truth. At any other time Lizzie's smile could infect him but tonight, he couldn't afford the luxury of letting her get too close. He'd been alone with her on the trail and it hadn't been as easy as he'd hoped to keep his thoughts pure. "Forget it."

Lizzie set down her crystal water glass with infinite care and looked him square in the eyes. She spoke on a whispered breath. "If I live to be ninety, I'll never forget you said that."

Chance stared at her. His mouth was creased tight. He shook his head at his own calamity, but Lizzie didn't seem to notice. Her mood brightened and from then on, she chattered incessantly. He didn't know the girl had so much to talk about, but she filled his ear until it was time for dessert.

Lizzie ordered tea cakes and hot cocoa, claiming she'd never had either before. Chance had vastly more experience with desserts than Lizzie, but his tastes never strayed far from cherry pie or apple cobbler. Tonight he chose the pie with a dollop of cream.

Afterward, Lizzie said, "I'm so full I swear I won't eat another bite for days."

"Seems I've heard that somewhere before." Chance grabbed his dainty coffee cup and swallowed down the contents in one hearty gulp.

"This time I truly mean it. Everything was delicious, Chance."

Lizzie had that look in her eye again. A warning shiver ran up and down his body. "You want to turn in? It's getting late."

"I suppose." Lizzie sighed and leaned back, rolling her shoulders and stretching her body like a contented cat. Her chin came up to expose the slender recesses of her throat.

Chance swallowed and looked away. Unfortunately he met the gaze of the two men still gawking at Lizzie. Blood boiling, he sent them a cold glare and rose from his seat, keeping his eyes trained on them as he set his hat on his head. They had the good sense to change the focus of their attention. He tossed cash down on the table and then took Lizzie's elbow, helping her rise. He escorted her out of the dining room. "I'm in need of a drink."

"But we just had—"

"Not that kind of a drink, Lizzie. If I deposit you in your room, I need your promise you'll stay put all night."

Her arm tensed under his hand. "You're locking me away?"

"Keeping you safe."

She pulled her elbow out of his grip with a yank.

Her eyes sparked with blue fire. "You're going to the saloon?"

It wasn't any of her concern what he did the rest of the night. Chance kept on walking until he reached the carpeted staircase in the lobby. "That's what men do at the end of a drive."

Lizzie was a step behind. Quickly, she caught up. "I… What about what women do at the end of a drive?"

Chance wasn't in the mood for her petulance. He was attracted to her, which baffled him to no end. Seeing two suited men with bowler hats show her some interest knocked something loose inside that gnawed at him. "I don't rightly know, I've never been on a drive with a gal. I suppose they go to their rooms and sleep."

"I'm not promising you that I will."

Those same two men who'd been staring at her, walked past and Lizzie turned her head with an upturned chin to smile at them.

Blood pounded in his skull at her stupidity. She'd defied him deliberately. He circled his hands around her arms and brought her up close. They were almost nose to nose. Her eyes grew wide. He lowered his voice to a rasp wrought with warning. "Don't be a fool, Lizzie. You're in a strange town. You don't know what the night will bring."

The fire in Lizzie's eyes died and her body went limp. She gazed at him and spoke with a plea in her voice. "I could say the same to you, Chance. You're a stranger here. What if…what if…" Her voice trailed off and a fearful look stole over her expression.

The scent of lilac filled his nostrils, calming his temper some. She had a look on her face now that beckoned his protective urges. What was she saying? That she cared about him and worried over him? No one had cared for his safety in a long time. Actually, the last person to do so was her grandfather.

His hands fell away and he took a step back. He couldn't go soft on her. She had enough to lose already and he was trying to protect her from more harm. The saloon enticed him with mind-numbing whiskey and the attentions of a saloon girl who wasn't an innocent, a woman who could satisfy his lust enough to keep his impure thoughts of Lizzie at bay.

"You doubt I can take care of myself?"

She shook her head without much commitment. "No, it's not that."

"Then what is it?" He folded his arms across his chest and waited for her explanation.

Her face flamed and she struggled, but finally she said her piece. "I don't want you to…to…to lie with a woman tonight."

Chance inhaled sharp. Sometimes, Lizzie truly amazed him. Only Lizzie would be so honest. Only Lizzie would shed her pride to admit something like that.

"That's what you were gonna do," she said, searching his eyes now.

Chance wouldn't deny it, but he wouldn't speak the words, either. He, too, didn't know what the night would bring. He stared at his boots, trying to choose the right words. "Lizzie, you and me…you can't go thinking…"

"I…don't. But you gifted me the dress and then we had a fine meal."

"We halfway argued through it."

"Seems to be what we do," she said. Sometimes,

Lizzie made a world of sense. "Tonight, I forgot about my troubles, Chance. It was kinda nice."

He snapped his head up to find eyes filled with both hope and desperation. He couldn't rightly ignore her plea. "I'll make you a deal. You go on up to your room. And I'll go over to the saloon for a drink. *Only* a drink. I'll knock on your door to let you know I'm back."

She sent him the small sweet smile she usually reserved for her grandfather. It shot his lust for a saloon girl to hell. He turned her toward the stairs and put a hand to her lower back. "Come on, I'll walk you to the room."

They climbed the stairs together and he put the key into the lock then pushed the door open. She entered and turned to face him with those bluer-than-blue eyes, looking pretty enough to make him forget his good sense.

"Lock your door, Lizzie," he ordered, reaching for the doorknob. The door whispered shut with his pull, blocking out her image. From behind the door, Lizzie turned the lock and Chance tried it once to make sure it was secure. Then he whipped off his hat, scrubbed his forehead and the headache developing there, figuring he'd not only earned himself a shot of whiskey, he deserved the whole dang bottle.

Chapter Eight

Sunshine poked its way into Lizzie's room, disrupting her sleep. The warmth spread through her and she rebelled against the morning by refusing to open her eyes. A feather-down mattress and soft sheets cradled her aching body in a cocoon of comfort granting her the best sleep of her life.

She raised her arms over her head and pointed her toes, elongating her body in a taut rejuvenating stretch. Her muscles cried with relief. She wiggled her toes and grinned. A sigh escaped from deep within her and her entire body relaxed. She had every intention of curling back into the luxury of the bed, when a knock sounded at her door.

"Lizzie, it's me."

She sat up. Her eyes popped open and she squinted from the sunlight streaming in. "Chance? Oh, uh, just a second. I'm not dressed."

She bounded up quickly and stubbed her little toe on the edge of the bed. "Ouch!"

"Lizzie, I'm waitin'."

She rubbed her toe. "I'm coming," she called out. She glanced at the wall clock as it chimed the nine o'clock hour. Heavens, was it really that late? For all her days, she couldn't remember another time when she'd slept this long.

Chance paced behind the door and knocked again. "How long's it take to get dressed?"

Lizzie washed her face and grabbed at the dress lying on the silk screen. Still a bit groggy, she fumbled with it, but managed to finally slip it over her head. Smoothing the gown out with haste, next she ran her fingers through her hair. Chance wouldn't wait much longer. They had to get to the stockyards and see about the herd. With any luck, they'd be on their way home before noon.

"Lizzie," he said, impatient, just as she yanked open the door.

"What?" Seeing Chance first thing in the morning wasn't a hardship, no matter how much she denied it. For one moment, she forgot she was mad as a hatter at him.

He strode into her room, taking the hat from his head. His eyes immediately went to the now-empty bed and the tangled sheets. "I see you slept like a hog in heaven."

"I did not!" He dared compare her to a hog.

He grinned.

"Wipe that silly smile off your face, Chance. You lied to me."

Chance's eyes narrowed to slits and his tone grew serious. "Don't be calling me a liar, Lizzie."

Her chin came up. "I will. We made a deal last night.

Bet you forgot your promise the second you walked out of the hotel."

He folded his arms across his chest and spoke with enough confidence to confuse her. "You'd lose that bet, Lizzie."

"You didn't knock on my door last night."

"That's where you're wrong. I knocked."

She'd waited for his knock. Each minute that had ticked by crushed her with disappointment. Finally, she'd slid into the comfort of the bed, waiting like a fool, for Chance to live up to his part of the bargain. "Well, I didn't hear anything."

Chance put his hands on his hips, peering at her as if she were a child needing a good reprimand. "That's because you were sleeping the sleep of the dead. I knocked, just like I said. Twice. I heard you snoring, so I walked off and went to bed."

"I don't snore, Chance Worth."

"You make noise when you sleep, Lizzie. And that's a fact. Same thing happened this morning. I came to get you. I knocked a few times."

Her eyes widened. She vaguely remembered hearing something like a bump or a knock as she dozed this morning, but she'd put it out of her hazy mind and gone back to sleep. Dawning awareness crept in, replacing her disappointment. The bed had been heaven to sink into last night and she might have drifted off quicker than she recalled. "You were here this morning? Why?"

"I came to get you. We had heifers to sell, remember?"

"Of course, I remember. I just… I just slept a little late. We can go now." Lizzie turned and grabbed her boots. She sat on the rumpled bed, and lifted one boot to her foot.

"There's no need to go now. I've already gone."

Startled by his triumphant tone, she asked, "What? You went without me?"

"I sure did and it's a good thing, too. Met a cattle broker eager to buy the entire herd. Seems the big sale they'd expected this week didn't happen. One of the herds ran into trouble along the trail. That's why the stockyard was empty yesterday. Bad news for them. Good news for us."

Lizzie lifted off the bed, her heart beating like crazy. "How is it good news? Tell me, Chance. Tell me!"

Chance pulled a paper from his vest pocket. He took his time unfolding it. Lizzie grabbed the note from his hand and quickly read the bill of sale. The calculations jumped off the page. Those numbers were all she noticed. She stared at them, then her entire body began shaking, her hands trembling so badly she could hardly hold on to the note. "But, but… This is three dollars a head more than we expected!"

Chance nodded with a broad smile. "Yep, it is. All we need is your signature."

This meant a whole new beginning for the ranch, for her and most importantly for her grandfather. Tears stung behind her eyes and a burden lifted from her shoulders. She flung the note aside and bounded straight into Chance's arms. "We did it! We did it, Chance."

Chance didn't return her embrace at first, but Lizzie clung to him, not caring a dang bit about her display. Then a rumble of pure laughter rose up from his throat and his arms came around her waist. Her senses heightened. His soapy-fresh scent wafted down as he held her to his chest. She laughed, too, and felt herself being lifted from the ground and twirled into a wide circle until her toes came off the floor and her gown flowed in a moon-shaped arch. Her heart swelling with joy, when her feet hit the ground again she stared into Chance's eyes. Lifting herself up, she pressed half a dozen kisses to his cheeks murmuring, "Thank you. Thank you. Thank you."

Chance had a smile on his face, too, but his expression changed with that last peck to his cheek. It was a look she'd not seen on him before. His lips straightened to a fine line. His gaze, fastened to her mouth now, turned molten like steaming hot molasses. Every nerve jolted in awareness and pure desire bubbled up inside her. She shivered with a need too powerful to ignore. She wouldn't stop to think about what she was doing. She wrapped her arms around his neck and lifted up again, brushing her mouth to his cheek once more, slowly this time, savoring the taste of him on her lips, drinking in the feel of his taut skin and manly stubble, breathing in the subtle scent of earth and soap. His name whispered from her throat. "Chance."

She stood poised there, with her lips so close to his mouth, her heart beating nearly through her chest. His hand came up to her head and he spread fingers through her hair. He made a sound, a low, deep guttural groan right before he turned his head toward her mouth. Their lips hovered dangerously close.

Kiss me, Chance. Kiss me like a man would kiss a woman.

"Lizzie," he rasped. "Don't tempt me like this."

She gazed into his eyes and he seemed lost, searching. For a measure of time, she feared he would reject her. Feared that he would back away with a reprimand. She prayed it wasn't so. His hand tightened in her hair and he lifted her face ever closer as he bent his head down to her. Anticipation swarmed in her belly. He inhaled a sharp breath and then his lips bore down on her mouth.

His mouth was rough on hers, like a thirsty man who couldn't get enough to drink. He held her tight, giving her no choice to deny him, no choice but to kiss him back. It was heaven, being in his arms, having him devour her this way. His body pressed close. His big hand wove through her hair. The swarming in her belly grew intense. Tiny impulses prickled her below the waist. She'd never met with these sensations before. She'd never been kissed before. She didn't know for certain if what she was experiencing was normal or expected. There was so much she didn't know.

Yet kissing him this way and pleasuring him seemed natural. It seemed right. Instincts took over and her body surrendered to Chance. She would give him anything he asked. Her spirit was buoyed by the notion and her kisses deepened with his urging.

"Lord above, Lizzie," he whispered between kisses and then something miraculous happened. Something powerful and unexpected. Chance parted her lips and as her mouth fell open, he drove his tongue inside. The first brushing of their tongues shot through her like a jolt of lightning. The impact was startling, a new revelation, and Lizzie experienced a sense of womanhood, maybe for the first time in her life. Stirrings gripped and surprised her. A tiny moan of gratification escaped her throat and Chance immediately drew her up closer, telling her the sound had pleased him. Her dress rustled against his trousers as an achingly slow pressure began to build below her waist. Her bosom swelled, making her nipples bud to upturned peaks. Even through the layers of their clothes, the intimate position spurred a sense of femininity and desire.

While she was soft as jelly, Chance's body grew hard. His thighs were unyielding as they brushed hers, his chest, a wall of power. His mouth, though, was giving even in his boldness as he took liberties with her. She wouldn't think to refuse him. Not when he brought her such immense, unexpected pleasure. His tongue probed the hollow depths of her mouth and she welcomed the intrusion. Their tongues met and danced and entwined, enveloping her in a lusty frenzy that spun her mind. Dictated by her body's impulses, she moved closer. A stampede of tingles pricked her skin and the pressure building inside intensified until Lizzie's legs could barely hold her upright. She wobbled, but Chance gripped her tight against him, protecting her from the fall.

Their hips smacked against each other and he let out a helpless groan. Lizzie's pulse raced and her breathing defied nature. Chance struggled to keep a distance between them, but Lizzie pressed herself to him once again. Her female instincts, ones she could not yet fully describe, took over her body. A need grew and the unrequited throbbing frightened her some, but at the same time, made her wish for more and more.

Chance took that moment to release her mouth from the kiss and the loss was almost too much to bear. She caught her breath and so did he, then his lips moved over her chin to brush more kisses to the underside of her throat. His hair brushed her chin and tickled her there, but she didn't giggle. No, she could only breathe in his soap scent and fill her nostrils with it as he worked his capable mouth down to her shoulders.

At the same time his lips moistened her skin he brought his hands around her waist and slid his palms up the sides of her torso. His thumbs caressed the outer swell of her breasts and the peaks lifted in response, straining against the gown's material.

"Chance, touch me there."

Heaven above, she hadn't meant to plead aloud. She gasped, not from humiliation but because he obeyed the command.

His lips moved along her shoulders, moistening her bare skin, while his thumbs pressed the side of her breasts. Pleasure shot clear through her. She held her breath and her pulse pounded hard against her chest. He brought his mouth achingly close to the top swell of her breasts as his thumb moved closer and closer. Anticipation grew, her nipples puckered and when his thumb flicked her pebbled peak, waves of sizzling heat scorched her belly. He rubbed her there, circling around the most sensitive area and Lizzie grew faint with need. It was as if the material hadn't provided a barrier. As if she felt his wondrous touch, skin to skin. Her entire body was attuned and waiting for more. "Oh…Chance," she whispered, her throat barely working. "Don't stop. Please."

He froze. She sucked in a breath, willing him to continue, to move his hands over her body, to kiss the very tips of her bosom as she so wanted. This time, her plea had a different effect. He appeared to have come out of a daze. His lashes lifted in several blinks and his mouth whipped away from her chest. The strong hands that had pleasured her expertly dropped to his sides. A look of recrimination stole over his features. His stare brought shivers of dread to her stomach.

He stepped back quickly, as if she'd lit him on fire. "Chance?"

There was the slightest shake of his head, a quick dismissal. Lips that had greedily taken hers, tightened to thin lines. "Go ahead and sign the note, Lizzie."

He bent to pick it up from the floor.

"Chance, you can't…you and I…we…" The sweet pleasure he'd inflicted still hummed throughout her body. She never wanted the feeling to go away.

Chance folded the note then tucked it into his pocket. "Never mind. You'll sign it at the stockyard."

"It was my first kiss," she said quietly, standing there watching him pull away from her.

He winced, his face twisting for a split second, before he set his expression back to stone. He picked up her boots and set them in her hands. "It was just a kiss, Lizzie. Just consider it one more lesson I've taught you on the trail."

She blinked, fighting off sudden disappointment, then lowered down on the bed and laced up her boots. Chance strode to the door, waiting. The thrill of being in his arms hadn't diminished, neither had her joy over selling the herd for a lucrative amount of money. Her pulse still pounded and her flesh still ached for his touch. She hadn't wanted that kiss to end.

Once her boots were snug on her feet, she marched toward him. Chance still wore his stone face when he opened the door. She hesitated. She'd never been one to hold back from speaking her mind. "I wanted more," she said.

His eyes snapped to hers. "Got the best deal I could."

"I'm not talking about the herd."

Chance inhaled sharp. "Lord above, Lizzie. Don't go saying things like that."

"You wanted more, too," she said softly, refusing to think for a minute that Chance hadn't enjoyed kissing her. He may *regret* kissing her, but he took as much pleasure in that kiss as she had.

He shook his head, leading her down the stairs. "I've said it before, you got a vivid imagination."

"I know what I felt."

Lizzie bumped into him when he stopped abruptly and turned on his heel. He glanced around the hotel lobby. Not a soul was around. His hands wrapped around her upper arms, getting her attention. His face resembled a block of granite as he peered into her eyes. "Don't go getting fool notions about me, Lizzie. I'm here, because Edward asked it of me. No other reason. That kiss wasn't about you and me, it was about me not easing my lust last night. You'd know that, if you weren't so dang inexperienced. I won't tie myself to anyone. Not the way you need. It's best you know that."

He let her go and stalked off. Lizzie's heart just about broke. Her eyes burned as she held back tears. She didn't know for sure, but she presumed that for most young girls, a first kiss would mean something to both parties partaking and that maybe the thrill would be shared. Lizzie had proven again she wasn't like most young girls. Up until now, there hadn't been anyone she'd wanted to kiss, much less allow to take such intimate liberties. With Chance, it had been different. She'd wanted more from him and his rebuke struck her pride.

But the hurt went deeper than humiliation. A sense of keen loss hollowed out the pit of her stomach.

Yet, she couldn't forget the reason she'd come here or the good the cash earned would do when they returned home. She fought her tears and gathered her strength. Pulling her shoulders back, she lifted her chin and hurried her pace to catch up with him.

Chance quickened his steps, heading toward the stockyard. Thoughts of Marissa Dunston entered his mind. The girl had caused him a wagonload of trouble since the moment she'd stepped foot on the Dunston spread. Her mother, Belinda, had married Alistair shortly after his first wife Clara had died. It had been plain as day, even to a young orphaned boy, that Clara had been the one who'd wanted a son. She would have mothered Chance and accepted him as family, earning his loyalty and love. Once she was gone and Alistair remarried, he'd barely recognized him as an adopted son. Pretty little Marissa, five years younger and deceptively sweet, had taken Chance's place, if he'd ever had one, in Alistair's affections.

Chance had known enough to stay away from Marissa. Unfortunately, she had other plans for him. She'd followed him around on the ranch and gotten him into more trouble than any female was worth.

Lizzie Mitchell was a different kind of trouble. She didn't manipulate. She didn't have female wiles to coax a man to do her bidding. No, Lizzie was too darn innocent for any of that. He didn't have to look at her walking beside him to know he'd disappointed her. If he was smart, he'd continue to disappoint her. He wasn't going to kiss her again. He wasn't going to touch her.

Nope, she wasn't that kind of girl. Unfortunately for him, Lizzie wasn't experienced enough to know that the way she offered herself to him might have provoked a coupling that she would regret. Chance had lost himself in her beautiful eyes and in her sweet surrender. He'd let his body take control of his mind. Good things would never come of that with Lizzie. It irritated him to high heaven that she hadn't known enough not to tempt him. It meant that he'd be alone in keeping her reputation intact.

He had to marry her off.

For Edward.

He planned to honor that vow and send Lizzie to her marriage bed, untouched.

They crossed through town, Lizzie's shoulders high, but her face a mass of confusion. Westerly breezes brought dust whirls up. It was a good excuse to keep his mouth sealed tight. Lizzie did the same. The walk to the stockyard was silent, and that suited Chance just fine.

They strode past the Mitchell herd corralled in pens. They were the only cattle taking up space and Chance was glad of it. He led Lizzie into the office. The same white-haired man Chance spoke with this morning rose from behind his desk to shake hands. Chance stepped forward in a quick greeting.

"The little lady sign that paper?" he asked Chance.

He turned to her standing behind him. It tickled him to see her mouth angle down and her eyes shoot daggers at the cattle broker. She stepped forward and jutted out her delicate chin. "I'm owner of the Mitchell Ranch. Elizabeth Mitchell."

The broker's gray eyes wrinkled. He probably

thought she wasn't old enough to broker the deal, but the man was desperate. He put on a jolly smile. "Steven Turlington. Glad to meet ya."

He covered Lizzie's small hand with his, giving her a fatherly pat.

She pulled her hand away, her voice as stiff and formal as royalty. "I'm glad we could come to an agreement on the herd, Mr. Turlington."

Turlington was too grateful to notice her snooty behavior. "Your man here got a good deal outta me."

Lizzie nodded. "Yes, he's quite useful that way."

That little ingrate. Chance covered his surprise and gave her a warning glance. She darted one right back, then put out her hand. "The paper, please?"

He plastered it onto her hand, and with hoity-toity airs, she made a big to-do about sitting down at the desk and signing the bill of sale. A sale that would see her out of poverty.

Once the deal was done, Lizzie walked out of the office and Chance followed her, cursing under his breath. He took note of two cowboys in the stockyards, eyeing Lizzie. As soon as they noticed him, both men nodded with a tip of the hat. Chance met their eyes dead on. They looked familiar. He'd seen them at the saloon last night.

"Hold up, princess."

Lizzie slowed her steps.

He brought himself up real close, blocking out the wranglers' view of her. "Hand that cash over to me."

Her mouth gaped. "No."

"Don't be a fool. You can't go walking around with all that cash exposed like that."

"You didn't bring the saddlebags."

Her accusation stung. He couldn't hold on to his temper. "You got me so dang—"

Lizzie's brows lifted expectantly. "I got you so dang what?"

"Nothing." He wasn't about to tell her that kissing her had knocked the sense clear out of his head. He hadn't the wiles to pick up the saddlebags from his room. He'd wanted to get himself out of her hotel room and away from a temptation that would lead him straight to hell. Chance had already been there. He didn't want to go back.

He ground his teeth together. "Just give me the cash, Lizzie."

She thought about it for a moment. With a sideways glance from under the brim of his hat, Chance took notice of the two male figures turning and walking toward the far pen, but not before he'd caught them watching again. "Well?"

Her face finally relaxed. It was a far more pleasant sight than the stubborn set of her chin. "Here you go."

She set the bills in his palm. He folded them in half and jammed them deep into his pocket. He inhaled sharply then released the breath. "Come on. Let's get us some grub before we hit the road again. This time it's on the Mitchell's coin. I think I've earned it. What'd you say to Turlington?" he asked. "Oh, that's right. I'm downright *useful*."

Chapter Nine

The skies overhead were blue and the trail back to Red Ridge not nearly as dusty as when they were driving the herd. With a saddlebag full of cash, the string of horses behind her and Chance riding ahead, Lizzie thoughts flowed free. Her first priority was Grandpa's health. Soon as she got a doctor to fix him up, they'd make a fresh start with the ranch. Once Grandpa had regained his strength, they could buy a few heifers and a bull. Grandpa knew all there was to know about raising cattle. It wasn't his fault her father died when he did, leaving the brunt of the work and worries to Edward. He'd raised her and kept the ranch going. He'd done a fine job with both, in her estimation, and if it wasn't for some bad fortune with the herd they'd have done just fine. It would be slow going starting up the ranch again, but Lizzie didn't mind. Hope filled her heart that life would get better now after the successful trail drive.

She still smarted from Chance's utter refusal to give her so much as the time of day since they'd left the hotel room. He acted as though he hadn't kissed her for all she was worth or caressed her in private places she'd never been touched before. Thinking on it brought gooseflesh to her arms and made her stomach flutter, so she shed herself of those thoughts as best she could.

Three hours later, Chance double backed to ride beside her, his gaze following the darkening sky. "Gonna be dusk soon. You ready to settle for the night?"

Her rear end screamed for mercy. She'd been ready to soothe her sore muscles two hours ago. "I could go another mile or two."

Chance narrowed his eyes, glancing at the terrain and then up at the sky again. His contemplation worried her silly. She sent up a batch of silent prayers. *"Please, don't let him agree with me. Not this time."*

"No," he said. "We'd best make camp here."

She shrugged a shoulder, thanking all that was merciful that her fool mouth hadn't gotten her another bruise on her backside. "Suit yourself."

He leaned forward in the saddle, his mouth quirking up. "I always do."

They made camp right there, near a cropping of trees.

"Build a fire, Lizzie," Chance said over his shoulder as he led the horses away to feed and bed them down for the night.

She was so grateful to be rid of the saddle she didn't comment on Chance's bossy command. She did his bidding, rounding up twigs and dried branches she found nearby. She was getting good at trail fires. Back when her father was alive, she'd never been given the chore and figured now, after watching how it was done for so many years, the building of a good fire was a skill one acquired from experience. Once she got it started, flames licked up in a blaze then settled to a crackling even heat.

After the horses were fed, Chance walked back with two saddlebags slung over his shoulders. One held the cash and their clothes. The other held supplies and food. He tossed them down then walked over to the horses again. He came back with two new blankets and cooking equipment he'd purchased from the mercantile in Prescott.

He laid out one blanket facing the fire and the other one clear across on the opposite end, at least ten feet apart from each other. The blankets were good-sized, made of wool, but softer looking than the old ones, that now covered the horses for the night.

Chance bent low to set a pan on a metal triangle and opened a can of beans onto it. Lizzie unwrapped a loaf of bread and uncovered a big chunk of fresh cheese.

"Fire looks good, Lizzie. You're getting the hang of it."

"Thank you," she said, plopping onto one of the blankets. Chance hadn't said much to her today, so she wouldn't sour at the compliment. She'd missed his conversation. "I guess I'll be the cookie on our next drive."

Chance slid her a sideways glance, knitting his brows together. "You got such high hopes."

His skeptical tone prickled her senses. "I didn't… not until today."

"High hopes never got me anywhere."

Lizzie broke off two chunks of bread and handed Chance the cheese. He sliced off two pieces with a knife and handed them back to her. She filled their plates and waited for the beans to warm.

Lizzie couldn't fathom not having some sort of

hope. Even with all the Mitchells had gone through, she couldn't have possibly given up. "I'm sorry about that. But if you don't have hope, what do you have?"

Chance bite into the cheese and chewed, thinking. "Just what's real, I guess."

"I bet you didn't always feel that way. You must've had some—"

He shook his head. "I can't remember that far back, if I ever did."

"Why…can't you?"

Chance wrinkled his nose then ran a hand down his face to rub his jaw. His eyes squeezed closed just for a few seconds and then he faced her with the full force of his dark haunted eyes. "My parents were murdered when I was a boy. Don't have much recollection of them. Just a few flashes enter my mind every so often. I hear their screams though, even to this day. I'll never forget those. My mama hid me away from the thieves in the root cellar. She took the ruby necklace off her throat and handed it to me. Her eyes were bright and clear, even through her fear. She said she had to help my daddy. She took up a rifle and kissed my cheek. That was the last time I saw her alive." Chance looked out over the fire. "I wasn't much more than five."

"She protected you," Lizzie whispered, a weight pressing her heart. She ached for the little boy who witnessed the death of his parents. Lizzie had no recollection of her mother but she'd had the love of her father and grandfather for many years. She'd been more fortunate than Chance. "It was a sign of her love for you."

"No matter," Chance said abruptly, stuffing food into his mouth. "It's over."

Lizzie wanted to cry for him. But Chance wouldn't want her pity. They ate the rest of their meal in silence, Chance deep in thought and Lizzie sorry she'd made him recall such a bad memory.

After the meal, the weather took a turn. The air cooled considerably. Lizzie shivered and put on her jacket. She nestled herself inside its warmth and after she'd cleaned up the dishes and stoked the fire, she took her place on the blanket. Her unruly dark hair fell onto her face as she stared at the golden licking flames.

From the other side of the fire, through a cloud of smoke, Chance sat upright on his blanket, his gun belt beside him on one side, the saddlebag holding the cash on the other. He was intent on gazing into the fire. She began combing her hair. There was a slight shift in his movement, and as if the fire, the distance and the smoke formed a barrier between them, he turned to watch her.

She put the ribbon tie in her mouth and ran the fingers of both hands through her unruly curls. Her hair fell across her chest over her right breast. There was a hint of lilac still on her hair and she struggled to catch the clean scent. She continued to separate the hair with her fingers, her movements slowing as she met with his intrigued gaze.

Chance touched her in ways she couldn't fathom. He touched her heart. He made her mad. He touched her soul. He confused her. He made her feel things she'd never felt before. Wonderful, glorious sensations that now, she was sure, were more than physical.

He watched her still. And she stared back. Her pulse raced so hard, a throbbing in her throat pounding against her delicate skin.

There was a movement that broke the spell. Chance

lifted from his blanket and she held her breath. Their gazes met again as he straightened to his full height. She prayed he would come to her, to lie with her and kiss her again. She wanted it so. Her hope died when he turned his back and stalked off.

"Chance," she called out.

"Get some sleep, Lizzie." His voice was strained, deep with regret. "Gonna check on the horses. I'll be back later."

Her shoulders slumped and all hope drained from her body. She finished tying up her hair, then lowered down covering herself with the big new woolen blanket. Chance had walked away from her. She should be accustomed to that by now. He was forever walking out, denying her. But this loss was keen and made her ache much more than the unforgiving hard-packed ground and her sorely bruised bottom. A tear dripped from her eye. And then another. She sniffed and held her body stiff, using all of her stubborn will to keep from breaking down into a sullen cry.

And minutes later, once she heard Chance's footsteps approach to stoke the fire, she eased the painful burden with much-needed sleep.

She stomped on wildflowers glistening under a strong sun. Daddy chased her and she giggled. Grandpa was there beside her mother. She waved from the front porch of the ranch house, beckoning them to come in for supper. Her mama wore an apron with the prettiest of tiny yellow flowers on it and Lizzie thought she looked beautiful. She took her daddy's hand and together they ran toward her smiling mother.

But then Daddy's hand covered her mouth and she

tasted sweat and rough leather and pressure enough to bruise her mouth. Lizzie snapped her eyes open just as she was being hauled up, out of her bedroll. One powerful gloved hand came around her stomach and the other, the one over her mouth, forced her head back, so that her face angled up toward the moon. The stench of alcohol and filth invaded her nostrils. Instantly, cruel dread wakened her from her peaceful dream. Her back was jammed against a man's body. She squirmed and kicked her legs, trying to free herself. Muted protests escaped her throat, falling short of her intent.

Across the camp, low burning embers cast light on Chance seated by the fire, being held at gunpoint by another man. She kicked harder and managed to put the heel of her bare foot to her attacker's shin. "Ow! Damn it. Stop your wiggling or you won't live to see another day."

The man aiming a Winchester rifle at Chance wore a hat low on his forehead and a dark bandana over most of his face. Only the glint of his eyes shone through.

"Let her go." Chance's voice broke with dangerous warning, sending chills up and down her spine.

The man yanked her against him like she was a rag doll. The handle of his gun touched her cheek in a rough caress. "Maybe I will and maybe I won't."

She was trapped in tight arms, pressed against a hard body. "Maybe I'll take her back behind them trees and show her a good time." He covered her breast with a hand and squeezed her hard through her jacket. His touch made her want to puke. She struggled in his arms, until he eased up the pressure.

Chance bounded to his feet. "Touch her again and I'll kill you."

"Sit down!" The sound of the rifle cocking froze Lizzie in her place. She shook her head at Chance. He couldn't die today. Not because of her. She trembled, fear overpowering her until the shaking was noticeable. Chance met her gaze, his eyes reassuring her, before he turned an icy glare on her attacker. Slowly, he sat down, never taking his eyes off the man holding her.

"Seems to me, you can't do much of anything right now but watch," he said, gleeful.

"Shut up," the rifleman said. "We ain't here for that."

"Yeah, but she's sorta pretty. Wouldn't take but a few minutes."

Chance showed little fear, facing the rifle. "What do you want?"

"The cash. You got a lot of it. I'm guessing it's in that saddlebag you're sleeping with." He pointed his rifle toward the saddlebags then back at Chance. "First, shove that gun belt over here."

Chance hesitated. The tip of the man's toe lifted the corner of the blanket hiding Chance's gun belt. "Yep, that one. Go on. Shove it right over to my feet."

Chance tossed the belt. It landed by the fire.

With the rifle trained on Chance, the attacker bent to pick up the gun and tuck it under his belt. "Now the saddlebag. Open it. Let me see what you got in there."

Chance pulled the straps from the leather binding and opened the bag. The man nodded, satisfied when he saw the cash. He slid his partner a quick glance. "Give her the rope, Quinn."

Her attacker shoved a rope into her hands. The coarse threads scraped against her fingers and she fumbled with it.

"Now go tie him up."

Lizzie's feet refused to budge. Her heart pounded. She felt inadequate, trembling with fear. She looked at Chance. His eyes were hard, his expression unreadable and she hoped he was figuring a way out of this.

"Well, git." The thief's hand landed on her back with an unforgiving push and she stumbled forward.

Lizzie had no choice but to walk over to Chance. "Tie his hands behind his back. Make it good and tight."

Both men watched, with guns pointed at her and Chance. She lowered down in front of Chance and lifted her gaze to his.

"Do as they say." His voice soothed and encouraged her, even as she saw no way out of this. She crawled behind him and he brought his hands in place to his back. She took his hands in hers and squeezed gently. Praying to the Lord, she hoped this wasn't their very last memory together. "I'm s-sorry."

Chance drew oxygen into his lungs and said so quietly, she strained to hear, "Don't let him touch you."

"I'd rather die," she whispered.

Chance swiveled his head to meet her eyes. "You're not dying."

There was such certainty in his words, for a moment, Lizzie found a shred of hope. She made a theatrical effort of tying him up, keeping the ropes from cutting his circulation, but tight enough to satisfy the thieves.

The rifleman walked over and eyeballed the ropes, making sure not to get too close to Chance. "Get up," he said to her.

Lizzie rose slowly, standing next to Chance.

"Take the money and go," Chance said. "You got what you came for."

The man ignored him. "Tie her up, Quinn. Let's get out of here."

Quinn sauntered up. There was a sickening gleam in his eyes. "Sure, I'll tie her up. You let their horses go."

The man looked over at the horses, then nodded. He tossed the saddlebag over his shoulder and stalked off.

A coyote howled off in the distance and she heard horses shifting as the stranger approached. "Put those hands behind your back," he said, but he didn't wait for her to do his bidding. He grabbed her wrists and a cry of pain broke from her lungs as he lashed her wrists behind her back. "You're coming with me."

"What? No! No!" Her mind screamed as the words tore from her throat. "Don't take me."

He slapped her face and the shock of it muted her cries. She tasted her own blood. "Shut up, you little bitch." He turned to Chance with an evil smirk. "I'm gonna get me a taste of what you been gettin'."

Lizzie couldn't see Chance's face any longer. Her eyes stung with unshed tears. Quinn dragged her away by the rope at her back. Her skin burned from underneath the binding at her wrists. As he pulled her along, leaves from low-lying tree branches scratched her face. She dug her heels into the earth and wrestled, trying to break free of his hold, but he was too strong. He stopped abruptly, sheltered by surrounding trees and shoved her down. She hit the solid earth with a thud. Her arms twisted behind her. She struggled to loosen the binds. They wouldn't give. She was trapped.

It was frightfully dark. She strained to focus, kicking at him with all her might. But he quelled her with his weight as he straddled her. She hated being helpless and small and weak, but she'd fight until she died.

He whipped off his mask, yet she couldn't see anything but his beady eyes. "You can scream your head off, but if you fight me, I swear I'll go over there and shoot that man dead. I know you don't want that. It's your choice," he said calmly, as if he was buying a sack of flour.

The fight left her. Quinn was the devil and he would go to hell when the time came. She truly believed that he'd kill Chance. She couldn't imagine his blood on her hands. She couldn't live knowing she might have saved Chance's life and didn't.

"Yeah, that's it," he said, his voice low, purring with satisfaction. "That's it, girl. How old are you? You might be my youngest ever."

She squeezed her eyes closed and swallowed, turning away.

He spread her jacket open. She was fitted between his knees and couldn't move much.

Bile rose up in her throat. Her body stiffened. He touched her stomach, the flat of his hand pressed to her belly. She wanted to vomit, yet she allowed him to touch her. She didn't know how much more she could take. She didn't know if she could save Chance's life.

Out of the darkness, a form appeared, grabbing Quinn's shoulders. He was lifted and tossed in the air. She heard his body hit the ground three feet from her with a thud.

Lizzie was free of him. The weight pinning her down was gone. She trembled with immediate relief and scrambled to her knees, struggling to keep her balance.

"You son of a bitch!"

It was Chance. He was on Quinn, striking his jaw

and pummeling his chest. It took a few seconds before Quinn fought back. Lizzie couldn't figure how Chance got away from the rifleman, but he had. He'd come for her.

The fight moved out of the range of her vision. The sounds of scuffling grunts and fists smacking filled the night. She strained her ears to listen and scoured the ground hopelessly for something sharp or solid she could use as protection.

A shot rang out. Chance's groan echoed against the trees.

"No!" She struggled to stand but fell down onto her backside in a twist. She lay there, trying to wrestle her wrists free from the ropes. Her pulse raced so fast, she thought she'd die right there on the spot. Her chest pounded and pounded and tears sprang from her eyes. "No, no."

Another grunt, this one short and final, broke through her cries. She closed her eyes, praying harder than she had in all her life. For Chance.

Don't take him. Don't take him.

Footsteps approached and she tried to still, listening, yet her body shook with defiant rage. Fear no longer gripped her in its claws. She was ready to die fighting, if she had to. She'd kick and bite and elbow the vile man, giving him no peace.

"Lizzie?"

A gasp whooshed through her lips and she froze in place.

"Lizzie?"

It was Chance. He wasn't dead. Her body sagged with relief and her teeth unclamped from their tight grind. The sound of his voice was a beautiful song to her ears.

It flowed through her body like a harmonious church hymn. "C-Chance?"

He appeared out of the darkness, his face battered, his shirt torn, holding his shoulder as blood seeped through his fingers. "Oh, Chance, you're alive."

He went down on his knees in front of her. "I'm alive." He scoured her body with sharp concerned eyes and then drew her close with one arm. She needed no more encouragement. She melted against him. "You're gonna be alright." His lips whispered against her forehead. "You're gonna be alright."

She wanted to crawl right up into him but he held her away from the wound on his shoulder. Yet he comforted her, stroking his free hand through her hair, over and over.

She nestled her face into his chest and took the comfort he offered. Her heart still raced, but the pounding in her chest ebbed to a pace that allowed her easier breaths. Chance was alive. He was safe. She was safe. That's all that mattered for now.

"Let's get your hands free."

He pulled away and a bloody knife appeared. He wiped it clean against his shirt then lashed the rope around her wrists. She brought her hands to the front and rubbed at them to bring back her circulation. Her wrists throbbed, but she ignored the raw pain. "Thank you," she said, tears spilling down her face.

Chance lifted his good arm again, to brush her tears away. His fingers caressed her cheeks with tender care as he ducked his head down so that his eyes were level with hers. "Are you hurt?"

She shook her head. "No, he didn't…" She bit her lower lip and looked away.

Send For
2 FREE BOOKS
Today!

I accept your offer!

Please send me two free
Harlequin® Historical novels and
two mystery gifts (gifts worth
about $10). I understand that
these books are completely
free—even the shipping and
handling will be paid—and I am
under no obligation to purchase
anything, ever, as explained on the
back of this card.

246/349 HDL FMP5

Please Print

FIRST NAME

LAST NAME

ADDRESS

APT.#   CITY

STATE/PROV.   ZIP/POSTAL CODE

Visit us online at
www.ReaderService.com

"He's dead, Lizzie. He won't hurt you."

Lizzie snapped her head around. "He shot you."

"Son of a bitch pulled a gun. The shot grazed my shoulder."

The shot could've killed him. Her body trembled, this time for what might have occurred. "You're bleeding."

"I'll be fine."

Blood seeped from his shoulder and Lizzie's stomach clenched. She could only imagine the gory scene just steps away with Quinn poked through by Chance's knife, lying in a puddle of his own blood. She pushed that thought out of her mind. Living on a ranch, the sight of blood usually didn't bother her except when it spilled from a person she cared about. Chance was doing the bleeding and that made all the difference.

She ripped the hem of her riding skirt, tearing off a long strip. She folded the corners to form a square bandage. Her hand shook terribly when she raised it to Chance's shoulder. She dabbed at the wound, thanking the Lord the bullet had only grazed him. "H-how d-did you get away?"

Chance's face twisted tight when she applied pressure to his shoulder and she cringed knowing she'd caused him pain. "I keep a knife under the blanket when I sleep. Wasn't too hard to get loose between the knife and the embers in the fire."

"The fire?" Lizzie blinked and then took his bloodied hands in hers. Slowly she turned his palms up. "Oh, my Lord, you're burnt." His hands and wrists were scorched and white little blisters were starting to form.

"Yeah, they're stinging a bit right now. I had to get to you fast and the knife was taking too long."

"So you set your wrists over the fire to burn the rope off."

He shrugged his shoulders and the gesture made him wince again. "You were screaming, Lizzie. Nearly tore out my gut." Chance rose then and reached for her with one hand, while he used the other to keep the pressure bandage on his shoulder. "Let's get to camp. See if the horses came back."

"The rifleman is dead, too?" she asked, her nerves wrought. Chance hadn't mentioned him. She figured he'd killed him.

He shook his head. "With me all tied up and his partner not paying attention, he took off with the cash. The greedy bastard double-crossed his own man. Soon as that happened, I got myself loose."

Lizzie shivered down to her bare toes. It was a miracle both of them were alive—a miracle due to Chance. He'd told her she wouldn't die tonight. And he'd nearly died protecting her.

Lizzie talked Chance out of going after the thief. How could he anyway? It was dark as pitch and the gunman had run the horses off. On foot and in the dark, tracking the thief would be impossible.

After a time, Chance insisted she sleep, but Lizzie couldn't imagine sleeping in the same campsite where they were attacked so they searched for the horses. She stayed close to him. He took to whistling, loud and short bursts, stopping every so often to listen for pounding hooves. They wandered the grounds for several minutes, never straying too far from the site and sure enough, Joyful appeared. Chance said he knew she would. She was a loyal horse and he stroked her mane even with his injured hands, glad to be reunited with her. The other horses were nowhere in sight.

They led Joyful to a cropping of mesquite trees and settled their gear. Chance didn't build a fire. He leaned against the trunk of a tree on a blanket and summoned her. It was dark, almost moonless now that dreary clouds filled the sky. "Come here, Lizzie. You need to sleep."

"Don't think I can," she said. Her nerves were jumpy and though her body was fatigued, her mind wouldn't settle. She dropped down beside him and covered herself with the blanket.

"Try. I'll be right here. Next to you. I'll stand watch." They didn't say it, but both were thinking that he'd stand watch in case the rifleman returned.

"You should let me wrap your hands."

"Can't shoot with a wrapped hand."

Lizzie accepted that. There was no talking Chance out of some things and she wasn't sure she would even try tonight. He had a gun, ammunition and a knife, in case he needed them.

He tucked his good arm around her shoulder and bundled her close. She rested her head on his chest and snuggled in. "Chance?"

"Hmm."

"They were the men from the stockyard, weren't they?"

Chance paused, contemplating with a long inhale of breath. He began rubbing her arm, soothing her with slow tender strokes. "Yeah. The man lying dead looked like one of them we saw today. They must've followed us."

Lizzie's body sagged and a notion filled her head.

Sudden guilt—the same as when she'd lost her dolls in the lake—seized her in a choke hold around her throat. The words tore from her lips in a quiet hush. "They were watching me with all the money in my hands. You said so…"

"They'd have known you had cash whether or not they saw it, Lizzie. You made a deal at the stockyard. My guess is that they were drifters hired on for a spell. They saw an opportunity and followed us."

"I was easy prey for them."

Chance didn't agree or disagree. "We're gonna have to double back to Prescott in the morning. Report the theft to the marshal. Have him come out and pick up the body."

The body? A shiver stole what was left of her warmth. Bile rose in her throat. It tasted bitter and burned on the way up. She swallowed hard to shove it back down.

Chance must have sensed her feelings. His words tumbled out with gentle ferocity. "Don't you go feeling guilty about anything. None of this is your fault."

She honestly wished she could believe that. But the bitter truth was that she was the cause of this robbery and the cause for most of Chance's troubles. Didn't make her feel too good, knowing that if she'd been more discreet maybe they'd be heading home with hard-earned money, instead of reporting a death and theft to the law.

Chance was quiet for a time and then he started up again as if he had some confessing to do. "I should've heard them coming. I should've kept an eye out. Fact is, when you stopped screaming I thought I was too late. Hearing that silence scared the stuffing outta me. It was worse than your screams."

His revelation might have brought her joy—that he cared for her—but the circumstances were too desperate to find any slim measure of good cheer. "Oh, Chance... he said...he said he'd kill you if I struggled. He said... he didn't mind the screams. I think he," she whispered, squeezing her eyes closed, "I think he liked hearing it... so I stopped."

Chance lifted his head, hinging his body up. His sudden movement caused her to snap her eyes open. She met his earnest stare. "You mean you were sacrificing yourself...for me?"

"To save your life," she said softly with a nod.

Chance shook his head and kept on shaking his head. An incredulous expression stole over his face and he searched her eyes for a long time. She couldn't look away. She could barely see him through the darkness, but she saw enough.

He leaned against the tree again and pulled her close to his chest. He spoke with deadly intent, forcing air from his lungs. "Wish I could've killed him twice."

The truth slammed at Lizzie from all directions. She'd nearly had her pride taken tonight. She could have been sorely abused and killed. And Chance might have died, trying to save her. He'd been forced to stab a man to death to protect her. That was enough to send her to her knees to pray to the Lord.

She would count her blessings later, but now her dire concern turned to the ranch. The much-needed cash was gone. What would become of her grandfather? All her dreams of getting him doctored and making him well again were gone. She'd banked his recovery on that money. She'd hoped for a miracle to save him. The ranch was as good as ruined. The thief who'd attacked them had not only stolen her cash, but pillaged every shred of hope she'd had.

She'd failed Grandpa again.

A sob rose up from her throat. And then another. She couldn't stifle them. The harder she tried, the more forceful they became. Her body shook all at once, and a flood of tears ran like a river from her eyes. She nestled into Chance's chest and soaked his shirt clean through with her sobbing.

"Ah, Lizzie." Her name rose from his throat with a deep sigh. He brought her tight against him and ran his hand through her long hair. His fingers sifted the strands with tenderness making her squirm to get closer to him. She couldn't seem to get close enough. She wanted to inch up inside him and stay there, forever safe, without thinking of her loss, without feeling anything but his powerful gentle arms around her. She clung on to his shirt, and cried as hard as she'd ever cried in her life.

Chapter Ten

∞

They took the road back to Prescott in silence. Lizzie rode atop Joyful and Chance walked some of the way. After a time, he mounted the mare and they rode double. His breath, familiar now, warmed her throat and his body curving around hers no longer worried her. She leaned against him and absorbed his strength. She'd been doing that lately, relying on him, but she couldn't much help it.

Her dismal circumstances filled her every thought. She was sick inside. It was as if someone had come through her body and swooped out all that was good, all that was hopeful, leaving her empty but for the ache.

Chance was deep in thought himself. Killing a man, no matter how good the reason, must weigh heavily on the soul. Even for a man like him—who'd lived life the hard way, as Grandpa would say—the taking of a life must have some profound effect. Chance said he'd wished he could have killed him twice, but Lizzie didn't think he meant it. If he'd had any other choice, he would have taken it. He'd stabbed Quinn to save their lives, plain and simple, but she wasn't looking forward to the retelling of the story to the town marshal. Nope, she surely wasn't.

"Lizzie, you alright?"

She nodded and sat straighter in the saddle, giving up the wall of Chance's chest as her backboard.

"Not like you being so quiet, but I suppose you got a right."

"I thought you liked it when I kept my lips buttoned."

Chance chuckled, his laugh small but rich enough to lift the corners of her mouth. She didn't have much else to smile about. "I do."

"So stop complaining."

From behind her, she sensed his mouth pulling up in a wide grin. The kind that infuriated her, but now it just seemed fitting. "That's my Lizzie."

She wished she was his Lizzie, but Chance made it perfectly clear she wasn't. Her mood was distressed enough without giving in to such silly notions right now. She wouldn't allow her mind to wander to a time that took Chance off the ranch and away from her. He was the first man to kiss her. That was a memory she would forever hold to her heart. And with what they'd been through together on this trail drive, she would even look upon Chance Worth as her friend.

He'd never admit that, but she knew it for a fact. And Lizzie needed a good friend right about now. More than she ever had in the past.

The ordeal in Prescott took less time than she'd thought. Chance made his statement to the marshal. They'd ridden over to the stockyard and questioned the proprietor, Steven Turlington, who'd bought their herd and sure enough, those two men, Quinn Martin and his friend, Buford Lang, were new hires, who'd only worked at the stockyard little more than a week.

Turlington told Chance and Marshal Hopkins all he knew of the two men. It didn't seem like much and all she could do was to hope the Marshal would get a lead as to where the other man might have gone. He promised to go back and try to follow the man's tracks from the robbery point.

Chance looked as though he wanted to go on that manhunt. He kept shooting glances at her as if making a tough choice. Finally, he left it in the marshal's hands.

She couldn't wait to rid herself of this town. Her nerves jumped while waiting for Chance to purchase supplies they'd need to get them home. As they exited the mercantile, he said, "Good thing I keep cash in my boots."

The robbers hadn't looked on their person. Buford, the man that took off was too smart to stick around overly long. He'd already gotten a wagonload of money. He'd double-crossed his partner and came away with the loot and his life. The other man had met with a violent death.

After making good headway out of town, they set up camp early to rest Joyful. Lizzie sat by the fire, hugging her jacket to her chest. "You would have gone looking for the thief, if it weren't for me."

"I have to get you back to the ranch." His voice was flat, deliberate as if there wasn't a doubt in his mind. He'd made a vow to her grandfather and so far, Chance had owned up to his side of the bargain. And he'd protected her with his life. She couldn't fault him for the robbery. That guilt she saved for herself.

She ached to see her grandpa again even as she hated facing him with another failure. He was all she had left in the world.

After they ate a quiet meal, Chance handed her the gun. "Think you can stay awake until dark? I'll get some shut-eye for a couple of hours then take the night watch."

A shiver of panic whispered through her body, but she wouldn't let Chance see her fear. She wouldn't think about her attacker tonight. Fear would not keep her down and yet another shiver claimed her nerves. "I'll do that."

He laid out his blanket by the fire, directly next to hers. "Stay by my side." He forced her to meet his eyes. "You got that?"

She bobbed her head. There wasn't a chance in hell Lizzie would stray. She took a swallow. "I got that."

She spent the time while he slept listening to every tree branch rustle, every snort Joyful made and every haunting howl of a coyote. She heard it all and jumped every time, the gun at the ready.

She glanced at Chance as he slept. His hard features seemed softer. His eyes were beautiful, fringed with dark lashes and perfectly arched brows. The angles of his face looked almost boyish as he lent himself to sleep. He snored, but she wouldn't tease him…well, maybe she would, if the subject came up. But his noisy sleep meant his exhaustion had gotten the better of him. She was equally as tired, with a mental strain that was never far from her thoughts. She continued to sit on the blanket, even as the peace of the sun's setting made her edgy.

Darkness descended on the land and Lizzie shivered, not from the cold, but from memories of the night before. Images that she'd been able to keep away in the brightness of the daylight hour, now threatened to fill her mind full as night crept in. Pure evil had a name in Quinn Martin and though she'd most likely go to hell herself for her harsh thoughts, she prayed the man was burning now in the devil's eternal bonfire.

It was quiet for a long time. The surrounding silence of the night frightened her. The campfire embers burned low. And except for a smidgen of moonlight, the sky above was as dreary as it was fathomless. It was times like these that Lizzie felt alone in the world and so intensely small, much like a sole sliver of grass amid a vast prairie.

"Who. Who."

She startled at the sound and grabbed up the gun, aiming it at the trees off in the distance. The big hoot owl that hadn't made a peep in half an hour now was making his presence known. *"Who, who, who, who."*

Lizzie set the gun down by her side, her shoulders sagging. She'd probably get in trouble for not waking Chance, but he slept so soundly beside her that she didn't have the heart to wake him. Minutes ticked by and Lizzie tried to think of happier times to block out the night sounds.

"Who, who."

She jumped and aimed again.

A hand came out and gently pried the Colt .45 from her grip. "How many times you gonna shoot that old owl, darlin'?"

She turned to the voice in the shadows.

"You're awake."

Chance checked the gun barrel then pinned her with

a firm look. "I should throttle you for letting me sleep this long."

She cocked her chin, feeling more like her old self than she had for days. "I'd like to see you try."

Chance grinned and even through the darkness, she found a disreputable gleam in his eyes. "It'd be something to see." His gaze drifted to her mouth.

Lizzie watched him through her lashes, her heartbeats speeding. "You want to kiss me again?" she blurted. She had a terrible way of spitting out exactly what was on her mind.

Chance twisted his face, making himself look altogether less appealing for half a second. "I didn't want to kiss you the first time."

Lizzie gasped. Chance wouldn't admit he enjoyed kissing her, but he had. It couldn't be one-sided, not when her insides had wrapped themselves into a tight knot after that first kiss. "If that's true, I'd like to be around when you want to kiss me. Mercy, can you just imagine how powerful that would be?"

Chance did a double take and then swallowed.

Satisfaction, pure and deep, uncurled in her belly, as she watched him take that notion to heart.

"You need to sleep, Lizzie. We have a long day ahead of us tomorrow."

He was good at changing the conversation when he didn't want to face facts.

"If we push hard, we might make it home before dark," he added.

Her shoulders slumped and the fight left her. "And what a homecoming that will be."

"You want to see your grandpa, don't you?"

"Yes, of course. I miss him. But, I'm still worried."

Chance patted the blanket she sat on, gesturing for her to lie down. "You don't need to worry. You'll be safe. I'll stay up the rest of the night to watch over you."

She knew she'd be safe. Chance would protect her with his life. She snuggled in and he helped cover her with the blanket. Turning her body toward him, her eyes closed and she honestly tried to shut off her mind, yet her worries wouldn't go away. She had no fears about Buford Lang returning, not with Chance on the lookout and the marshal on his trail. Her fears were of the unknown. She'd be returning home, empty-handed, and the future of the Mitchell family looked bleak. She couldn't figure a way out of this dilemma. All she could do was pray that Lang would be caught and the money would be returned.

It was a pitiful hope from a girl who had little faith anymore.

After half an hour of her restlessness, Chance said, "Lizzie, calm down."

"I can't."

"Try"

"I am." He was so dang infuriating at times. Acting as if she actually wanted to toss and turn the night away.

"Try harder."

"You could help, you know."

"How?"

"You could do me a favor."

Chance darted a few glances around the perimeter. "I won't kiss you good-night, if that's what you're asking."

"Don't be silly, Chance." She rose up, bringing the blanket with her. "That wouldn't calm my body at all."

Breath blew out of his lungs and his eyes opened wide. He seemed truly surprised by her honesty and a little bit flustered. She thought a reprimand was coming, but Chance's expression changed when he gazed at her mouth again. Her breath caught in her throat and heat began to build in her belly. Chance noted her interest with a long stare at her lips, and fanciful thoughts entered her head. His gaze lifted to hers. "That much is true, Lizzie. You'd enjoy it and get all worked up again."

"And…you'd enjoy it, too."

He didn't agree or disagree. Instead, he simply leaned back on his elbows and gazed into the night, his eyes alert to the surroundings. "Ask your favor."

Lizzie laid down again, her head pillowed against a saddlebag. She turned toward Chance. "Talk to me. Tell me about your childhood."

A frown pulled his lips down. He whispered quietly, "My life's hardly a bedtime story, Lizzie."

"I know. But I want to hear it. It'll help me to…to fall asleep."

His mouth twisted and he eyed her with skepticism.

"Just for a few minutes… I promise not to ask one question."

He shook his head. "I'll believe that when I see it." And a few owl hoots later, he began recounting his life.

Sometime during the night, Lizzie curved her body around him. She made herself comfortable and snuggled in. Her hair tickled his throat and her head nestled onto his chest. He'd held her with his good arm draped around her shoulder and rubbed her arm as she slept. She was safe and warm underneath the blanket. She still looked more like a child than a woman in her petite form, but Chance didn't for a minute think there was anything childlike about Lizzie anymore.

She made a little sound, a rebelling moan against waking. Chance wouldn't disturb her sleep. The sun had just peeked over the horizon. Soon the warming light would do enough to wake her.

He surveyed the land as he had all during the night and sighed with regret at how things had turned out. When that depraved bastard had Lizzie tied up, dragging her away, something snapped inside him. His body quaked with rage. There was no way he would let anything happen to her. He'd summoned all of his strength and focused his mind solely on one thing, getting Lizzie to safety. He'd have burned all his fingers off trying to get free, if it meant saving her from that man's brutal attack. When he'd finally unbound his restraints, he'd found her trapped and helpless, with that worm of a man on top of her, pinning her down. Chance had gone a little crazy and Quinn had fought him hard, but Chance had grown up fighting to survive. He'd had to, and he knew all the tricks. He wouldn't stop until Quinn Martin met his maker and got his just deserts.

Regrets stretched over his mind. He wished he could have gone after the bastard who'd run off with the Mitchell money. He wanted to catch that man for Lizzie's sake. And to repay his debt to Edward. But Lizzie's safety had been his first concern.

Lizzie stirred and rubbed her face against his chest. He groaned, willing his body not to take what Lizzie would volunteer so freely. Lizzie had been through an ordeal that would have destroyed most women but she'd forged on. She was safe and he would keep her that way until he could turn her over to the man she would marry.

She wouldn't make it easy, but he was determined to see this through.

Joyful shuffled in the background. She was restless. They'd have to hit the road soon. They'd get back to the Mitchell ranch before nightfall. Lizzie would have her own bed to sleep in and Chance might even get more than a few hours of rest himself.

Sleep was something he'd learned early on to live without. In the orphanage, he'd often wake at night from frightful dreams. They had haunted him as a young boy. His mother's screams. His father's grunts as he tried to protect his family. The helplessness he'd felt from that one night had stayed with him all these years. He'd been a little boy, too young to really understand the evil that entered the Worth homestead that day. But his shocking dreams reminded him time and again.

Lizzie made a little growling sound of protest before lifting her head several inches from his chest. She seemed a little dazed at first as she registered her surroundings. With furrowed brows she angled her head toward his face. Inky dark hair fell full around her head, those bluer-than-blue eyes, hazy from sleep, captured his attention and her rosy bowed lips nearly touched his. She smiled and Chance remained still. What he wouldn't give to wake her out of her melancholy mood with a morning kiss. If he allowed himself the indulgence, he could teach Lizzie so many things.

"Morning, Chance," she whispered sweetly, gazing up at him. Lizzie didn't know the temptation she posed to him, he was certain, but she had a way of looking at him that puffed his chest and made him glad he was a man.

Last night he'd fought a battle of demons as he stood watch over her, recalling the sweet taste of her giving mouth when he'd kissed her. He remembered how her innocent gasps of pleasure had spurred his desire. He relived touching the soft mounds of her bosom and the powerful jolt it awarded him. She was slight, but full in his hands, enough of a woman to satisfy him. He had itched to touch her bare skin, to caress her without barriers. She'd responded to him with trust and passion. She would have done his bidding no matter what he asked of her.

Knowing that she would give herself to him without question filled his head with notions of claiming her, of stripping off her clothes and burying himself deep inside her body. His manhood stiffened as he played it out in his wicked mind. He'd make it good for her and bring her a woman's pleasure. The more he'd tried to banish those heady thoughts, the more his body ached for want of her.

Only the reminder of his debt to Edward had saved him. It was like a splash of icy river water to the face. That man trusted him with his granddaughter. He'd not given him one warning in regards to Lizzie's reputation. Edward had more faith in him than he'd had in himself. It was a sobering thought.

He dropped his hand from around her shoulder and sat up slowly, stretching his arms above his head. The movement gave her no choice but to scoot out of his way.

From his stretch, he slid her a sideways glance. "Mornin'."

Disappointed, she looked at him as if he'd kicked her in the gut.

"You ready to head out?"

It was the last day he'd have to spend with her in such close quarters. Once back on the ranch, he'd take to sleeping in the dilapidated bunkhouse again. It would prove a helluva lot less dangerous than sleeping beside her every night and fighting off the uncanny temptation he hadn't seen coming.

She drew in a breath and released it slowly. "As ready as I'll ever be."

"Don't you worry. Things'll work out."

Lizzie stared into his eyes. "You didn't paint such a rosy picture last night."

"My life isn't a fairy tale, Lizzie. I told you that already."

He'd shared his most honest feelings with her last night. She'd listened, but Lizzie couldn't contain her questions, even though she'd promised to. She'd asked question after question, and Chance hadn't minded answering them as much as he thought he would. He didn't know why it was, but revealing his life to her had lifted his spirit. He'd told her things he'd never told another living soul and the weight lifted made him feel lighter than air last night. Maybe he shouldn't have done it. Maybe he should have held back as he was wont to do, because now Lizzie looked at him with a new glint in her pretty eyes.

"I'm sorry for it, Chance."

He shrugged and rose from the blanket. Standing, he gave her a shrug. "Just told you so you'd sleep. You weren't gonna settle down otherwise."

Lizzie's lips lifted just a little. "Still, I'm glad you told me about your folks and your time at the orphanage and how you got taken in by Mr. Dunston. He wasn't a very nice man."

"I survived it all, so don't pity me, Lizzie."

"I don't pity you," she said, quietly, gazing at him with a gleam in her eye. "I…I admire you."

With a shake of his head, he blew out a breath. "Well, don't. I'm not all that admirable."

"You've saved my hide a time or two. How can I not admire that?"

"I had to." Chance picked up his gun belt and fastened it around his hips. It sat low on his waist and felt right being there. It was a part of him and he wasn't proud of it. He'd had to defend his life too many times to count. He'd shot men before. He'd brutalized them with his fists when he had to. There wasn't anything admirable in that.

Lizzie's face fell and she looked down at the ground for a moment. "Because you owed my grandfather a debt?" Her voice was small as if the answer would pound her already beaten spirit into the ground.

Chance should let her go on believing that. It would make dealing with Lizzie easier. But her heart was already broken and he had no illusions about what she faced when they returned to the Mitchell spread. "I'm not gonna let anyone hurt you, Lizzie. Just accept that as fact."

She gazed at him from her seat on the blanket, a question tearing from her throat. "What if you're the one hurting me the most?"

Ah, hell. It was just like Lizzie to confuse his actions. His brows gathered and he formed his words carefully so as not to injure her pride. "It's not my intent."

They stared at each other for a time. Chance wouldn't go soft on her. She had a future waiting, one that he would see to the end, and one that didn't include him. He pointed to the blankets. "Roll them up and let's get going after breakfast. We don't have time to waste."

Chapter Eleven

Lizzie walked beside Joyful onto Mitchell land as the sun began its descent behind the Red Ridge Mountains. In years past, upon her return home after a trail drive, she'd jump down from her horse to race up the steps, homesick in that very moment and needing to find all things familiar inside the house. But there'd be no racing today. There'd be no joy in familiar surroundings. Today, her heart bled with disappointment and failure as she ambled toward the house to give her grandfather the bad news.

Chance dismounted and ground tethered Joyful, then put his hand to Lizzie's back as they climbed the steps and entered the house together. The instant she walked inside, her heart dipped with dread. The curtains were pulled closed, shutting out light, and an eerie silence filled the house in the darkness.

"Grandpa?"

Chance's spurs jangled as they moved farther inside the room. "Edward?"

Lizzie glanced at Chance. His pulse ticked on the side of his jaw.

"In here," Grandpa called out.

The strain in his voice gave her a start.

She dashed to his bedroom and gasped when she saw him lying across his bed, as ashen as the pale hair on his head. She rushed to his side and kneeled by the bed. He managed a smile for her and shakily reached for her hand. She grabbed his hand with both of hers and cried inside for the frailty she found in his grip.

"I'm glad to see you, my girl."

"Oh, Grandpa." Lizzie kissed his hand, holding back tears as an ache began in the pit of her stomach. Her grandpa watched her, as if he couldn't believe she was there.

"I love you, Elizabeth."

She bit down on her lip and gasped. The words tumbled from her mouth. "I love you, too."

She couldn't take her eyes from his face. He looked so weak she thought he'd vanish into the air.

"You got the herd sold off?" he asked with a strain in his voice. "All...went well, then?"

Lizzie squeezed her eyes closed. Above her, Chance's voice carried in the quiet room. "Yes, Edward. We've sold off the herd. All is well."

Lizzie shot him a quick look. He gazed down at her, giving a silent warning not to contradict his purposeful lie.

"That's g-good." Grandpa coughed for a moment and even the violence of the coughs had mellowed to bare stolen breaths. He whispered to Chance, "Appreciate all you've done, boy."

Chance took a swallow and nodded. "You got nothing to worry over, Edward."

Grandpa closed his eyes. "That's…all I need to hear."

"Grandpa!" Panic swam in her belly and she turned to Chance.

Chance whispered to her. "Let him sleep, Lizzie."

Lizzie turned to her grandfather. He'd fallen asleep, his breaths shallow but his body restful. She didn't want to leave him, but before she could protest, Chance lifted her from her kneeling position. Her legs quaked as she stood. From behind, he braced her shoulders, steadying her, and spoke quietly in her ear. "I need to talk to you."

He guided her out of the room. She went reluctantly, keeping her eyes on her grandpa as she walked away.

Outside his door, Lizzie's tears finally spilled over onto her cheeks. "He's so weak."

"Yeah, he is." Chance's face pulled into a frown. He sighed with regret and she could see how shaken he was, too. "I'll go into town and get the doctor."

She searched his eyes. "We lied to him." The accusation was aimed at herself, as well. She hadn't the courage to tell her grandfather the truth.

"No, we didn't," Chance said. "We sold the herd. And all will be well."

She shook her head back and forth, the long tail of her braid whipping from shoulder to shoulder. "Nothing's right. Nothing. How can all be well?"

Chance wiped tears from her eyes, collecting each drop with a fingertip. "Listen to me, Lizzie. You got nothing to worry over. I'm going into town and when I come back, we'll show Edward the money. It'll ease his mind."

"W-what money? You g-gonna rob the bank?" She sniffed. Had Chance gone delusional?

Chance inhaled deeply and looked her straight in the eyes, his voice firm as granite. "I'm selling the ruby necklace."

"No! You can't. You can't. It's all you've got left of your mother's memory."

Lizzie wouldn't let him do it. He couldn't possibly make such a sacrifice for her. Chance had nearly lost his life preserving that necklace. It was all he had of his family.

"You got no say in what I do, Lizzie. Much as you think otherwise. You need that money more than I need to hold on to the necklace. I made Edward a promise and I aim to see it through."

"Not with that, Chance. Not with that."

"Listen to me. I wouldn't be here if it wasn't for your grandfather. That's the plain truth. Now I'm going to fetch the doctor. If there's a chance to save Edward any pain, we're going to take it."

Lizzie's world was crashing down around her. She was lost and aching so badly, she thought her heart would shatter.

Chance softened his voice. "You can stay with him. Watch over him. When he wakes, he'd like to see you there."

"But—"

"Be strong, Lizzie. I know you are. I'll be back as soon as I can." Chance grabbed her forearms gently and she lifted her eyes to peer deep into his determined brown eyes. "Do as I say. It's gonna be all right."

Lizzie had no choice. She knew that once he set his mind on something, he wouldn't back down. Everything inside her went slack and she didn't have the will to protest. She nodded and watched him open the curtains to bring the last of the day's light into the room. Then he walked over to her mother's sideboard and opened the bottom drawer. He grabbed the wooden box engraved with the Worth *W* and lifted the lid. His gaze lingered on the jewel for a stretched-out moment, then he sighed, deep in thought. He caught her attention, his gaze intense. "Good thing I left it here or it might have been stolen, too. Maybe this was the true purpose for Edward to store this for me all these years. "

Lizzie didn't believe so. That necklace belonged to Chance. It was his legacy, but she couldn't make him see that. Instead, she watched Chance snap the box closed, walk out of the house and ride off the ranch with the promise to return with the doctor.

Chance kept the ruby necklace tucked inside his vest as he rode the few short miles into town. The sun had set, but there was enough moonlight to guide his way down the road toward Red Ridge. Joyful was tired, and normally he wouldn't push her. But this wasn't a normal situation. This was a mission to help Edward one last time. Chance had no illusion that Edward would recover, but he sure as hell wanted to keep the man from any more misery and pain.

As he entered town, he asked the first person he saw on the street—a rotund man wearing a hat and walking with a cane—where he could find the doctor. The man gave him directions and less than fifteen minutes later Chance met with Dr. Finnigan Jones at his home, introducing himself as the Mitchell-ranch foreman.

Dr. Jones nodded his head and kept on nodding when

Chance told him about Edward's ailment. Sadness stole over his features. "I'm aware of Edward's case. I'm afraid there's no cure for consumption. All I can do is offer him laudanum to ease his pain. How is his grand-daughter holding up?"

"Not too well. He's all the family she has."

"Yes, I remember. Lizzie, is it?"

Chance nodded.

The doctor wiped his spectacles with a cloth then examined them in the light before tucking them into his vest pocket. "I'm afraid I haven't been able to convince her that Mr. Mitchell was quite ill and recovery wasn't likely. Poor girl. She held on to misguided hope. I'll finish up here and make the trip out to the Mitchells' within the hour."

"Appreciate it."

Somewhat relieved that Edward would get treatment tonight, Chance left the doctor's home. Now it was time to sell the necklace. In all the towns he'd been to, the wealthiest men were the saloon owners and the bankers. Chance headed for the saloon first with the idea of making a sale and quenching his thirst with a bottle of fine whiskey. He was saddle weary, grimy from the trail and feeling piss-poor in general. A swig or two might lift his sour mood.

Chance entered the saloon and took a look around. The place was half-empty. There was a low hum of conversation. Men and a few saloon girls sat around tables, sipping their drinks. In one corner four men played cards, while in the other, a woman dressed in green satin with a feather in her hair whispered to the piano player.

Chance sidled up to the bar and ordered a bottle of

the finest whiskey they had on hand and within seconds, the bottle and the whiskey glass appeared before him. Chance poured himself a shot. Leaning back, he sipped the golden liquor, savoring the slow burn going down his throat.

The woman in green laughed, throwing her head back and for a moment, the barkeep's eyes gleamed as he watched her.

"Does she sing?" he asked.

The barkeep turned to him for a second. "Like a songbird sent from heaven. Maisey's got a pure voice." He went back to staring at her.

"That her husband? The piano player?"

The barkeep shook his head. "Nope, her brother. They're an act. Been playing here for about a year now. They just live down the road a ways."

He studied how the bartender watched her. He would make a lousy poker player. His eyes gave him away and Chance saw his opportunity. "You own this saloon?"

The bartender turned to him, his brows gathered into a fine line across his forehead. Once he focused on Chance, his friendly voice took a dubious tone. "I do. You got a complaint?"

"Not a one. Whiskey's real good." He lifted his glass in salute.

Tension released from the barkeep's face. "You're the man working over at the Mitchell spread, right?"

Chance nodded. He wasn't surprised that this man knew who he was—strangers in town were always being sized up by the local folk. "I am. Chance Worth." He put out his hand.

The barkeep walked over and shook his hand. "Nice meetin' you. John Lancer. I know Edward Mitchell. As decent a man as they come. They've hit on some hard times out there."

"I can't disagree with you. Fact is, I'm trying to help them."

"You working for free?"

"Something like that," Chance admitted. "But they're cash poor. They need a little boost. Maybe you know of someone wanting this."

Chance turned his body to hide the jewel from prying eyes and pulled the box from inside his vest. He opened the lid slowly and showed off the gem. "It's a genuine ruby. Biggest I've seen."

Lancer's eyes widened when he caught sight of the pear-shaped red ruby. Then he met Chance's gaze with brows that lifted his forehead. "Where'd you get that?"

"It's a family stone. Came to me legitimately, if that's what you're asking. My mama cherished the gem. Any gal would love having such a fine piece." Chance swiveled his head toward the woman in green across the room. "Yep, any fine lady sure would love to get this here necklace as a gift. For some special occasion or something."

Lancer followed the direction of Chance's gaze to see Maisey step up onto a four-by-four platform. The piano player started in with a lively tune and the gal's voice broke through the din of noise, garnering everyone's attention.

Lancer appeared fully captivated, refusing to serve anyone until the song was finished. Chance understood why the man was smitten. Maisey's soft tender voice could stir even the least saintly of men and bring them to their knees. She mesmerized the audience with an innocence and purity that saloon patrons rarely were privy to. She belonged in a church choir, not a smoke-filled room, and by the look of admiration and pride on his face, Lancer seemed to know it.

Lancer twisted his mouth and sighed. "How much?"

"Two hundred."

The barkeep stilled and a storm brewed in his eyes. "You got guts, Mr. Worth. I'll say that."

"It's worth double that." He snapped the box closed and began tucking it away.

"Now, hold on. Hold on," the barkeep urged. He stole a longing glance at Maisey who was ready to sing her next tune, before leaning close to Chance over the bar. In a lowered voice, he asked, "How about one-fifty and free drinks for a month?"

The idea of free whiskey made him silently smile and though tempting, he shook his head. He needed hard cash. "Not a chance."

After a few minutes of negotiating, Chance was able to seal the deal for the amount he'd wanted. That cash, along with what he had left of his own money, wouldn't come to half of what was stolen, but it was enough to keep Lizzie secure for a few years. Now if he found her a husband, his worries would be over.

Lizzie woke up in a chair beside her grandfather. Stiff from her awkward sleeping position, she pulled her arms up and stretched out the kinks. She rolled her neck back and forth, then hinged her body forward, away from the quilt that did little to add comfort to the ladder-back chair.

Early dawn light streamed through holes in the worn-thin curtains. Morning smells of fresh earth and crisp air brought her out of her sleepy haze. She focused on

Grandpa again. Seeing him sleep restfully now gave her new hope.

The doctor had brought medicine to ease his pain last night and her grandfather had had a good night. She knew once he woke, he'd feel a lot better. Now that she was back home, she'd see to his recovery and though she hated the thought of Chance selling his precious family gem, the money would go a long way in easing her grandfather's burden. He would finally have some peace of mind and the lack of worry would aid in his healing.

She was sure.

The door opened with a creak and she saw Chance standing there. He hadn't shaved since Prescott and the stubble looked scratchy on his face. His hair was overly long, brushing his collar. He gestured for her to come to him and she rose, noting that despite his lack of grooming, he was handsome enough to make her skin tingle. He'd slept in the bunkhouse last night after returning from town. It was the first night in days that they'd slept apart. Though her purpose was clear, to see to her grandpa's needs, Lizzie had to admit she missed sleeping beside Chance last night.

She gave her grandfather a quick examining glance before tiptoeing out of the room. She followed Chance to the kitchen where the delicious scent of hot coffee wafted to her nostrils.

"How is he this morning?" Chance asked, pouring them each a cup from the coffeepot.

"He slept peacefully all night. The laudanum is working."

"Good," Chance said, then lifted the mug to his mouth for a sip. "Edward deserves to be out of pain."

Lizzie took her cup into her hands and the heat warmed her. "I think he's going to be fine in a little while. He just needs rest like he got last night."

Chance winced, his face growing tight. "Lizzie." Slowly, seeming to muster patience, he set his cup down on the table and turned to meet her eyes solidly. "That's not what the doctor said. You gotta face facts. Edward is very ill."

"Chance, don't you go preaching doom to me. Don't. Once he sees the cash and knows we're gonna survive this bad spell, his spirits will lift."

Chance stared at her such a long time, her heart nearly stopped. She didn't want to hear what he was about to say. The debate flashed in and out of his eyes, until finally he sighed. "You need to eat. Sit down. I'll fry up some eggs."

"I'm not hungry."

"You'll eat. Those eggs are going down into your gullet one way or another. I'm not about to watch you faint dead away."

Lizzie didn't fight him. She didn't have an appetite, but he was right about sustaining her health. She needed to eat. She plopped down onto the chair and they ate eggs and drank coffee in silence.

Chance walked outside to see to Joyful. After a time, Lizzie heard hammering out by the bunkhouse. Chance was making some sort of repair. The notion of fixing up the ranch ran through her mind and brought her a measure of joy. She finished cleaning up the kitchen in a short time, then checked on Grandpa again. She lowered down beside him on the bed and watched him breathe. He looked frail but soon he'd be right as rain. He had to be.

His eyes shuttered open and he actually smiled when he saw her. She took it as a good sign. "Lizzie," he said, his voice quietly calm. "Open the curtains, girl. I want to see you in the light."

Lizzie did as he asked and stole a glance out the window. She watched Chance working on the bunkhouse door for a moment and then turned with a big smile for her grandfather. "Good morning, Grandpa."

He lifted his head from the pillow and the effort seemed to sap most of his strength. "Mornin', dear girl." His gaze raked over the room. "Where's Chance?"

Before Lizzie could answer, he rasped in a soft voice, "Will you go get him?"

"Surely, Grandpa. I'll be right back."

Lizzie called for Chance from the doorway then returned to the bedroom. "He'll be right in. Grandpa, he made a good deal with the cattle buyers." Lizzie pulled out the stack of bills from the bedside drawer. She took a breath, praying for forgiveness from the Lord for lying, and once again, thanking Chance for his sacrifice. "We got us enough to build the herd again. Just look at all this cash. You and me, we'll be all right."

Chance's boots scraped the floor as he strode into the room. He sidled up to her and darted a questioning glance from Edward to her. "Mornin', Edward."

"Boy." There was tenderness in the way he called Chance "boy," as though he was someone who held a special place in his heart. There was no doubt he did, Lizzie had to admit. Though Chance was stubborn as a mule, hard to deal with, bossy, overconfident and just plain rude at times, Lizzie would never forget what he'd done for her family. He owed Grandpa a debt, but many men wouldn't have honored that debt the way Chance had.

Edward took a moment to gather his strength before he continued. "I got to thank you," he said, his voice rich with sincerity, "for coming and helping us."

"I'd do it again, Edward."

Grandpa's lips lifted in a smile. He managed a nod, too.

He put out his hand for Lizzie. She grabbed onto it and again was struck by the absolute failing in his grip. He took shallow breaths now. "You're my beautiful granddaughter and I... I will always love you."

"I'll always love you, too, Grandpa."

"Elizabeth," he whispered her name.

Lizzie glanced at Chance. His face was hard, but his eyes...his eyes shone with sympathy and sadness. Lizzie's stomach squeezed tight and panic she couldn't control rose up, swarming her with terror. She watched Grandpa close his eyes then, softly, easily, giving up to the pain that had consumed him. His breaths stopped soon after and his face...his beautiful, old, sweet face lost expression. His hand dropped loose of hers.

"Oh, no."

Color quickly drained from his skin. She couldn't bear to see the life seep from his body. She couldn't bear to see him so very still. She turned her head away, the pain of seeing him gone forever too much to take.

Tears spilled silently from her eyes. She wept and wept.

Two powerful hands touched her shoulders and turned her around. She fell against Chance, sobbing. He held her firm, like he always did when she needed him. He didn't shush her, or say anything to make her feel better. Nothing would—the pain in her heart was wicked and sharp and Chance knew. He knew and he let her cry until she didn't have another drop of moisture left.

"Edward is at peace now," Chance said, an hour later.

Lizzie nodded, sitting on the sofa, staring soulfully out the window. She hadn't said a word since her grandfather died. It was as if all the bluster inside was washed clean away, hollowing her out. Her heart hurt. It ached like it never had before.

"He was struggling for months, Lizzie." Chance's voice cracked and she looked at him, standing by the window, sipping whiskey. He took a swallow and then walked over to sit down beside her. He took another sip then turned to her. "He loved you something fierce."

A lump formed in the throat. She didn't think she'd ever be able to swallow past it. "I...know."

"He waited until we returned...to let go. He was a remarkable man."

Lizzie didn't have any more tears to shed. She nodded, then looked at the bottle he clutched in his hands. "Can I have some of that?"

Chance glanced at the amber bottle with puzzlement, then looked at her, his eyes lit with slight amusement. "You ever tried it?"

She shook her head. "But if there was ever a time, it would be now." The whiskey would help wipe the pain away. Chance surely thought so. He'd taken several swigs already.

"Yeah, I suppose you're right."

Chance rose from his seat and retrieved a glass from the sideboard. The tumbler was sized for water or lemonade and when he returned, he poured a splash of liquor that rose an inch high. "Drink it slowly. Might burn when it goes down."

Lizzie brought the glass to her lips and sipped. The whiskey tasted pleasant at first as she swirled it into her mouth. When she swallowed, a lingering heat scorched her throat on the way down to her belly. That's when it hit her. The burn lit low and flamed up, building like a budding fire across the prairie. She coughed once and Chance put his hand to her back.

"You alright?"

She caught her breath and nodded. Oddly, the sensation soothed as much as it caused turmoil. She turned to Chance. "It's strange-tasting."

He took the glass from her hand. "It's not for young ladies."

On instinct, Lizzie reached for the glass again, brushing fingers with Chance, and their eyes met in a lingering stare. She witnessed his pain, though he tried to shield it from her. He would miss Edward Mitchell, as well, of that there was no doubt. They watched each other, with fingers entwined on that tumbler and something changed between them in that moment. She'd experienced many firsts with Chance. He'd been the first man she'd slept with, in that horrible storm. He'd been the first man to kiss her. He'd been the first man to touch her body in ways that should have been wicked, but only made her crave more. He was the first man to share grief with her when someone they'd both loved had passed on.

Now, he was with her as she experienced her first drink of pure alcohol. "You know I'm not that young. I'll finish it," she said softly.

With reluctance, Chance released his hold and watched as she took the rest of the liquor into her mouth.

"Sort of eases the pain," she said after a time.

"Dulls the senses, darlin'."

"Do you often need your senses dulled?" she asked, looking down at the empty glass in her hands.

"There have been times when I wanted to forget. Yeah, it helps."

"Did you drink because of a woman?" she asked.

His quiet chuckle filled the room. "Maybe, a time or two."

"I wonder if a man would ever drink because of me," she said, a sweeping sense of wistful longing grabbing her. She sighed and stared out the parlor window.

She sensed Chance's gaze on her. Then he lifted the bottle to his mouth and took another swig. "I'm sure you'll make some man crazy enough."

The comment didn't really sink in. She turned his way. "Chance?"

"Hmm?"

"My head feels muddled. Is that the dulling?" Lizzie swayed toward him on the sofa.

Chance grabbed her shoulders and leaned her back against the cushions. "Yeah, seems to be working overly fast on you. You're such a little thing."

"I'm not that little," she said in protest, but the sound coming out of her mouth was almost breathless.

Next thing she knew she was being lifted from the sofa. She felt light as air, floating, as Chance carried her across the room. Her head met with the soft pillows on her bed, her eyes blurring as she glanced up at Chance. His handsome face appeared twice in her vision. Two Chances. She smiled.

"Take a rest, Lizzie," he was telling her. "I'll make arrangements for Edward."

"You're not leaving me," she said, feeling the need for panic, but unable to muster that emotion. Everything seemed so fine right now as she closed her eyes.

"I'll be back before you wake up, darlin'. I promise."

Chapter Twelve

Edward deserved a proper burial and Chance made sure he got one. Nearly half the townsfolk came to the hillside that overlooked the Red Ridge Mountains to pay honor and bid farewell to a decent man. One by one, they approached solemnly, climbing up the rise and then making their way down to level land beside the gravesite. The casket lay above ground, ready to be hoisted down after the minister said his piece and prayers were spoken.

Dressed in a dark shirt, trousers and string tie, Chance stood by Lizzie's side. She looked downright maudlin dressed in black, wearing a dark-ribboned bonnet that covered a severe bun on her head. Today, she looked every bit of her nineteen years. Her face was swollen from tears, her cheeks reddened and those bluer-than-blue eyes, looked so sad.

Chance felt the loss keenly himself. It was as if he'd lost a father all over again. He'd not given a soul his trust after his folks were killed. Even as an orphan, he'd been on guard, protecting himself against feeling any more loss in his life. Then Edward Mitchell came along, saving his life and making him realize he was worthy of fair and honest treatment. Edward had given Chance something powerful in that and he'd always be obliged. But he'd also felt something strong for the older man, a devotion and respect he'd not given anyone else in his adult years.

Lizzie stirred beside him. He turned his head to make sure she was holding up, but found her eyes wide and lit with joy. The look baffled him, until he followed the direction of her gaze and saw Mrs. Finch walking down the hilly rise with a young man beside her, dressed in a fine wool suit. Lizzie dropped the bouquet of wild-flowers she held in her hands. She picked up her skirts and hastened toward the two figures, her bonnet falling from her head, held only by the ribbon tied at her throat. She appeared oblivious to anything but getting to them. Once she reached the young man, she barreled straight into his arms.

"Hayden," she said loud enough for all to hear. "You're here. You came home."

"Course I did, Lizzie. I told you I would." He embraced her lightly out of respect for the solemn occasion, but his quick smile was genuine and all for Lizzie. Then his expression changed. "Just sorry I came home to Mr. Mitchell's passing. It's a sad day."

Chance moved closer to pick up on the conversation. Hayden Finch coming home now might be the best thing for Lizzie.

She stepped out of the young man's arms and nodded her head. "It is, Hayden. The saddest of days. It's been horrible. My heart is just about broken."

Mrs. Finch put a hand on Lizzie's shoulder. "You dear child. You've had to endure this all alone. I had no idea Edward was in such a bad way. You should have told me. I would have come by more often and helped you."

"Thank you, Mrs. Finch. I wasn't exactly…alone." Lizzie turned to Chance as he moved into their circle to greet the Finches. Lizzie made quick introductions and they shook hands.

Hayden thanked him for watching out for Lizzie and Mrs. Finch greeted him with a cautious eye. Chance had seen that look before. She was wary of him and thought he posed a threat to her son's happiness. That much, Chance knew for fact. But her worry was unfounded. Soon, she'd see that.

The minister cleared his throat and called the mourners to cluster closer to the gravesite. Fast-moving gray clouds had appeared and the wind had picked up, putting a bite in the air. Chance stood on one side of Lizzie, while Hayden stood on the other, hats in hand. They bowed their heads and prayed as the minister paid homage to a fine man.

Lizzie made it through the ceremony, sniffling but without a barrage of tears, and Chance was relieved. Her crying cut straight through him and made him want to protect her from anything that would do her harm. It was obligation, he surmised. His vow to Edward that made him react that way.

Most of the mourners walked up to give her their regards before taking their leave. Lizzie stood over the casket long after they were gone. Only Chance and the Finches remained by her side.

Gently, Chance took the batch of wildflowers she

clutched out of her hand and set them on top of Edward's casket. He gave Lizzie a quick smile, but she didn't acknowledge it. Her eyes were the saddest he'd ever seen. "You ready to go?" he asked quietly.

Lizzie simply stared at the casket and the flowers lying there now. She stood still as stone as if she hadn't heard him. Chance understood her not wanting to let go. He'd felt that way as a young boy, staring at his parent's grave markers, clinging to the life he'd once known and fearing what the future held for him without them.

Saying goodbye was difficult. Lizzie was brave and she'd survive though he wished he could make it easier on her. He understood how a body grieved. Time healed yet the loss, no matter how long ago, always left a scar.

"Come on now, Lizzie. Say your last goodbye," Hayden said quietly.

She glanced at the blond-headed man. He had a pleasant enough face and didn't have to bend to look into her eyes. He put his arm around her shoulder and brought her close with a slight squeeze, encouraging her. "It's time to go."

Lizzie stared at him and when Chance was sure she would protest, she nodded her head and let Hayden guide her away from the gravesite.

Chance's gut lurched seeing Hayden consoling Lizzie, seeing the trust she had for him, seeing his arms snug around her. Just a few minutes ago, he was thanking all things holy that Hayden had returned home. Edward had hoped Hayden would be the man for Lizzie and that meant Chance would be free of his obligation toward her. If he could trust the look he saw in Hayden's eyes, Lizzie would soon have a beau, and maybe a husband. So his tightening gut didn't make a lick of sense.

Chance said a final farewell to Edward with heaviness in his heart then strode up the hill, meeting the three of them at the top. Mrs. Finch stepped forward, her tone formal. "After such a day, Lizzie might find some solace spending time with us. And I'm inviting you, as well, Mr. Worth, to have a meal with us."

Chance glanced at Lizzie's hopeful eyes. It was better to let the Finches console her without him in the way. They'd take good care of her. "I appreciate the offer, Mrs. Finch. But I've got to see to some things for the ranch." He turned to Lizzie. "I'll come by for you later."

Lizzie snapped out of her quiet mood. "But, Chance you have—"

"Sorry you can't join us," Mrs. Finch said quickly with an overly polite smile. "Come along now, Lizzie. You must be famished."

Lizzie began another protest, "But—"

"Like I said, Lizzie," Chance said firmly, "you go on. Spend some time with the Finches. I'll come by for you in a few hours."

The look in her eyes reflected deep disappointment. She stared at him and then with a slump of her shoulders, she sighed wearily. Exhaustion had gotten to her and she was too grief-filled to argue. Chance turned and headed toward town without a look back. It was best this way for both of them, but that notion didn't prevent his guilt at disappointing her on such a sad day, from slicing clear through him.

"I'm sorry I didn't finish the meal, Mrs. Finch." Lizzie glanced at the fried chicken, dumplings and squash sitting on her plate. Not only hadn't she finished it, she'd barely taken three bites. The food went down hard and Lizzie had barely tasted anything. She didn't have the heart to eat.

"It's fine, dear. You'll have it later. You've been through a great deal, but now that Hayden is back, you won't feel quite so alone."

Hayden sat beside her, his plate empty. "Lizzie, things will get better now. I just know they will."

Lizzie nodded, though she didn't feel such optimism. She was hollow inside, missing her grandpa overly much. She lifted her gaze to Hayden, finding some comfort in his return. She needed his friendship now more than ever. "I'm glad you're home. It was a lift to my spirits seeing you today."

"I just arrived last night, Lizzie. And I have plans. Big plans. When you feel better I'll tell you about them."

Lizzie didn't want to hear his plans. He was going to find a girl and get married. He'd told her a dozen times before he left for Illinois that when he got back to Red Ridge, he'd be ready. Another bout of sadness tore through her heart. How long would he be her friend? Would he abandon her once he found his lady love?

"Hayden is planning on expanding my shop," Mrs. Finch said, sitting taller in her chair. "He's got wonderful ideas to build an emporium."

Hayden glanced at his mother and spoke softly, "Mother, she doesn't want to hear about it now."

"No, no… I do. I do, Hayden," Lizzie said, sending a tentative smile to Mrs. Finch. "Go on, tell me."

Hayden smiled warmly and began, "We're going to break down the walls of the millinery and build up the store to more than twice the size. Hats are only a small part of what we'll sell. Once the emporium is complete, we'll sell everything from clothing to jellies.

We'll allow some townsfolk to put their wares in our store and we'll sell them on consignment."

"Consignment? What's that?" Lizzie glanced at Mrs. Finch, then back at Hayden. "You sure did learn some big words in Illinois."

"Lizzie," Hayden said with such excitement, it reminded her of years past, when they'd race along the lakeshore, the anticipation being nearly as much fun as the race itself. "Well, if you, for example, decided you'd like to put your dolls in our store, we would sell them for you and we'd take a small share in the profits. It's being done in the East all the time now."

"Oh, I see."

"Hayden has a lot of good ideas, Lizzie," Mrs. Finch repeated. "I'll take our plates now and bring in dessert."

Lizzie immediately rose. "I'll help you."

Mrs. Finch gestured for her to sit down. "Nonsense, dear. Hayden will help. Won't you, son?"

"Sure thing, Mother."

"Lizzie, do you think you can eat a bite or two of peach cobbler?" she asked.

"Oh, uh…yes, Mrs. Finch." She'd have to force it down, not to offend her. "Thank you."

An hour later, Lizzie sat on the back-porch swing with Hayden. She'd always liked the Finch home. It was located just outside the main part of town and had a pretty whitewashed fence and flowers in the garden.

Her stomach ached a bit. She'd managed to eat half the portion of her dessert and it lay like lead at the bottom of her belly. Oddly, the swinging made her feel better, so she leaned back and enjoyed her time with her friend.

They sat in companionable silence for a long while,

but Lizzie could do that with Hayden. They could sit, or play games, or talk to each other for hours, and all of it felt right. They'd argue, too, but in the end, Hayden would always give in. Sometimes, that would aggravate her. She liked winning, but only when the fight was hard-won.

Maybe he'd changed, she thought. Maybe he wouldn't have time for her with his fancy new idea for business. Maybe he'd outgrown their friendship. In her heart, she knew nothing remained the same for long. But she dearly hoped her friendship with Hayden, unusual as it was, wouldn't be among them. He'd been gone for two years—an eternity to someone like her with scant amount of friends—and she'd counted the days until his return. That is to say until Chance had shown up on the ranch weeks ago, causing havoc and making her question everything she'd held dear.

As much as she'd protested, Chance had made her face facts she didn't want to face. He'd been upfront and honest with her. With a certain amount of shame, she admitted to herself that she hadn't pined for Hayden's return once Chance Worth stepped foot on Mitchell land.

"Oh, no!" Struck by a sudden thought, Lizzie lifted partway from the swing. "Chance doesn't know where you live."

Hayden shook his head and reassured her. "No need to worry, Lizzie. He'll find us. Everyone in town knows where we live."

She relaxed against the back of the swing. "I guess you're right. Nothing will stop that man from doing what needs doing."

Hayden stared at her. "Tell me about him, will you?"

"Chance?"

"Yes, tell me how he came to work at the ranch."

Lizzie spent the next thirty minutes explaining how Chance had met her grandfather. She told him everything...well, almost everything. She heeded Chance's warning not to speak to anyone of the night of the storm when they'd slept under the same blanket nearly naked. And she'd kept the kiss they'd shared from Hayden, as well. But not because she'd promised Chance she'd hold that secret, but because she wanted that memory to be hers and hers alone.

Not even her dear friend Hayden would be privy to the details she held close to her heart.

"Do you like him, Lizzie?"

The question startled her. She sat stiff in her seat and took a big swallow. She glanced at Hayden, who seemed to be genuinely interested in her answer. "I...uh." What she felt for Chance went deep, but she couldn't say for certain what those feelings were. There were times she thought she was half in love with him and then there were times when she wished she'd never met him. "He's helped at the ranch and all." He'd saved her life a few times, too. "Grandpa thought him a good man."

"But you don't?"

"No, I do." Her revelation shouldn't surprise her. But it did. When Chance had first come to the ranch, Lizzie had been hell-bent on making him feel out of place. She hated him coming, disrupting her life. But after a time, she'd seen in him what her grandfather had. A man who'd had a tough life and had survived by sheer will and smarts. It left him unable to trust or to open himself up to anyone. But he had honor. That much she knew about him and she admired him for it.

Her brows furrowed as she tried to sort out her feelings in her head, but nothing seemed clear. She turned to her friend. "Hayden, why are you being so nosy about him anyways?"

Hayden drew a quick breath. "Now, Lizzie. You're not gonna like what I have to say, but I'm just gonna say it. Mother mentioned about the two of you staying alone at the ranch. It's hardly proper."

Lizzie bolted upright, her fury overtaking her exhaustion and grief. Fire fueled her indignation as she turned to glare at him on the swing. "What are you saying exactly? Do you want me to give up the ranch and the land? Or maybe you want me to do all the work by myself without anyone's help? Lord knows, I did my fair share when Grandpa took sick. And so now I'm not allowed to have a ranch foreman, for fear of my reputation being ruined. Well, I don't have the convenience of choosing, Hayden. I just don't."

Hayden rose to his feet and met her gaze straight on with apology in his eyes. "Calm down, Lizzie. I didn't mean to upset you any more than you are already. Honest. I'm just trying to protect you."

"Well, I'm sick and tired of men trying to protect me." She flung her arms up in the air. "All of you."

Hayden gripped her arms, which had gone limp. "Sit down and take a breath."

She slumped down into her seat and stared straight ahead, when she wanted to march straight out the door.

"I'm sorry, Lizzie. Truly."

She shook her head. "I wouldn't let Chance hear you say any of this. He wouldn't take kindly to it. He's been respectable to me." She turned to him, her voice gravelly but determined. "Do you think I'd stand for anything else?"

Hayden squeezed his eyes shut. "No, of course not."

"If people talk, they talk, Hayden. I've got a ranch to run." Or rather to build, with Chance's help. Once she got the ranch going again, Chance would leave. The thought just added to her distress.

"I shouldn't have said anything at all. I don't want us to fight. I never want that." He gave her a moony-eyed look. "Please forgive me."

Her temper cooled some. His apology was sincere. She trusted that he only wanted what was best for her and she could never stay mad at him for long. "I'll forgive you, if you promise not to talk about this again."

"I promise," he said quickly.

With a bob of her head, she said, "Then, I do forgive you. Now, tell me about your time away. I want to hear everything."

An hour later, Lizzie stood with Hayden and Mrs. Finch enjoying the shade of the front porch when Chance rode up in a wagon pulled by Joyful and another sorrel. There was a keen look in his eyes. Immediate excitement stirred in her belly. She let her grief go for a moment and forgot about Hayden's upsetting comment earlier. Her heart raced wildly as she bid Mrs. Finch and Hayden farewell on the porch steps, thanking them for their kindness.

She strode purposely toward Chance and faced him, hoping she was right in her assumption. "You bought us a wagon?"

Chance nodded and jumped down from the buckboard. "You ready to go home?"

"I am," she said. She didn't think anything would

pull her out of her sad mood, but this…this was something.

Chance helped her up, holding her hand as she
climbed onto the seat. He tipped his hat to the Finches,
climbed onto the wagon, took the reins and together
they rode off.

Lizzie ran her hand down Melody's chestnut mane
and whispered good morning to her. You like it here,"
she said, "don't you, girl?" The mare gently shuffled
closer, her big round eyes expressive, apparently enjoying the attention from her side of the corral fence.

Lizzie broke a carrot in two and immediately Joyful
ambled over from the far side of the perimeter. She
shared the carrot with the two mares giving Joyful a
loving pat on the shoulder as she chomped on her treat.
"Good girl," she said, grateful Joyful had accepted
Melody so easily. Chance said that she would welcome
the lively company. Poor Juniper didn't have much
energy anymore. For a ranch the size of hers, there
weren't very many animals. At least there were chickens
in the henhouse.

Bringing Melody to the ranch had lifted Lizzie's
spirits some. The past two days had been lonely without Grandpa. Chance wasn't around much. The day
he'd surprised her with Melody and the buckboard
wagon, he'd also bought lumber and supplies enough
to see to the repairs to the ranch. Most of his day was
spent out on the range, repairing fences or replacing
the old ones that had fallen down. He worked from
sunup to sundown. Lizzie did what she could around
the house, her usual chores enough to keep her busy

most of the day, but it didn't stop her heart from aching from her loss.

Nights were the hardest. She'd sit across from Chance at supper and glance at the empty seat at the head of the table. Her heart would ache, but Lizzie fought her sorrow. Having Chance there helped some, though after he'd take his last bite of the meal, he'd dash off to the bunkhouse claiming fatigue.

"Ouch, damn it!"

Chance's angry voice carried all the way to the corral. She whirled around putting the sun behind her and strode toward the backside of the barn.

"Chance?"

"Ah, hell."

Lizzie stopped short, seeing blood spurting from Chance's hand. He was crouched by the barrel in front of a shaving mirror, bare chested with soap on half his face, wielding a long blade in his left hand. Tiny spots of blood dotted his face, too. A gasp escaped her throat as she rushed to his side. "What happened?"

"Lost my grip and nearly sliced my hand open."

"Let me see." She grabbed his right wrist gently and turned it palm up. Her stomach pitched at the inch-long slash. His hand was steady, but bleeding like a stuck pig.

She grabbed a small stool and shoved it under him. Punching her finger into his good shoulder, she ordered, "Sit down." He plopped down. "I'll be right back."

She rushed inside the house, making a quick sweep of the supplies she needed.

"You've done it good now, haven't you?" she asked when she returned moments later.

An angry growl rose up in his throat in answer.

"Hold this with your good hand," she said. Chance balanced a bowl on his lap as she dunked his injured hand inside the clean water. She dunked her hand in, too, and put firm pressure near the wound. The water was cool and would help ease the pain he must be feeling. His hands had barely healed from when he'd warded off her attacker. She hated to see Chance injured again.

The bleeding stopped, thank the good Lord.

Lizzie didn't release his hand, though. She kept on holding it under the water, applying pressure, unwilling to move away.

He kept his focus on her hand over his, then lifted his eyes to hers with a look so intense, her toes curled. He said quietly, "I got work to do, Lizzie."

She stared at the hand she held underwater, shaking her head. "Not today, Chance. Not with this here right hand."

She didn't know how it happened, but next thing she knew their hands were out of the water, the bowl had dropped to the ground and their fingers had entwined. The contrast of his weather-bronzed hand up against her pale one, big to small, rough to soft, sent shivers through her body. His touch made her shiver uncontrollably and the power of it shook her to the core.

She took a swallow.

Water dripped from both their wrists now. Lizzie's pulse pounded.

Joyful nickered from the corral, breaking the silence.

Chance spread his legs wider and drew Lizzie closer, their gazes fastened as they stared for countless moments into each other's eyes. Chance glanced at her lips, a quick flicker that she couldn't miss. He could easily pull her down onto his lap and kiss her senseless. She wouldn't protest. Not one little bit.

His gaze stayed on her. "You look pretty, Lizzie."

They were the kindest words he'd ever spoken. She'd saved the blue dress he'd given her in Prescott for a more fitting occasion. She wouldn't wear bright colors until a respectable amount of time of mourning had past. But she had taken extra care with her hair, pinning it up in a new fashion with loose tendrils falling on her cheekbones, and was wearing a newly sewn brown blouse tucked into a pleated shirt of the same color. "Thank you."

"You going somewhere special today?"

She smiled. "It's Sunday, Chance. I'm going to church. You could come with me."

"Now how can I go with my face half shaved?"

"I'll shave you," she said softly. They were inches apart. His warm breath mingled with hers. "I could do it. I would shave Grandpa at times, when he was too weak to do it himself."

His eyes filled with hunger and want and then he lowered his gaze to stare at her lips. She parted them and a deep groan rose up from his throat.

Throbbing heat pulsed below her belly. She was beginning to recognize the unfamiliar sensation that only surfaced when she was near him.

He said quietly, "I can't have you touching me that way, Lizzie."

She blinked. "But it's only a shave."

He pulled his fingers from hers and dropped his hand. "No, Lizzie."

"Are you saying you don't want me touching you?"

He rose from his seat and she was forced to back up

a step to give him room. He grabbed a cloth and wiped the soap off his face, then wrapped his hand. "That's what I'm saying."

Her hope shattered. She thought for sure he would kiss her again. She thought for sure he wasn't going to turn her away. Not after all they'd been through. "Why do you keep doing that?"

He didn't pretend ignorance. He gave her a straight-forward answer and pierced her with a genuine look of regret. "I keep forgetting who you are, Lizzie. I forget sometimes that you and me just won't work."

"Because of your vow to my grandfather."

"We've been through all the reasons," he said flatly, ending the discussion. It infuriated her when he did that, as if she was a child and he'd put his foot down, giving her no regard at all. "I'll take you into town in the buckboard and you can ask Hayden to drive you back later. I'm sure he'll be at church. Seeing as I can't do much work today, I'll get me a real shave and stay in town for a while. Don't wait up."

Lizzie glared at him. How could he be so kind in one moment, and so bullheaded and dense in the other? "Fine. Hayden asked me on a picnic after church. I'll be out late, too. At least he's one man I can count on."

She stomped out of the yard and slammed the door behind her, leaving Chance standing there, probably mad as a hatter. At least it seemed that way, with all the cursing he was doing.

Chapter Thirteen

Lizzie stared at the ten yards of fabric spread out on her parlor floor. It surrounded her with color and brightness, lending some life to a room where she'd known a world of sadness. Her decision, once made, to begin fashioning her dolls again, had helped her deal with her loss.

She ran her palm across each one of the fabrics, reveling in the feel of soft calico cotton, smooth satin and rougher burlap under her fingertips. She owed one little girl a special doll and she had other orders to fill that would help bring cash to the ranch.

This time, though, the fashioning of her dolls would be more joy than obligation, and it would help fill the loneliness of the nights. Heaven knew she'd cried herself to sleep many a night, wishing for comfort that never came. Thinking that the comfort she sought in her heart of hearts would come from the man who slept in the bunkhouse just fifty steps away.

Chance was polite to her lately, which made her

extremely wary. She couldn't say he didn't pull his weight on the ranch or deserve the rest he sought after dinner. Still, he wasn't much of a companion. Most times, it was like pulling a stuck steer out of mud to get him to talk to her at all.

I can't have you touching me that way, Lizzie.

And she hadn't touched him or been touched in nearly two weeks. Not even a slight brushing of shoulders. Chance gave her a wide berth lately, keeping himself otherwise occupied when she was around. The one thing he had done was to encourage her to work on her dolls to fill the time. She'd heeded his suggestion, after assurances from him they had enough funds to buy the necessary items.

Chance had hopes for the ranch and that helped to boost her spirit. In the two weeks since Grandpa's death, aside from making a good deal buying widow O'Dougal's wagon, he'd obtained a wily bull that had caused a lot of damage to the Bar T Ranch. The owners were only too glad to be rid of him and Chance had struck another great deal. The bull was dangerous in inexperienced hands, Chance said, but he'd dealt with his type before and assured Lizzie he'd be no problem. After the bull came the purchase of a dozen heifers and yearlings, bought from a rancher eager to move out of Red Ridge.

The unexpected sound of Hayden's voice interrupted Lizzie's reflection, giving her a start. She peeked out the parlor window, noting him speaking with Chance, who had just ridden in from the pasture. Curious, she walked to the door and opened it as Hayden and Chance were shaking hands. "Glad you could make it."

Lizzie stepped forward and both heads turned her way. "Afternoon, Lizzie," her friend said.

"Hayden, hello." She tried to keep surprise from her voice. It's good to see you."

Chance had a lopsided grin on his face. "I asked Hayden to supper today when I stopped in town. Too bad his mama couldn't join us."

Lizzie's eyes widened. Not that she wasn't happy to see her friend, but she hadn't expected Chance to do the inviting and not tell her until the guest had shown up.

"Chance said you were lonely, Lizzie. He thought I could cheer you up," Hayden said.

Lizzie slid her eyes to Chance. He kept his expression blank. "Of course I'm glad to see you, but I'm managing okay," she said.

"Well, I'm sorry I haven't stopped by more often, Lizzie. I've been busy working on the expansion of the millinery."

"I saw you at church this past Sunday." That was five days ago.

"Yes, we had a nice visit." Hayden wore the silliest moony-eyed expression.

"Lizzie, why don't you take Hayden inside the house? I'm sure he'd enjoy some lemonade on such a warm day."

Lizzie sent Chance a glare before turning to Hayden with a smile. "Would you like a drink?"

"Sure thing, I would." Hayden puffed out his chest. "Thanks for the invitation today," he said to Chance. "It's good to see the ranch again."

"I'm sure Lizzie would agree that anytime you want to stop by for a visit, you're welcome."

"Thank you, Mr. Worth." Hayden climbed the steps and Lizzie let him inside the house. Before she closed the door, she peered at Chance, who was grinning like a fool. Then he walked away with Joyful following loyally behind.

Lizzie slammed the door shut, muttering.

Hayden froze, with his arms half in, half out of the brown jacket of his suit. Ever since he'd returned home, he'd taken to wearing fancy clothes, and now as he glanced at her with a question in his eyes, she covered her chagrin with a faint-hearted smile. "Wind kicks up this time of day out here, always slamming the door clear shut."

His eyes honed in on her. "You sure that's all it is?"

"I'm sure," she fibbed.

Hayden accepted her lie and she stirred uneasily with a smidgen of guilt. She didn't need to bore him with her trials regarding Chance Worth. Her friend stepped into the room, finally taking his jacket off and slinging it over one shoulder. He focused his attention on the fabric strewn about the room. "My gosh, Lizzie. Look at all this."

She hastened to gather up yards of material, enough to make a walkway toward the kitchen. "I'm going to be working on my dolls again."

"I see that. You planning on making a hundred of them?" When he laughed Lizzie saw the young boy she'd grown up with reflected in his eyes and his friendly face.

"Not exactly a hundred, but quite a few." She'd also set out to replace worn, holey curtains and to fashion herself a few pieces of clothing. Every one of her skirts were either ripped at the hem or patched where they'd been torn.

She set the piles of yardage down on the sofa and gestured for him to sit at the kitchen table. She took his jacket and hooked it on the peg Grandpa had always used. With a sigh, she turned to pour them each a glass of lemonade. He waited for her to sit and then took a sip. "Nice and tart. Just the way I like it."

"We don't sugar it. Never did."

"I remember." His gaze flowed over her. "Lizzie, you sure have grown since I left. You're even prettier than I remembered."

Heat rose up on her cheeks and throat, not from the comment, but from the way Hayden was looking at her. She'd never seen that particular expression on his face before. "You don't have to say that, Hayden. I know I'm not pretty."

"But you are," he insisted. "Your eyes, they light your whole face."

"Same eyes as always, Hayden. Same girl you used to torment."

Hayden's lips quirked up. "I'm glad you're the same girl. And you did your share of tormenting me, as I recall."

Lizzie grinned at the memory.

"But we had the most fun when we were tormenting mean old Mr. Gilroy," Hayden said, with a note of mischief on his face. They'd throw rotten apples at his house and then run for the hills. They'd steal vegetables from his garden and make faces behind his back. "Sometimes, I think on that with shame. We shouldn't have pestered him so much."

"He deserved it," Lizzie said without pause. The

grouchy man owned the lumber mill and wasn't fair-minded at all. "He didn't know a smile in his whole life. He never had a kind word for anyone and didn't take kindly to my grandpa. They'd argue over the price of lumber and he'd call my grandpa all sorts of vile names. One time, grandpa had to cover my ears, protecting me from his foul mouth. I think he would've come to blows with the old man for being so disrespectful, but Grandpa walked off, teaching me the value of turning the other cheek."

Hayden laughed heartily. "That's one lesson you never learned too well."

Lizzie straightened in her seat, ready to protest, but Hayden was right about that so she could only agree. "I'm not a bad person, Hayden. But I do believe in an eye for an eye, like the good book says."

"Lizzie, you're not bad at all." Hayden reached over to touch her hand. His fingers were gentle on her skin and she found comfort in that. "You're a good person and you've been strong with all you've had to go through on your own."

Lizzie was grateful for Hayden's friendship. "Thank you, Hayden."

During supper, Hayden entertained Lizzie and Chance with stories of his escapades at Lake Forest University and the friends he'd made while studying there. He told tales of living in Illinois and how much he'd learned. His exuberance overflowed and Lizzie caught Chance smiling a time or two while they ate hearty beef stew with panfried biscuits. After supper, Lizzie served the two men leftover berry pie and coffee.

"But as much as I enjoyed my time away, I missed Red Ridge," Hayden said. He set his coffee mug down to stare powerfully into Lizzie's eyes, yet he spoke ever so softly. "My life is here now."

Out of the corner of her eye, she noticed Chance watching her. He'd been darting glances at her and Hayden all evening. Chance finished his coffee with one huge gulp, his throat straining to push the liquid down. She was forever noticing things about him that fully mystified her. Right now, she couldn't figure why his swallowing was so darn appealing? Why did seeing his Adam's apple bob up and down put goose bumps on her flesh?

His chair scraped against the floor as he pushed away from the table and rose from his seat. "Thanks for the meal, Lizzie." He patted his stomach. "Filled my belly near to bursting." He turned to Hayden. "She's a fine cook."

"I agree," Hayden offered eagerly.

Chance's compliment, aimed at Hayden, annoyed her.

"Well, I best be getting to bed. Got me a busy day tomorrow."

Lizzie scowled at her foreman. She'd hear him tinkering around in the bunkhouse after supper. He never went straight to bed. "Tomorrow's no different than any other day, Chance." She was tired of him making excuses for jumping up and leaving after supper. It was as if the man was deaf and dumb for all the conversation he'd offered lately.

"There's a lot to do to get this place in shape," he answered with a solemn look in his eyes. It was the same lecture she'd gotten most every night from him.

Chance tipped his hat and bid them both good-night.

Lizzie silently fumed at him. Once her dear friend

Hayden took his leave, she worked on cutting fabric into the late-night hour. Fashioning her dolls lent her comfort and gave her a distraction from a very distracting man.

Lizzie looked out at the lake as crystal-blue waters rippled under the morning sun, spreading out like a wide Spanish fan. It was kind of strange how something so beautiful to look at on a clear day could pull you down and drain the oxygen from your lungs, nearly killing you on another day. With a shiver, she recalled the first time she'd met Chance, right here on this lake. It had been the first time he'd saved her life.

The lake was peaceful and quiet now as she secretly watched Chance swimming. It was soundless from here, as he cut across the water. He came up then dove in again causing ripples to disturb the surface. The next time his head came out of the water, he was ten feet from shore, rising up and heading her way. He hadn't noticed her yet. Droplets of water rained down his chest, his dark hair straight and slicked back. The sunlight bronzed his skin and Lizzie drank in the sight. She should be used to seeing him half dressed, but Chance wasn't the kind of man a girl got used to, no matter what he was wearing or not wearing. It wasn't until he was standing to his full height that he noticed her. "You gonna turn your head or see me in my underdrawers?"

Lizzie pressed the package she held tight to her chest and watched him approach. She could hardly tear her eyes away. Goose bumps rose up on her arms as her eyes dipped down below his waistline.

He caught the direction of her gaze and stared into her eyes with a cocksure smile. "I should have known. Never give Lizzie an option. She'll always take the wrong one." But Chance had no malice in his voice. He was teasing.

Once out of the water, he dropped behind a tall bush and when he appeared again, he was wearing pants and tying the gun belt around his waist. "So, Lizzie, what brought you out to the lake this afternoon? You spying on me?"

"Me, spying on—" Lizzie's face went flush and heat burned her cheeks.

Chance grinned.

Lordy, he smelled fresh and clean and he looked so darn handsome. "You wish."

He tilted his head to the side, his gaze locked on hers. "Maybe," he said softly.

Her eyes widened at the admission. She'd missed seeing him lately. Missed the once-fragile friendship they'd developed on the cattle drive and missed the comfort he lent when her grandfather had passed on. It had been weeks since they'd had a real conversation. She'd spent her time doing her part on the ranch and working on her dolls at night.

Lizzie should be happy things were going so well. The ranch was going to survive, she knew it down deep in her bones and her best friend was home and spending a little time with her. Yet, nothing seemed right and she finally figured she was lonely for Chance's company, so much so, her heart grew heavier each and every day.

"I, uh…" She stared at his chest and the tiny hairs drying under the warmth of the sun. She took a swallow and tried to stifle the sweet hot swirls in her belly, but they kept on coming. "Here," she said, putting the package in his hands. "I made you something. I just finished it and I was—"

He held up the package. "This is for me?"

Lizzie nodded.

"You hunted me down to give this to me?"

She felt like a fool for wrapping it and tying the gift with string cord. She stood there, wondering what excuse she could give him. Nothing came to her mind but the truth. "It's your birthday today, Chance."

Chance blinked, as if just recalling and his gaze drifted off in the distance. "How did you know?"

"Grandpa always posted you a letter for your birthday."

Chance gazed down at the package he held. "He did at that."

"Would you like to open it?"

"Let me go get my shirt and—"

She set a stopping hand on his upper arm. "No, no. Don't get your shirt," she said.

His gaze traveled to her hand. Lizzie, too, focused on the thick cord of muscle underneath her fingertips. A forceful jolt flowed through her slight frame, making her dizzy. Her heart was working hard not to pound straight out of her chest.

"J-just go on and open it. I'm…I'm anxious to see what you think." Her hand fell from his arm.

His eyes narrowed at her request before he nodded. She watched as he untied the string and pulled out the indigo three-button shirt she'd been working on for two full nights. He stared at the garment in his hand. "You made this?"

"Yes."

He held it up to the light to admire her work. "It's nice. Real nice," he said and from the sincere tone of his voice, she believed him.

Carefully, he pulled it on over his head. Lizzie watched him fit his powerful arms through the sleeves and tuck the lower end of the material into his trousers. He straightened his shoulders and the fabric stretched across his chest.

"It fits." Lizzie couldn't contain her smile. She was immensely pleased.

"It does," he said. He ran his hands up and down the front of the shirt. "Feels real good, too. Thank you, Lizzie," he said and stepped closer, taking her face in the palms of his hands. With the slightest pressure he lifted her face to meet his eyes. "Means a lot." With the gentlest touch, he brushed a kiss to her mouth.

The touch of his lips on hers stunned her so, she backed away from the sheer wondrous shock. She'd dreamed about him kissing her again. Dreamed of him touching her and making those sweet hot swirls in her belly turn into a full-out twister.

Instantly, she closed the gap between their bodies to circle her arms around his neck. She lifted her eyes to his. "Happy birthday, Chance."

She brought her mouth closer and gave him a true kiss, one filled with every single heartaching emotion she felt for him. A kiss that eased the pain of her recent loneliness and told him without a doubt that he was someone special in her life.

She'd been fighting it for too long. Maybe because he'd never given her a reason to believe he'd ever want a woman like her and maybe because she'd been unsure of what she'd really been feeling. But now, without any doubt, Lizzie knew in the pit of her stomach and from the very depth of her spirit, that she loved Chance Worth.

She loved him so much, she nearly burst with joy. She poured everything she had inside into her kiss. Oh, how she'd missed being near him and breathing in his scent, tasting from his mouth and feeling his body harden with need.

Heat and moisture pooled between her legs. She relished the sensation, no longer afraid of what she was feeling. No longer timid about the changes her body went through when she was with Chance.

His tongue stroked hers now. She couldn't name the exact moment when Chance took over the kiss, but she fell into it and let him take the lead. Chance grabbed her around the waist and drew her smack up against him. Their hips met and she felt the extent of his desire against her thighs, the pressing of his manhood a thrill that shut down her mind to all rational thought.

Chance breathed heavily against her mouth, the temptation that constantly surprised him hard to contain. His voice rasped over her lips. "I could take you right now."

Hope registered on Lizzie's face, an expression that any man would take pride in noting on a woman he was ready to seduce.

Except that Chance couldn't seduce Lizzie. He'd regretted the words the second he'd uttered them. He spoke aloud what he'd been thinking and that had always gotten him into trouble. Truth was, he longed for Lizzie in the worst possible way. He was keenly aware of her, every minute of every day and he'd been doing his darnedest to keep his distance from her.

Edward Mitchell would approve of Hayden Finch for his granddaughter. Lizzie and her friend were becoming close again. It was the way it should be. Hayden was smitten with Lizzie. He was the better choice...the only choice for her. Clearly, he could provide for Lizzie and give her a secure life with no worries or struggles.

But lately, none of that seemed to matter to him. He'd come to admire Lizzie's unflinching spirit. When he fully expected her to wallow in grief, she'd shown strength and put all her efforts into building the ranch again. Her days were filled with hard work and during the nights, her lamps were lit into the late hours as she created her dolls. He'd seen her at her best and at her worst. Lord knew, she was surly and disagreeable at times, but now as he gazed into her beautiful eyes shadowed with lust, Chance couldn't talk himself out of wanting her.

He couldn't talk himself out of the fierce emotions roiling around in his gut, either. Though she acted contrary and annoyed him almost daily, he couldn't deny that she was sweet in her own way. She'd remembered his birthday, something Chance was happy to forget. His birth didn't amount to a hill of beans, except to Lizzie.

Her gift touched something deep and solemn inside. He wouldn't steal her innocence.

She deserved better than that. Better than him.

The realization dawned on him, that he wasn't making this sacrifice for Edward's sake anymore. He was doing this for Lizzie. Because he truly cared about her.

With deep regret, he unlocked his hold on her and stepped back. "Forget I said anything."

Lizzie stood frozen, as if she was still in his embrace. Her eyes opened and a look of utter befuddlement dawned on her face. She blinked several times, comprehending what had just happened. Then she shivered in disbelief.

He expected her to rant and give him a good chewing out, but she only stood there, with her chin up, her head held high to look past him toward the lake waters. The lips that gave to him so generously a moment ago were pinched tight but her words slipped out quietly despite the firm lock. "There's a barn dance at Petey Donavan's ranch in two weeks. It's ladies' choice."

Her head moved the inch it took to face him directly. Sad blue eyes beseeched him with the slightest flicker. He knew what she was asking. Knew what she wanted to hear. He'd already injured Lizzie enough for ten lifetimes. A shudder ran through him, knowing in his gut that his next words would seal his fate forever. This time though, she would never forgive him. "Ask Hayden."

Her eyes shone with accusation and Chance died a little bit inside. He'd never intended to cause her such pain or make those pretty eyes turn hard with hurt.

She nodded with little quick bobs of her head that told him she'd expected no less.

She'd expected him to disappoint her.

The notion was like a knife gutting him.

She turned from him, her skirts swishing against the ground as she left the clearing by the lake and marched off.

"Wait, Lizzie!"

But she didn't wait. She kept on going and Chance could only let her go, because he had nothing to say that would make her happy.

"Damn it," he muttered, staring at her retreating form until she was out of sight.

His body ached in need of her.

He glanced at the lake and the glistening waters that beckoned him. Within seconds, he'd chucked his clothes and took the long strides to find his way back into the water. Once he was chest deep, he dove under, hoping to ease the lust of his body and wash away the pain surrounding his heart.

He wasn't sure the dunking would do much good.

The hell of it was, he wasn't sure of anything anymore.

Chapter Fourteen

Lizzie hadn't had a female influence in her life for a long time. She didn't have the benefit of motherly advice. As a result, she'd managed to do things her own way, whether it was proper or not and without too much thought if her way was acceptable. She'd had no choice in the matter and often she'd wonder what it would be like to have her mama here to primp her, help her dress and fuss over her hair for a barn dance that Lizzie wasn't even sure she wanted to attend.

She had procrastinated in asking Hayden to the dance. Her heart simply wasn't in it, but Mrs. Finch told her flat-out, he was looking forward to going with her. He'd made polite excuses to Haddie Jones and Abigail Westhaven while waiting for Lizzie's invitation. She'd felt obligated after hearing that. She wouldn't disappoint Hayden for the world, though he'd been giving her long looks that made her feel a bit uncomfortable lately. Sometimes, he'd put a hand on her arm, or brush his fingers over hers. As hard as it was for her to believe,

Hayden might be interested in her as a woman. But she wouldn't dwell on that at the moment. She'd had enough perplexing thoughts, thinking about Chance these past few weeks.

If she was excited about one thing regarding the barn dance, it was that she'd be wearing a new dress.

It was the first gown she'd ever made for herself. She'd chosen a striking blue material made of imported silk that glimmered under the light. She'd put delicate lace around the sleeves and made several tucks under a bodice that pushed her small breasts up, giving her a womanly shape. At the waist, the gown flared out in folds that reached the ground. She wore no jewels, because she had none, but the rivulets of curls that fell onto her shoulders and caressed her upper chest added the adornment she'd needed.

"Goodness, Lizzie," she said, taking a final look at her reflection in the bedroom mirror. She barely recognized herself.

She heard rustling outside, so she left her room to peer out the parlor window. Hayden's two-seater buggy was hitched to the post in front of the house. It was just like Hayden to be early. He'd been so eager about this dance; he'd gone on and on about it when she was with him.

She took a deep breath and made a vow to have fun today. She hadn't danced in years, but Hayden knew how and he'd promised to teach her.

She opened the door and found Hayden there, smiling, holding a batch of soft pink lilies in one hand. His gaze flowed over her with admiration. "You're…you're." He took a swallow and began again. "Lizzie, I don't think I've ever seen you look so beautiful."

Lizzie flashed a true and genuine smile, happy to receive a compliment. "I'm glad you like the dress. I've been working on it after supper all week long."

"I do," he said, his eyes gleaming. "But it's not the dress, Lizzie. It's the woman wearing it."

"Thank you, Hayden. I don't know what I'd do without your kind words." He was truly a blessing in her life.

"You'll never have a need to find out." Then he remembered the flowers. "These are for you. For the drive over to the Donavans'."

He handed her the flowers and she put them to her nose. A slightly sweet scent wafted up her nostrils. "That's very thoughtful of you, Hayden. And I must say, you look very handsome today."

He wore a tan vest underneath a dark suit that fit his frame perfectly. He looked worldly, dressed much like Governor Tritle, who'd once visited Red Ridge on his way to an inaugural ceremony in Phoenix. Sometimes when Lizzie looked at Hayden now, she had to remind herself of the boy he'd once been, who'd tug at her braids and cackle with laughter, then run away so she would chase him.

"Are you ready to go?" There was boyish eagerness in his eyes.

"Yes."

With a sweep of his hand, he gestured for her to walk out first, then he reached back to close the door. They'd made it to the buggy when Lizzie remembered something. "Hayden, I almost forgot. There's one hook at the back I couldn't reach. I swear I was a fool to sew it in." She tilted her head to the side, giving him access to her exposed shoulders. "Could you? It's the top one."

He blinked his eyes and hesitated. Lizzie wondered if she'd embarrassed him by asking the favor. "If you don't want to, maybe I can ask—"

"No, Lizzie," he said, his voice a bit shaky. "I'd be happy to."

He walked behind her and fumbled a bit with the material.

Chance turned the corner of the barn then, coming forward with a stack of fresh-cut wood in his arms. Immediately, he took note of the buggy. And when he spotted her with Hayden standing close behind, fiddling with her dress, he stopped dead in his tracks. His mouth dropped open.

His gaze traveled over the full length of her, from her upswept hair to the very hem of her fancy gown, but he did a double take at the heart-shaped bodice. Her chest swelled from the unabashed blaze in his eyes.

Hot tremors ricocheted through her body. Her breath caught, causing a little gasp to escape.

"Sorry, Lizzie. My hands are clumsy," Hayden said, mistaking the sound she made as impatience.

"It's okay," she said quietly, watching Chance.

With a flick of his eyes, Chance turned his attention to Hayden. The look he shot him was so fierce, so hard, that Lizzie shivered noticeably, yet Hayden was unaware of his presence.

"There, finally got it," he said triumphantly, giving her shoulders a little pat.

By the time Hayden lifted his head, Chance had already turned away, dumping the logs into the wood pile and striding off.

Lizzie was completely shaken. Chance had wanted this. He'd been hard-nosed and stubborn, hurting her pride for the very last time. He'd told her to ask Hayden to the dance. But judging from the look on Chance's face and the glint of steel in his eyes, he seemed to want anything but. Lizzie had never been the object of a man's jealousy before. But Chance had no one to blame but himself. He'd been pushing her away, denying her any credence, since the day they'd met.

"Are you ready?" Hayden asked, coming to stand in front of her.

She nodded. "Yes, I'm ready. I can't wait to dance until my feet ache."

He grinned wide and helped her up onto the buggy. "I think I can surely oblige."

Lizzie tamped down her ill ease and smiled at her best friend. If anyone could make her forget her heartache, it was Hayden Finch.

Chance chopped wood.

He chopped wood until his arms ached, his shoulders went stiff and his mouth became parched. Then he chopped wood some more. A tick worked at his jaw with each blow of the ax, with each damn splintering of lumber.

No matter the strain to his muscles or the pain to his back, the vision of Lizzie looking beautiful in that silky gown refused to be forced away. The notion that he couldn't dismiss her any longer plagued him until he thought he'd go crazy.

After an hour, he ceased his chopping and leaned heavily on the ax handle. He'd been thunderstruck seeing Hayden's hands on Lizzie today, seeing the way he touched her as he fixed her dress.

His mouth twisted in disgust.

He'd never been jealous of a man in his life.

Chance put down the ax and sat on a haystack. He reached for the bottle of whiskey he'd brought from the bunkhouse, stretched his legs and leaned back so that his head rested against the barn wall. It wasn't too dang comfortable, but in a few minutes, he wouldn't know the difference.

He wasn't going to chop any more firewood or mend another broken-down fence. He wasn't going to muck the horse stalls or pitch another bale of hay. Nope, his workday was officially over. He raised the liquor to his lips and drank, pouring whiskey down his gullet in a big gulp.

I wonder if a man would ever drink, because of me.

A wry chuckle escaped his throat.

He'd told Lizzie one day she'd make some man crazy enough. It must have been a premonition, because he was going a little loco right now.

The sun dipped toward the western horizon. Lizzie had been gone for hours now, probably turning young male heads and making poor old Hayden Finch sweat.

"Ah, hell." Much as he tried, he couldn't stop imagining Lizzie dancing in Hayden's arms, laughing, her blue eyes sparkling like two bright gems.

Feeling prickly, Chance rose abruptly. The alcohol hadn't numbed him sufficiently. He was too restless to wallow in pity anyway. What he needed was a long hard ride. He grabbed his gun belt and fastened it as he strode over to the barn to retrieve his saddle. The barn was dry from the day's heat and the scent of animal droppings, straw and packed earth rose up to greet him. They were familiar smells that on any other day would bring him comfort. Today, nothing much was helping.

At the corral, he set his saddle down and with a sharp eye spotted Joyful at the farthest fence. He gave her a whistle. The mare trotted over. He had his hand on the gate, when he heard footsteps approaching. The sound of hysterical crying reached his ears at the same time he swiveled around to find Lizzie racing toward the house. He had to blink his eyes twice, making sure he wasn't seeing things. Her dress was torn at the shoulders, her upswept hair was in a shambles and her dirt-smeared face looked as if she'd been through a dust storm.

"Lizzie!" he called out.

Without giving him a glance, she climbed the porch steps and pushed through the door. "Leave me alone, Chance Worth!" The door slammed shut behind her.

"What the hell." Chance ate the distance to the house in long strides then yanked the door open and entered the house.

Lizzie whirled around, her eyes red and swollen. She'd been crying a long time.

His pulse pounded in his throat seeing the look of misery on her face. "Go away, Chance."

"Not until you tell me what happened."

"This is all your fault!"

"My fault? What are you talking about?" He approached her slowly. She wasn't making any sense. "Why are you crying?"

Tears continued to spill down her face. "It's… Hayden."

Hayden? He rocked back on his heels. Chance took another look at her dress, almost in tatters now and falling off her shoulders. Dirt smudged her face. "Hayden did this to you?" Chance put a hand on his gun. He'd only known this kind of fury when that bastard Quinn

Martin had taken Lizzie into the brush. If that mama's boy Hayden Finch dared to hurt Lizzie, he'd make sure he'd never come near her again. Chance took her arms, holding her firmly, and searched her eyes for the truth. Protective instincts poked at his nerves. "What did he do?"

Lizzie's face wrinkled tight. "He…he…"

Chance had murder on his mind, as he coaxed the truth from her. "Go on, darlin'."

"He…" She bit down on her lower lip. The tender skin there puckered. More tears fell.

She was torturing him. "Lizzie, tell me."

She glared at him, her face once again filled with accusation aimed at him. "He…kissed me."

Chance blinked and let that sink into his skull for a minute. Newfound jealousy burned in his gut. For her sake, he kept his voice steady. "Is that all he did?"

"No, t-that's not all!" Her bluster overtook her misery. "Look at me." She stepped back for him to see her, gesturing with a sweep of her hands over her dress. "I'm a mess! And I feel like a fool."

He had a fierce need to protect her. "If he abused you he'll answer to me. Where is he?"

"No! It's not Hayden's fault."

"Lizzie, you're not making a lick of sense." Chance's patience was at its limit. He'd been in a sour mood before she came home, but seeing Lizzie so distraught now made him want to pound his fist into a wall—or into Hayden's face.

"This is all your fault, Chance. Don't go blaming Hayden." Blue fury sparked in her eyes as she tried to catch her breath. "Hayden k-kissed me and I was so… surprised. Lately, he'd started looking at me as a woman and it…it confused me. But I never once thought he was coming home for *me*. He loves me, Chance. He wants to marry me!"

She squeezed her eyes closed and shook her head fiercely as if reliving something awful. "I hurt him. I hurt him so bad. I'll never forget the look in his eyes when I pushed him away. When I told him it felt strange kissing him. When I told him… I couldn't marry him."

"So he attacked you?"

"No! He didn't touch me after that. He… His face sort of crumpled. He was so very hurt, pleading with me to change my mind. But I couldn't, Chance, and I told him so. That's when he… He told me we couldn't be friends anymore. That he loved me too much to be my friend. I ran all the way home from the Donavans. I fell a few times, ripping my dress, but I kept going fast as I could trying to erase the wounded look in his eyes from my mind. It was like…like I'd betrayed him."

"You didn't betray him," Chance said, greatly relieved he didn't have to knock the stuffing out of Hayden.

Again she lifted swollen tear-weary eyes to him. "His touch never put flutters in my belly or made my heart pound so hard it felt like it's gonna burst clear through my chest." She shook her head, her admission guileless. "It isn't like when you touch me, Chance. Not like when you kiss me. Nothing's ever felt so good in my life and…and—"

"Lizzie." Her name escaped his throat.

"I know you're gonna tell me to—"

Quick as the snap of a whip, Chance curved his hands around her slight waist and drew her up against him. "I'm gonna tell you to be quiet, so I can kiss you."

He claimed her mouth in one quick swoop. He didn't give her time to protest. He didn't give her room to pull away. He held her tight and went on kissing her, letting the warmth of her giving lips tear down every barrier he'd built in his mind. Letting her sweetness seep into his soul and touch every place he'd sheltered for so long. He wasn't going to deny he wanted her with a need so fierce, he was ready to murder anyone who'd try to stop him.

"Oh, Chance," she whispered into his mouth. "I couldn't take it if you pushed me away."

"Not today, Lizzie," he said, stroking her unruly long hair away from her face and looking deep into the prettiest eyes he'd ever seen. "Not ever again. Today, I'm gonna make you mine."

He lifted her in his arms and looked her straight in the eyes. "This is what you want?"

She nodded, without a bit of hesitation.

He nuzzled her throat and kissed her again.

Then he carried her into the bedroom.

Chance set Lizzie down on her bed gently. Her pulse pounding, she watched Chance move to the curtains and close them, denying afternoon sunlight entry into the room. Everything dimmed. She kept her gaze trained on him as he strode to the washbowl on her dressing table. He dipped a cloth into the rose-scented water and came over to the bed. Lowering onto his knee next to her, he washed her face with the cloth.

"I look a mess," she murmured.

He shook his head. "You have a scratch on your face. A few on your shoulders," he said tenderly, dabbing them. Cool moisture met her bared shoulders and after he'd wash an area, he'd bend to brush his lips to her skin. Goose bumps prickled all over.

She was impatient for him to lie next to her. She'd missed breathing in his scent and rolling over to see him sleeping beside her. One night, he'd covered her body with his, to protect her from the freezing storm, but now it was different. Now, she saw the undeniable intent in his eyes as he kissed her tenderly, making her squirm on the bed and wish for more. "Slow and easy, princess," Chance murmured.

Finished with his ministrations, he set the cloth aside and unbuckled his gun belt. She watched him in the dim light as he lowered down onto the bed. She welcomed the dip of the mattress with a silent sigh.

They faced each other on the bed and she peered into Chance's handsome face. He was so familiar to her now. She knew every fleck of color in his brown eyes. She knew every sharp angle of his profile. She knew the powerful breadth of his shoulders. She loved every measure of him, every little part that made him who he was and the newness of her love made her giddy inside.

She could hardly believe that just a few hours ago, she thought her life was ruined. Losing Hayden as her best friend and knowing Chance didn't want her had been crushing blows, even for her strong, stubborn nature.

But now, her immediate future was hopeful. Lizzie would not make any further assumptions. She would simply treasure each moment she had with Chance.

His fingertip trailed a path along her cheek with the slightest of touches. A tremble coursed the length of her. His gaze was warm, shed of any defenses, shed of the guard that had hardened there since she'd met him.

"I won't hurt you, Lizzie. Trust in that."

She touched his cheek, her fingertips absorbing the heat of his skin. "I do."

His lips met hers again briefly and then his hands went to her back. "I want you out of this dress, pretty as it is."

With expert fingers, he unfastened the hook and buttons. The back of her dress fell open and Chance put his hands on her shoulders, carefully moving the dress down inch by inch.

His eyes stayed on his task as he tugged the material lower and lower.

"Lift up a little," he said, kissing her shoulder.

She arched and Chance guided the dress past her waist over her hips and down her legs.

He flung the dress to the floor and returned his attention to her.

She took a big swallow.

Her chemise and a thin cotton skirt covered her.

"If I do anything you don't like, you just tell me," he said.

"There's nothing you could do that I won't like," she said, breathless. Her body was a mass of trembles.

Chance smiled with warmth in his eyes. "Lizzie, you don't know what your words do to me."

He rose from the bed, his gaze staying with her as he unbuttoned his shirt and pulled it over his head. Her eyes dipped to the expanse of his powerful chest, bronzed from working in the sun. She drew in a sharp breath. She'd seen him this way, many times, only now, she would have the freedom to touch and explore, to sink her fingertips into his skin and relish each caress.

He came back to the bed and gave her a greedy kiss.

She wrapped her arms around his neck and drew him closer. Her fingers wove through the thick strands of his hair.

"So sweet," he said, between kisses.

"I'm not sweet," she said, laboring for breath.

"Don't argue," he whispered, his lips lifting in a quick smile as his tongue found hers with a deep stroke.

A soft moan spiraled up her throat. She ached now throughout her body, but the tip of her thighs fairly throbbed.

Chance seemed to know her needs, because he broke the kiss to remove the rest of her clothes. He was quick handed and before she knew it, she lay naked on the bed beside him. Every instinct she had told her to cover up. To hide her body from his eyes. She was sure he would find her lacking in many ways. But when she dared to peek at his face, his eyes held nothing but appreciation.

"You are beautiful," he said quietly, reverently, and this time, his tongue found the very peak of her nipple. He licked her there and then circled the tip round and round, until finally, to her shock, he took the upturned tip into his mouth.

Heat burned below her belly. She squirmed and squeezed her legs together as he suckled her gently. Her sensitized body seemed to move on its own accord now, following him wherever he would take her.

She gasped aloud from the tormented pleasure and put her hands on Chance's chest, her palms flat on his hot skin, her fingers gripping him.

"Touch me, Lizzie. Anywhere you want," he said urgently.

And she did. As he toyed with her, she explored him. She found joy and solace in letting her hands roam over his shoulders and back. She didn't know how strong and powerful he really was, until she'd been allowed to do her own uninhibited exploration.

He grunted as her fingers slid below his navel to the top of his waistband. He murmured for her to be careful. It was dangerous and thrilling to see Chance react to her touch as if he couldn't get enough of her caresses. As if, he, too, was on the brink of something much more powerful.

She kissed him freely now, moving her mouth over his body, licking his flesh with tiny strokes of her tongue in the same way he had done to her.

The warm gleam in his eyes changed then to a glint of raw desire. He pressed her down onto the bed with a gentle shove and she landed easily on her back. He moved his palms over her small breasts to fondle her over and over, causing a wonderful ache of need to shoot clean through her body as he kissed her.

Something was building inside, a new sensation that left her desperately wanting.

Anticipation grew stronger as he caressed her. His fingers splayed wide on her stomach then traveled lower and lower. Her female center burned with scorching immeasurable heat.

The throbbing intensified.

"Lizzie, stay with me, darlin'." He kissed her again as he wove his fingers through the soft curls that protected her center.

Her breaths were rapid, almost out of control.

She ached so badly.

And then he touched her. Where, she knew by natural instinct, he needed to be.

He stroked her once, twice, and the third time, a wonderful tension-filled moan escaped her lips. "It feels... so good."

"That's it, sweet princess," Chance said, reassuring her. "Let go."

And Chance continued his ministrations, stroking her, gliding his fingers in and out, building heat, building pressure until Lizzie thought she would completely burst from the glorious sensations gripping her.

Her breaths came out in little pants. She arched her hips and moved in harmony to his stroking. When she thought she couldn't take another second, Chance stopped suddenly and rose to remove the rest of his clothes.

He stood for a second, bare skinned and beautiful. She caught a glimpse of him below the waist and took another swallow of air. She'd never before seen a man fully unclothed. She was struck with awe.

As he approached the bed, he looked at her, the hot gleam in his eyes replaced by concern. "Don't be afraid, I won't hurt you."

She craved him and yearned to know what it was like to have that craving satisfied. Her body pulsed in need of him. But first, she had to ease the look in his eyes. She breathed on a bare whisper, "You know I'm not *really* a princess."

He smiled softly as he returned to the bed and kissed her soundly on the lips. "You should be treated like one."

With that, Lizzie fell even more in love with him.

"Are you still with me?" he asked, parting her legs and stroking her again.

She reacted to his touch with a drawn out sigh. "Yes." She squeezed her eyes closed.

Chance positioned himself over her and spread her legs wider. The tip of his manhood nudged at her entrance and she felt her skin stretch. He waited and she impatiently spread her legs wider in invitation. He moved slowly, allowing her to adjust to his size and strength, the restraint on his face proof of his keen will-power. He held back for her and she wanted so much to please him. With his teachings, she would soon learn how.

"Try to relax, darlin'," he murmured. Then he inched farther and farther with utmost care. Having him inside her and being connected like they were was strangely wonderful. Sharing their bodies this way, was better than she'd ever imagined.

The fire inside her kept building.

When he gently started to thrust farther, a shot of stabbing pain seized her. She flinched, holding back a scream, and then it was over. Her breaching had ebbed. Chance watched her carefully and she lifted up to kiss him, his concern warming her heart.

"I'm fine," she whispered, meeting his gaze.

He nodded and whispered her name. "Elizabeth."

Calling her by her real name was the best gift he could have given her.

He moved more freely now and she met his rhythm. They were in harmony with each other. Lips to lips. Hips to hips. Skin to skin.

Sweet hot sensations swept through her body. Seeing Chance above her, seeing his face tense with pleasure and knowing she could give him this, made each moment precious and sacred.

When his thrusts deepened, she arched her hips off the bed, straining for some unknown precipice. Her heart raced as she heaved short breaths, and when Chance gripped her waist higher, to drive deeper, long, sweet, unexpected sounds slipped from her throat as her body splintered apart.

Chance pumped into her one last glorious time, his face releasing tension, his body shaking in unabashed satisfaction.

The moment froze in time as Chance peered into her eyes. Sated and newly schooled in the bedroom, Lizzie could only stare at him in wonder. She knew then that she'd never give herself to any other man. She'd never lie with anyone else. Chance was all she'd ever need.

He lowered himself down onto the mattress and took her into his embrace. He kissed her a dozen times before relaxing on his side. "Are you alright?"

She was sore, but it was a wonderful kind of pain.

There was such worry in his eyes that Lizzie couldn't be fully truthful. She touched a hand to his face. "You didn't hurt me. It was…glorious, Chance."

He nodded, spent and seemingly satisfied with her answer.

She set her head against the pillow and gazed at the ceiling, allowing the aftermath of lovemaking to wash over her. "I never want to get up from this bed," she murmured on a sigh.

Chance wound an arm around her shoulders and kissed the top of her head. "I was thinking the very same thing."

Lizzie had never known joy like this. She hadn't known that her body could sing with pleasure and the hum of it could vibrate inside of her all day long. She hadn't known what love was truly like until Chance came into her life. She was filled with it and her bliss threatened to overflow in her smile and the bounce in her step.

Last night Chance had been protective of her and refused to touch her again until she'd had time to rest. They'd slept awhile in each other's arms and she'd gotten up briefly to bring supper to the bedroom, while he'd bedded down the horses and checked on the livestock. But this morning, they'd woken in each other's arms and his good-morning kiss had ignited another bout of lovemaking.

Now, he sat at the kitchen table, his eyes on her as she handed him a plate of scrambled eggs and bacon. She buttered a few biscuits and put a basket of them in front of him, next to a mug of steaming coffee.

"Looks mighty good," he said. "I'm hungrier than a bear."

"Feels mighty good," she said, and when his gaze narrowed in puzzlement, she added, "having you talk to me at breakfast."

"You know why I didn't, Lizzie." He put a forkful of eggs into his mouth.

"I suppose," she said, wondering about his code of honor. He'd been set and determined to push her into Hayden's arms. "I was lonely, and sick and tired of your please and thank-yous."

Chance glanced at her with a grin. "Were you now?"

"I was."

Just as she was ready to take a seat, he grabbed her hand and tugged. She fell onto his lap. "Oh."

Her arm naturally went around his neck. "You want to have breakfast like this?" he asked.

Lizzie was lost when he touched her. She was lost and never wanted to be found. "Sitting on your lap?"

"You won't get lonely." He said with a devil of a smile. Then he cupped the back of her head and leaned in to nuzzle her throat.

Stirrings awakened quickly as his lips traveled along her neck to her chin, then to her lips. He gave her a long, sweet kiss and when it ended, the look in his eyes made her breath catch.

Her immediate reaction made him hesitate.

"On second thought, that's not the best idea." He lifted her off him, his eyes smoldering as his gaze roamed over her.

"I thought it was a pretty good one," she said, regaining her breath to taunt him with the dare.

"Lizzie, we just… Your body needs a rest." He put a forkful of food in his mouth and chewed. "Someone's got to be sensible around here. Lord knows, you make me crazy with want."

"You're forever protecting me," she said softly, without complaint. He was right. They'd made love less than an hour ago and her body was still adjusting to him. She ached but she welcomed the pain and treasured his concern over her. "Thank you."

"Don't make me crazier by thanking me for anything, darlin'. I'll wonder what's going on inside that pretty little head of yours."

They laughed and finished the meal with pleasant talk. Lizzie washed the plates in the sink and Chance came up behind her. He circled her in his arms and set her hair to the side to kiss the back of her neck. "I'll be out on the range most of the day."

She nodded. "I'll be going into town this morning."

"I'll see you at supper."

She turned around and found herself locked in his embrace. He brushed a quick goodbye kiss to her lips, but the second their lips met, the pull was like two gale winds joining force and it was impossible to stop. The kiss went deeper and lasted long enough that they finally had to draw apart to take a sustaining breath. Chance backed up a step, displaying more willpower than she had, but his look of regret told her how difficult it was for him.

"If I don't go now, I'm likely to haul you back into the bedroom." He grabbed his hat from the peg on the wall and plopped it on his head.

The sweet strumming in her body intensified as she watched him walk out the door. She stood there for a few minutes, reliving yesterday and the delicious, desirable way Chance made her feel. For once in her life, she had no regrets.

Later that morning, Lizzie packed up her dolls, then hitched up Melody to the wagon and rode into town. She had several important calls to make this morning. Her first stop was at the Swenson house. She had a special doll for little Sarah.

The Swensons were home, and replacing Sally Ann with the new doll went better than expected. Mrs. Swenson was overjoyed with Lizzie's visit. Sarah had taken one look at the new doll, clothed in shimmery blue silk and lace, pristine and perfect, and she gladly handed back Sally Ann without too much fuss. She did place a sweet kiss on the old doll's head before turning her over. Both Mrs. Swenson and Lizzie were proud of her for taking such good care of the doll.

Her visit with the Swensons was brief. She had

other stops to make in town, but Lizzie, coward that she was, avoided the millinery shop, in fear of running into Hayden. She didn't want to rehash the argument they'd had yesterday. So much had happened since then, and she feared if he took one look at her, he'd know the truth, that she'd fallen in love with Chance Worth. It would probably crush him if he learned that she'd slept with Chance in the real sense, and that she was immeasurably happy.

No, she didn't look at the shop or slow the wagon as she drove by. And after she finished making doll deliveries, a great sense of pride swelled in her heart as she finally managed to fill all her orders despite that drastic episode at the lake. She'd also received orders for half a dozen more dolls, which meant extra earnings for the ranch.

Lastly, and perhaps most importantly, Lizzie had to visit an old family friend. Lizzie had a bargain of sorts to make with her, and she only hoped the woman would comply.

When Lizzie returned home with cash in her pocket, she unhitched the wagon and led Melody to the barn. She stood on a stool to currycomb the mare then wash her down. The tail end of a dust storm had caught her by surprise on the way home, and both she and the horse were layered with a thin coat of Arizona dirt.

She corralled Melody and was surprised to see Joyful was back in the pen, too. Her heart raced hard in her chest, knowing Chance was back already. She liked the days when he worked at home and she could see him fixing things around the house or dealing with the livestock as though he truly belonged here.

Lizzie went in search of him. She grinned when she

found him around the back of the barn, washing up by a water trough, his head down, hands covering his face.

She snuck up beside him and reached down into the water, scooping out two handfuls and tossing it at him. The water splashed his neck and shoulders.

His body shot upright. Stunned, he reached for his gun, which he didn't have holstered, and she backed away, cackling with laughter. The back of his hair and shoulders were soaked

When he saw her, his face split into a smile. His eyes twinkled devilishly. "You think you're gonna get away with that?" Before she could turn and run, he grabbed her wrist with one hand, trapping her, and reached down into the trough.

"No, Chance! Don't do it! Don't you dare!" She laughed, trying to squirm away but his grip was firm. He splashed water onto her hair, her face, her neck and her chest.

"Come to think of it, I think you need a bath."

Lizzie looked down at the water trough and began shaking her head, giggling. "No! I'm not going in that trough! I'm not."

"Oh, yes you are, Lizzie." His laughter loosened his hold on her and Lizzie broke free of his grip. She dipped her hand into the trough one more time to splash his shirt before she took off running.

Chance chased her and she ran as fast as she could around the corral and barn. When he finally caught up with her just outside the barn door, she was breathing heavily and was too exhausted to fight him. He grabbed her around the waist and she didn't try to squirm free. His hands on her felt too good.

With a triumphant smile, he lifted her in his arms.

"Gotcha. Question is, princess, what am I gonna do with you?"

"Anything you want," Lizzie whispered, her body tingling from his touch. Every second she was with Chance, her heart pounded and every nerve in her being became sensitive and alive.

He arched a brow and a hot gleam of desire sparked in his eyes. "I think we'll have us a bath *later*."

Chance carried her inside the barn and laid her down on a soft batch of straw. It was dark and cooler inside. The scent of damp earth and freshly mucked stalls filled her nostrils. She was cushioned on all sides with new hay and as she peered up, Chance met her eyes as he gently covered her body with his. They were both wet and breathing hard from the silly chase.

He looked into her eyes and then at her mouth. Her lips parted in anticipation and the gleam in his eyes intensified. Then he crushed a sweetly demanding kiss to her lips. She drank in his scent, his taste and kissed him back with the same such demand.

Soon their bodies were entwined with heat and passion. Chance touched her through her clothes and she bared his shirt to touch his chest. Her breaths came harder now and that yearning that deepened at the very sight of Chance surfaced with full force.

"This is crazy," he said, kissing her throat, neck and chin. "I can't get enough of you."

Lizzie felt power and pride that she could satisfy such a man. "I can't get enough of you, either," she breathed. Chance stopped for a second to gaze into her eyes. Then he grabbed her around the waist with both hands and rolled her over, so that she now was on top of him and his back was against the bed of straw. She straddled his legs and Chance murmured commands, stroking her beneath her dress, until moisture pooled between her thighs and she ached for welcome release.

He coaxed her with gentle words and taught her how to please him. Without shedding her dress, she took Chance inside her, guided by his hands on her hips until she found her own rhythm. She moved on him and the hint of soreness that had remained from last night lent itself to great pleasure. She moaned as she rocked up and down, feeling their exquisite joining to the hilt of her womanhood.

Chance rose up then, wrapping her legs around him and pulling her closer, to drive his manhood deep until they simultaneously splintered with thrilling, earth-shattering spasms. "Elizabeth," he murmured as he held her tight and fell back against the straw.

She could only smile, with a glow that beamed from the inside out.

A short time later, Lizzie sat in the bathtub Chance had brought into the kitchen. She'd warmed pots of water over the cookstove and scented it with lavender and he'd filled the tub for her. Now, he kneeled behind her and washed her hair, fingering the long strands and scrubbing them clean.

"The first time I saw you, all this pretty hair was sticking out every which way."

"Don't remind me," Lizzie said, "of that day at the lake."

He leaned over to kiss her cheek. "You hated me."

"I, uh…" Lizzie couldn't think straight with Chance grazing his fingers over her neck and shoulders. He was so careful with her now, his touch so gentle. "You were a brute."

He laughed and tugged at her hair. "You deserved my brutish ways. You were a brat."

"You don't think I'm a brat now, do you?"

Chance hesitated and Lizzie swiveled her head to gaze at him. "Do you?"

He feigned deep thought. "Depends."

"*Depends?* On what?"

"On whether or not you're gonna let me take a bath with you."

"There's hardly room for two of us in here. You're so big and—"

Chance began stripping off his clothes. His chest bared, Lizzie lost her train of thought. "I got caught in that dust storm, darlin'. I'm gonna need some good scrubbing to get clean."

Then he yanked off his boots and the rest of his clothes came next. He stood next to the tub, gloriously exposed, watching her. She couldn't look at his body without wanting him. "You're a devil, Chance Worth."

"Okay by me, if you get out and wash me."

"Is that so?"

"Just don't put on any clothes. I sorta like the notion of you sponging me without a stitch on."

The next few days floated by like a dream. Their time together was thrilling and amazing. Lizzie couldn't seem to think about anything but Chance. They'd get their chores done as quickly as possible and then spend their nights making love and talking afterward for hours. Chance shared stories of his time in the orphanage and she told him about her life on the ranch when her father was alive. Lizzie now looked at Chance as the man she loved, but as her friend, too. There wasn't anything she couldn't tell him. She hoped he felt the same way. He certainly hadn't mentioned leaving the ranch, which she viewed as a very good sign.

Lizzie couldn't remember a time when she'd been happier. And Chance, too, wore a smile for her every day. Their lives seemed to fit. The ranch was thriving. Everything was finally falling into place.

And best of all, Lizzie had a secret she held close to her heart. She could hardly contain her excitement. Tomorrow, she'd planned on cooking a fancy dinner and dressing up pretty for Chance before giving him her surprise.

Chapter Fifteen

New dawn broke through the curtains in Lizzie's bedroom, the early beams of light waking Chance. He rose quietly and grabbed his clothes as he glanced at Lizzie sound asleep in the bed. He leaned over to cover her shoulders with the quilt and brush a light kiss on her forehead. He wouldn't wake her, she needed rest. Last night, she hadn't been her usual self, her stomach cramping and upset. He'd held her during the night comforting her to sleep.

Chance strode to the door and as he grasped the knob, he stopped to take another look at her before walking out. His lips curved up in a wide smile. He'd never been so smitten with a woman that he needed to steal one last lingering glance before leaving her bed. His feelings for Lizzie overpowered him. He was in love with her. The revelation had hit him a few days ago and since then he'd been letting the notion seep into his brain and take hold. He'd never felt this way about a woman before. He'd never trusted himself with that emotion. But Lizzie had torn down the defensive walls that he'd built inside himself as protection. She'd wedged her way in with sass and grit. She was strong, a survivor, and the right woman for him.

He loved her from the bottom of his heart.

He wanted to marry her and live on this ranch and raise children with her. The idea had been brewing in his head ever since Hayden had asked Lizzie to marry him. Funny thing, for all those weeks prior, a proposal from Hayden had been exactly what Chance had been hoping for. But when it happened, Chance had realized what he would stand to lose. More than anything in his life, he needed Lizzie.

Chance dressed quickly and strode outside to feed the livestock. As a treat for his loyal horses, he hand-fed Melody and Joyful sugar cubes after they'd had their fill of oats. He mucked a few stalls and spread fresh hay down for the two horses that would help build this ranch. Chance had plans for the Mitchell spread. He envisioned him and Lizzie, chasing their youngsters around the yard as a thousand head of cattle grazed the land. He'd pull calves, and Lizzie would bear children. They'd work hard and build something for the future. His head was bustling with ideas.

Lizzie had promised him a fancy meal tonight.

It would be the perfect time to propose.

An hour later, he washed up before entering the house for breakfast. Lizzie was standing by the cook-stove, hunched over the coffeepot, her hand covering her stomach. He strode to her side. "Lizzie, what is it?"

"It's nothing." She moved very slowly to pour coffee.

"You're white as a sheet, darlin'. Your stomach upset again?"

She nodded. "It'll pass." She glanced at him, meeting his eyes. "It always does this time of month." A flush of color rose up her face. After all they'd been through together, Chance didn't think anything would embarrass her.

He took the coffeepot out of her hand and led her to a chair. "Sit down. I'll get the meal on the table."

She sat and braced her elbows on the table, her chin resting on her fists. "Just so you know, I'm gonna be cranky today."

"I'll forgive you," he said, concealing a smile and dishing up the eggs. He bent to kiss her cheek and then sat down to eat.

Lizzie picked at her food. Every so often, she would wince and rub her stomach gently. Chance didn't know much about a female's monthlies, but he could see she had some pain this morning. She appeared tuckered out and hadn't bothered to comb her hair. Her pretty eyes looked weary.

"I planned to go into town later today. If you're not feeling better—" he began, then stopped when he heard the sound of pounding hooves. Riders were approaching. "You expecting anyone this early?"

Lizzie's eyes lifted in surprise. "No, but that doesn't mean—"

"Stay inside," Chance said, rising to retrieve his gun belt. He strapped it on and checked his gun. It was loaded. "I'll see who it is."

Lizzie blinked, and a worried look crossed her features, but Chance didn't have time to ease her concern. Though he'd never had any trouble in Red Ridge, he knew enough to always be prepared. Hard lessons had taught him as much.

He walked out the front door and stepped into the yard, just as three riders greeted him. Chance gazed at their faces, recognizing each one.

"Alistair," he said. His adoptive father sat atop a pure black gelding. His graying hair and beard were impeccably groomed and the clothes he wore were those of a wealthy land baron. The other men, his lackeys, were on either side of him. All three honed in on Chance with eagle eyes.

"Finally found you, son."

Chance flinched at the way he said "son," sugary sweet, as if the reunion was a joyous occasion.

Chance took a second to meet with the other men's eyes, before turning back to Dunston. "What do you want?"

"A fine way to greet your father."

"My father died when I was five. You know the story."

Dunston's mouth twisted in a sneer. "You always were ungrateful."

"Why are you here?" Chance asked.

"I'm asking you to come home."

"Home?" Chance spit the word out. The notion of the Circle D Ranch being his true home was strange and foreign to him, now more than ever. A pang of dread sliced through his gut. Dunston never did anything for selfless reasons. He was up to something.

Alistair nodded. "That's right."

"I recall you saying once I stepped foot off the Double D, I didn't have a home anymore."

"I was mad as hell at you, Chance. You left when I needed you most."

Chance said dispassionately, "You never needed me.

You got twenty men working your spread. I was just another ranch hand to you." He pointed his finger back to the road that led off the property. "Turn your horses around and head out. You wasted your time coming for me. I'm not going back there."

Chance turned his back on them and approached the steps.

"You don't come home willingly, you're gonna pay. I got me an eyewitness to you stealing my payroll right outta the cash box."

Chance spun around, his ears ringing from the false accusation. "What? I didn't steal anything."

"Ole Larry says different. He claims you hit him over the head with the butt of your gun and took off running with all the cash. He had quite a headache for days. Didn't you, Larry?"

Larry jumped to attention, sitting up taller in the saddle. "Yes, sir. I sure did."

"That's a damn lie and you know it."

"I don't know anything for sure," Dunston said. "Except, I had a dickens of a time finding you. You hid yourself away pretty well. But you didn't figure on my connections with the local authorities, did you? I put out wires and one marshal up Prescott way recognized your name. Seems you killed a man."

Chance bristled. "That man stole from me and was ready to take my life."

"Well, I'm glad he didn't."

Chance shook his head, trying to figure why, after all these weeks, Dunston had gone to the trouble to find him. "I don't get it. Why's it so important to you that I come home?"

Alistair hesitated, darting a look behind him as a buggy ambled toward the house.

"Chance?" Lizzie's voice carried from the front porch. He should've known she wouldn't stay put in the house. "What's going on?"

"Go back inside, darlin'. I'll take care of this."

True to her nature, Lizzie did just the opposite. She came down the steps and stood beside him, gazing at the men on horseback.

Alistair's gaze went to Lizzie. His lips curled into a cruel smirk. "Don't tell me she's the reason you don't want to come home? Why, she's as sorry a sight as this dilapidated, pitiful excuse for a ranch."

Horrified, Lizzie gasped. Her hand went to her chest.

"You son of a bitch!" Chance lunged forward, ready to pound some sense into the older man, but Lizzie grabbed his arm, tugging him back.

"Chance, don't! Please…don't! It's alright." It wasn't her slight strength but the power of her plea that stopped Chance from grabbing Alistair by the throat.

"It's not alright. He owes you an apology."

"I don't need an apology," Lizzie said quietly. "I don't care what he says about me."

It was clear to him Lizzie was trying to calm the situation down, but Chance's nerves were bursting out of his skin. He put a warning threat in his tone as he looked at the old man. "I'm waiting for that apology, Dunston."

Alistair had the foresight to remove his hat and look contrite. "I'm sorry, miss. But if you care a hair about my son, you'll tell him to come home. I'm a generous man. I can forget all of this unpleasantness."

"Like hell I will," Chance said through tight lips.

Lizzie's chin jutted out, her eyes sharp on Alistair. "He didn't steal from you. I know that for fact. Chance isn't a thief."

The older man continued, "I'd hate to see my son thrown into jail. It's not a pretty place."

Lizzie raised her voice. "He won't go to jail."

Alistair rubbed his nose, hiding a smile. "Sorta hard to prove a man's innocent when there's an eyewitness. Truth is, Chance stole a lot of money from me and then ran. There were other men that saw him leave the ranch in a hurry after the robbery. They'll testify to it."

"He's innocent!" Lizzie raised her voice, seeing first-hand the unscrupulous nature of the man who'd adopted Chance.

"Is that so?" Dunston was a picture of serenity now as he nodded to the driver of the buggy that had come to a stop a short distance from the house. "Let's see if you still think so, once you hear from my stepdaughter, Marissa. Abe, go help her."

Marissa?

Chance thought he's seen the last of the spoiled girl.

He watched Dunston's lackey stride over to the buggy to get her. Dressed in the finest clothes, with flowing skirts fashioned with delicate lace, she looked as regal as a princess stepping down from the buggy. Her honey-blond hair gleamed like spun silk and curled in ringlets under a stylish hat. She held her head high as she approached, her jade-green eyes darting from Alistair to Chance.

Lizzie gave another gasp, this time one of awe as she stared at Marissa.

Chance let go a vile curse. Seeing Marissa turned

his stomach. She'd never been anything but trouble to him. "What the hell is she doing here?"

Dunston finally dismounted his horse to greet his stepdaughter, taking her by the hand. The two faced Chance. "Marissa is with child," Dunston said. "Your child."

Beside him, Lizzie's body visibly shook.

His gaze flew to the belly hidden under the vast amount of material of Marissa's dress. Sure enough, there seemed to be the slightest bump. But he had no claim to it. That was not his baby.

Now, his blood boiled over. "I never touched her." He sent the woman a sharp glare. "Damn it, Marissa. Why in hell are you lying like this?"

"I'm…not lying, Chance," she said, hesitating and glancing at Lizzie, before meeting his eyes again. "You're the father of my child."

He gnashed his teeth and shot her a hot glare. "That's not possible, Marissa. And you know it." Then he whipped his head toward his adoptive father. "So that's it, Alistair? The reason for the trumped-up charges. You're blackmailing me to come home, because of her. If I don't, you'll have me thrown in jail."

Dunston sent him a crafty smile. "You come home, son. Marissa's mother and I will welcome you back. You'll marry Marissa and raise your child under my roof. I'll make you foreman. I'm offering you what you've always wanted, Chance."

Chance scoffed and shook his head, too angry to speak.

Marissa closed her eyes briefly, as if to gather her strength. "Chance, please. This is all so very humiliating, standing here, begging you to come home and help me through this time."

Lizzie turned to him, her expression revealing her confusion. "Maybe you should speak with her private-ly."

"No, Lizzie. You can't possibly believe her."

Lizzie drew her lower lip in as her gaze went to Marissa. Beautiful. Feminine. Desirable. He could see Lizzie's mind working now, thinking about all the ways she didn't measure up. When the truth was, Lizzie was ten times the woman Marissa was.

"I'm about to faint from the heat," Marissa said, fan-ning her face with her hand.

"Why don't you go inside the house, Marissa," Lizzie said quickly. "Have a seat and cool off for a spell."

Chance fumed. "You're inviting her in?"

Lizzie nodded. "It's hot out here for her. And you should go inside, too. Talk to her, Chance."

"No, Lizzie. The only person I'm gonna talk to is you." He shot Dunston a hard look. "Alistair, take Marissa behind the barn. It's shady there and she'll be…*more comfortable,*" he nearly spat out.

The older man began, "That's hardly—"

"You shouldn't have brought her here in the first place," Chance said.

With that, he took hold of Lizzie's hand and led her inside the house, shutting the door good and hard, so he could talk to her.

"Listen, Lizzie. None of this is true. I swear—"

"I know you're not a thief," Lizzie said, bolstering her courage. "You don't have to convince me of that."

"I'm not guilty of any of it, Lizzie. Marissa's lying through her teeth."

Lizzie smiled sadly. For a few days, she'd been blissfully happy. She'd had everything she'd ever wanted. It crushed her to know it was all over.

She couldn't let Chance go to prison for her. And she believed, from the things Chance had said about Alistair Dunston, he would be vengeful enough to send him to prison for a long time if Chance didn't agree to leave with them. She'd seen the ruthless glint in that old man's eyes. He meant what he said. He was too wealthy and powerful for Chance to fight him. "She's beautiful, Chance."

"That doesn't make me the father of her child, Lizzie."

Lizzie squeezed her eyes shut. "I don't blame you, Chance. Really."

He backed away from her, shocked. His voice elevated. "You do believe her. You think I fathered her child!"

The look of betrayal in his face sliced her right down the middle. She couldn't meet his stare. She turned away for a moment, trying to hold back tears, trembling inside. Once she gathered her courage again, she forged on, turning to look him straight in the eyes. "You and I... We both know what it's like for a child to grow up without both parents. We've been through it. You, more than anyone—"

"Stop talking crazy, Lizzie. Just stop it."

She'd never heard that pleading tone in Chance's voice before. Pain seared through her stomach. "Y-you n-need to go with them."

"What?" Chance's eyes narrowed. There was pain on his face.

They were hard words for Lizzie to say, but once she'd said them she knew in her heart they were true. Alistair Dunston would make sure Chance rotted away in prison for a crime he didn't commit. It was better to break it off now. To let him think she didn't trust his word. To make him hate her. She lifted her chin. "I never thought you'd stay on here with me anyway."

"I never said I was going anywhere else."

"But you would have. Eventually. You wouldn't have stayed and where would that have left me?"

"Lizzie, damn it. I know what you're doing. You're trying to protect me, but I don't need your protection. I'm innocent. I won't go to prison."

"It's better this way," she said, ignoring his last statement. She'd have to ignore whatever he said and keep vigilant, while she was being ripped to shreds inside. "You need to go now, before… Well, I know I'm not with child. You don't have any obligation to stay."

He folded his arms across his chest. His face set with a stubborn expression. "I'm not leaving you alone here."

Lizzie met his dark eyes, hating the next words she would utter, but there was no hope for it. Chance had to believe her. "I won't be alone. I have Hayden. He's much better suited for me, actually. We know each other so very well. He'll make a fine husband. With him, I'll never want for anything. He'll make my life…easy. Your obligation to me is over, Chance. I'll prove it to you." Lizzie left the room for a few seconds, mentally fortifying herself. She was throwing away the man she loved and saving him at the same time. She had to do this.

When she returned, Chance was brooding. He looked

ready to kill. "Here you go." With a shaky hand, she gave him the box that held the ruby necklace.

"What's this?"

"I think you know," she said. "I got it back for you."

Chance opened the box. His jaw dropped and his lips trembled when the necklace came into view. The hardness on his face softened. "How did you—"

"It was going to be my surprise to you, Chance. I wanted… I owed you this ruby necklace. When you told me you sold it to John Lancer, I knew Maisey would have it. The entire town's been gossiping about the expensive gift John had given her. Maisey and I used to sing in the church choir as children. She was my friend and when she lost her folks, my grandpa was very kind to her and her brother. I paid her a visit the other day and told her what happened with the necklace. She's going to marry John Lancer. She's very glad of it, too. She offered the necklace back to me, but first she had to make sure John would be in agreement. He's so over-the-moon about Maisey, he'd agree to just about anything. I promised to pay him back over a good length of time. And I will. So now, you see, we're square. You and me. And I'm asking you to leave. Ride out of Red Ridge, Chance. I want you to go."

Chance put his head down. He didn't say anything for a long time.

Outside, she heard voices. The Dunstons were getting impatient.

Finally, he lifted his head and the look of regret and rejection in his eyes scarred her for life. "I'll go, Lizzie. If that's what you want."

"It is," she said without pause. "We'll both be better off."

With that, Chance nodded slowly. Then he took a last look into her eyes before turning on his heels and walking away.

Chapter Sixteen

~~~~~~~~~~~~~~~~~

She was dead in her heart, one hundred times over. The pain of Chance's leaving sent her to bed for two full days, during which she soaked the bedcovers with tears. She couldn't eat or sleep. She kept reliving their time together, both good and bad and branded those memories inside her head. Mourning the loss of her love, she vowed not to forget a moment of the time she spent with Chance.

After she'd given herself those woeful days to wallow in heartache, she forced herself out of her physical slump. Lizzie had learned early on that life went on, no matter the pain and suffering. She had a ranch to run and that meant hiring part-time help. It meant pretending to the world that she could do this on her own—that her life wasn't completely in ruins. That her hopes hadn't been shattered by the whim of a coldhearted, powerful old man.

Lizzie pulled biscuits out of the oven. They were burnt around the edges, the dough dry. She hadn't put much effort into her baking. It didn't matter. For the past week, nothing much tasted good to her anymore. She ate her meals because she had to in order to survive.

She smiled sadly. Chance had told her she was strong, a survivor. But Lizzie didn't much feel that way now. A part of her would rather just curl up into a ball and wither away.

The knock came at precisely noon. She knew he would come. Yesterday, she'd run into him in town and he'd asked if he might stop by for a visit. She moved to the entrance slowly, steadying her breath, and then opened the door to his familiar face. "Hayden. It's good to see you. Come in."

"Afternoon, Lizzie. Thank you for the invitation."

Hayden had taken one look at her forlorn expression at the Roberson's livery and had insisted on seeing her today. He'd offered to bring over a meal so they could talk in private. Lizzie had too much pride to allow him to bring his own food, so this afternoon she'd made a sorry attempt at supper. "It's not much. Fried chicken and gravy. Biscuits are a little burnt."

"I'm sure it'll be fine." Hayden stepped inside the house and took off his hat. He followed her into the kitchen where she gestured for him to take a seat.

He didn't sit, though. Instead, he helped her dish up the meal and put it on the table. Then he turned to her. "I'm awfully sorry for what happened between us. I shouldn't have presumed that you and me…that we were more than friends. I shouldn't have kissed you that way."

She gulped air, remembering her shock at Hayden's kiss. "I was surprised, is all."

"I know and it's my fault. I thought… Well, now I

know how you feel. I care for you, Lizzie. That will never change and I shouldn't have said we weren't friends anymore. That was my pride talking. I'm sorry for all of it. If you'll have me as your friend again, I promise to always honor our friendship."

He stared at her with genuine concern and Lizzie felt a measure of blessed relief. "Oh, Hayden," she whispered. "I want us to be friends again, too."

Hayden opened up his arms just like he did when they were children and Lizzie stepped right into his embrace. "It's been so h-hard," she said softly, against his chest. "With Chance gone."

"I know, Lizzie. I know you loved him. I guess I should have seen that all along."

"I sent him away," she said, tamping down guilt. She knew Chance couldn't fight Dunston's ruthless lies. "I had to."

Lizzie poured out her heart to Hayden, explaining how her feelings for Chance had grown into something she couldn't deny any longer. She told Hayden everything from start to finish, leaving nothing out about Chance's life and the awful man who had blackmailed him to come home. She told him about Marissa, too, how beautiful she was and how much trouble she'd always been for Chance. Then she blurted, "I laid with him, Hayden. You can think I'm terrible for it, but nothing felt more right in my life."

His face pinched tight and hurt entered his eyes. But his words, when they were finally uttered, soothed. "Ah, Lizzie, I'd never think terrible of you. Never. I promise."

"You really mean that?" She pulled back to look deeply into his eyes.

"Yes."

And Lizzie knew then what a wonderful friend she had in Hayden. She gave her head a little shake. If she and Hayden were to be close again, she needed to tell him the rest of it, so that there would never be any doubt as to her feelings. "I told Chance I was going to marry you, to get him to leave the ranch. I told him all the ways you and me are more suited. I had to make him believe that his leaving was what I wanted."

Lizzie stepped out of his embrace. Hesitantly, she raised her eyes to his. "It was a lie. Even if you would have me, I couldn't marry you or anyone else." Tears welled up as she whispered on an unsteady breath, "Not ever."

"You love him that much?"

"I do, Hayden. So very much."

Hayden closed his eyes for a second, absorbing that, and then opened them again with determination. "I'll always be here to help you, Lizzie. Just remember, you're not alone."

Hayden made her feel better and after they ate their meal, Lizzie told him her plans of hiring on part-time help at the ranch. Warren Roberson had two cousins who were just old enough to know ranching and just young enough that Lizzie didn't have to pay them adult wages. Having them around would give her time to fashion her dolls. Hayden would sell them on consignment in his shop and put them in a catalog he was planning on dispersing to neighboring towns.

That night, she made peace with Hayden and as good as it felt to have her friend back, once he left the ranch, Lizzie's heartache surfaced again.

It seemed to always return, due to her ever-present loneliness.

* * *

"It's nice to have you home and at our table again, Chance." Belinda Dunston gave him a warm smile as a servant filled the dinner dishes with meat, potatoes and creamed corn. The two older Dunstons sat at opposite ends of the rectangular table while Marissa and Chance faced each other.

Marissa's mother didn't have the foggiest notion about the scheme Marissa and Alistair had cooked up to get him to come home. Chance was a prisoner here, for all purposes, but he was sure Belinda didn't know that. She'd been sugary sweet to him since he'd returned, believing that he fathered Marissa's child. Chance suspected even Alistair didn't know the extent of his stepdaughter's lies.

For one week, Chance had given Belinda different excuses as to why he couldn't dine with the family in the main house. But he'd run out of them by day eight. Tonight, they received the best of his winning personality.

"I'm here, at the table. Don't know how nice it is."

Alistair glared at him.

Belinda looked a little confused and Marissa's back went up.

Chance returned the old man's glare, watching him stuff his mouth with creamed corn.

The Double D wasn't home. It never would be, but Chance had too much anger inside to think of any place as home anymore. He put Lizzie out of his head, for about as long as he could hold his breath. Then thoughts of her came flooding back and crowded his mind. He worked overly hard every day as foreman with the notion of falling into an exhausted sleep at night to gain some peace. Still and all, her image entered his head the moment he woke every morning. He was angrier at her than he was at any of the Dunstons. When he thought Lizzie the one person in the world he could trust, she'd betrayed him. She'd given up on what they'd had.

Belinda was now determined to make Chance part of the family. For years, she'd only seen him as a threat to her daughter's place in the Dunston household. Now, she'd repeatedly said that for the baby's sake, they should all try to get along.

The baby that wasn't his.

The minute the meal ended, Chance rose and excused himself from the table. All eyes were on him as he strode out the door. Once outside, he took deep breaths to tamp down his fury. The sun was beginning its descent and a sense of peace, when the workday was over and the livestock were quieted, had settled on the ranch. The distant horizon looked like an unattainable dream now. He toyed with the idea of running. Of getting on his horse and taking off for Colorado or Nevada, but the notion of having to hide out the rest of his life didn't sit right.

Chance couldn't live the life of a fugitive. No doubt, Alistair would falsify an even bigger crime against him and hire his own posse to find him. But the real reason Chance didn't want to leave, the reason that resonated in his gut and took hold with force was that he wanted Lizzie to be able to find him, if she ever needed him.

Fool that he was, if Lizzie should ever seek him out, he'd move heaven and earth to help her, despite his bitter anger at her.

Marissa caught up with him outside the stables. He took a look at her emerald gown, her fashionable hairstyle and her beautiful face, and hated the sight of her. "Go away, Marissa."

"Chance, you're being unreasonable."

"*I'm* being unreasonable? You're lying like a sinner at the gates of heaven and I'm the unreasonable one."

"I know I've been awful to you in the past, but this time it's serious."

He glanced at her stomach, growing with another man's child. "You should take it up with the baby's father."

"Shush," she said, lowering her voice. "I wish I could."

"What's that supposed to mean? Is he married? A man of the cloth? Why can't you—"

"No! Of course not. But I can't tell you anything more."

"What do you want from me, Marissa? Why'd you follow me outside?"

"My mama's expecting us to announce..." she began, then swallowed before finishing. "To announce our nuptials."

Chance had expected as much. Marissa wanted him to perpetuate the lie. "Sure thing, I'll get right to it... after I spit shine my boots."

"Chance...please."

He looked into Marissa's eyes. The shades of green were profound, the darkest one a rich tone of jade. Yet Chance found no beauty there, just desperation. He sighed wearily. "You know it might have been different between us if you hadn't been so conniving. We could have been like a true family. I would've looked out for you, Marissa."

She met his stare, stunned. "Oh…I, uh, I never thought—"

"You never thought of that, did you? That I might be a true brother to you? That I might be your friend? Everything had to be a competition between us. You spent your time casting me in a bad light to Alistair. You did yourself proud on that."

She drew in her lower lip. Her face blanched. "I'm sorry. I truly am, but there's nothing I can do about this."

"You can tell the truth. To your mother and Alistair… you can do the right thing, Marissa. What kind of man walks away from his responsibility anyway? What kind of man allows another man to raise his child?"

Marissa let go a sharp gasp, shaking her head. "Alistair would disown me if he found out and would do even worse to…to—"

"He really doesn't know you're lying?"

Marissa took a gulp of air. "No and I have to go now. Mama's expecting me to read with her tonight."

With that, she picked up her skirts and rushed into the house.

Two nights later, Chance lay on his bed, peering at the ceiling in his bedroom. He'd counted the tiles up there at least a dozen times already, trying to fall asleep. The room was one of twelve in the three-story main house and large enough to fit three big beds. Bitterly, he recalled wanting so desperately to live in this house as a child, but Alistair said a boy needed to earn his keep and that eventually he'd have a place here, once he'd learned enough about ranching. For a time, Chance thought Alistair was grooming him for a position running the empire, but that was a short-lived notion and one that had broken his heart when he realized he would always be living in the bunkhouse with the other ranch hands.

Every so often Chance's eyes would drift shut, then an image of Lizzie would pop into his head and he'd wake with a start. Restless, he rose and strode to the window. He unlatched a lever and as the shutters opened a soft breeze blew in. Stars filled the sky, twinkling over the vast Dunston empire, stretching as far and as wide as he could see. A soft knocking broke his thoughts and he moved to the door. "Who's there?"

"It's me, Marissa," she said softly, but with urgency.

"Go to bed."

"I can't." Her excited whispers reached his ears. "I really need to speak with you. Please…Chance… Open the door."

"Ah, hell," he muttered. He opened the door and she came rushing through, her skirts brushing his leg as she whirled around to face him. "What now?"

"I need to talk to you."

"So talk," he said, turning up the lamp a bit, casting them both in dim light.

Marissa took a moment, seemingly to gather her thoughts. "The other day, when you said you'd have been a true brother to me, did you mean that?"

Chance blew out a sigh. "Yeah, I did."

Marissa's eyes drifted downward. "I regret that now. I didn't see it. I was selfish and wanted Alistair to love me. I wanted to be his favorite."

"You succeeded."

Her eyes lifted to his with genuine apology. "I'm sorry for it, Chance. I really am."

"Yet you continue to torment me."

"I…I've decided to do something…for you and for me." She paused and nibbled on her lip. Chance waited with ebbing patience. "I told the father of my child the truth yesterday. He loves me. He wants to marry me but—"

"But?" She'd caught him off guard. He hadn't expected this.

"It's who he is that's stopping me. Alistair will never forgive me when he finds out about him. He'll probably disown me, but I'm willing to risk it now. If I lose his love, well then, so be it."

Chance was wary and too smart to begin to hope. "What made you change your mind?"

"You did, actually. Tell me, Chance. That woman you were living with in Red Ridge? Do you care about her?"

"Lizzie?" Chance furrowed his brows. "Why does that matter?"

"It may not matter at all. But I know one thing, the way women know other women. Lizzie gave you up to protect you. To keep you out of prison. She risked it all to save you from Alistair's wrath. *I saw it in her eyes, Chance.* She was terrified for you. She would have said and done anything to make sure you left with me. She knows you're not my child's father. She believes in your complete innocence. I saw that in her eyes, too. She's a brave woman. Fearless. And I'm hoping to learn something from her…and you. I've been a coward long enough. I need to tell Alistair that I'm in love with Brenden Groves."

"Groves? He's the child's father?" Chance couldn't believe it. Ten years ago, sixteen-year-old Brendan

Groves had shot Alistair in the shoulder during an argument about a heifer that had crossed their border through a faulty fence. Alistair had nearly died and the hotheaded boy was headed for jail for a long time, when suddenly Alistair dropped all charges against him. Rumor had it that Alistair blackmailed Brendan's father, a rival cattleman, garnering enough land and cattle out of the deal to make the Dunston spread the biggest in the territory. As a result, the bad blood between the two families had become common knowledge in Red Ridge.

"So now you can see why I did it," she said.

Chance shook his head. "I'll never see justification in that."

She sighed. "I know you're right. But I did tell my mother the truth today." She paused. "She wasn't happy with me though she finally gave me her support. Tomorrow," she said on a deep breath, "Brendan and I are going to face Alistair together. We're going to tell him the truth."

"It's the right thing to do, Marissa."

"I'm scared. But I'm determined. I'll make sure Alistair knows you're innocent. My mother and I will see to it that nothing becomes of those trumped-up charges." She walked over to Chance with tear-filled eyes and brushed a soft kiss to his cheek. "Maybe it will, in some way, make up for the trouble I've caused you."

Chance was truly amazed at this turn of events and proud of Marissa for the first time in his life.

She gazed into his eyes. "We can't go back, but from now on, I'd like to think of you as my brother. Is that alright with you?"

Chance struggled with the notion of letting go of

his anger and hostility. It was another sort of prison to him and once he managed to finally give Marissa the benefit of the doubt, he felt truly free. She'd just given him his life back. "From this day forward… You're my sister."

Marissa smiled and so did Chance.

Chance tied Joyful's reins to a tree branch and strode over to the shore quietly, watching Lizzie practice her swimming techniques in the middle of the lake. The girl didn't have the skills needed to be graceful in the water. She dove in several times and splashed around much like a hooked fish, before surfacing to tilt her face toward the sun. Her dark luxurious hair floated on the water's surface spreading out around her.

Seeing her again lifted his heart and made him grin.

Her clothes sat on a rock five steps from the shore. He grabbed her dress, the pretty blue one he'd given her in Prescott, and tucked it under his arm then leaned against a slender mesquite tree in the shade. She turned toward the shore and swam until her feet could touch the lake bottom. Bright sun beamed down and pristine waters glistened. As she walked out of the lake, the cotton bloomers and thin chemise she wore hid little of her body underneath. Chance sucked in a breath. His heartbeats quickened.

He stepped out of the shade and into view.

She stopped just at the water's edge. Her bluer-than-blue eyes went wide with surprise. "Chance."

The sound of his name on her lips gladdened his heart. "Elizabeth."

They stared at each other for a long moment.

Chance saw everything so clearly then. The body

he'd come to cherish—the face, lit by eyes more beautiful than the summer sky—a pure and honest spirit that would sustain him until the end of time.

A shiver ran through him.

"What are you doing here?" Her voice was guarded. Her gaze snapped to the dress draped over his arm.

"Watching you swim. You still haven't gotten the hang of it."

She narrowed her eyes, jutting out her chin. "I keep afloat."

His gaze traveled over her body once again and powerful yearnings swelled inside. "Not that well."

She took a step forward. "Can I have my clothes now?"

He lifted the gown to admire it. "Sure is a pretty dress."

"I'd like to get into it."

Chance grinned. "I sorta like you outta the dress. But I'll give it to you if you answer one question for me."

She trembled when a breeze blew by. Goose bumps broke out on her arms. "Ask it."

"You were never gonna marry Hayden, were you?"

She went still.

"Were you?" he pressed.

She blinked then ducked her head slightly. "No."

"Why?"

Slowly, she took the steps necessary to face him. Her gaze locked with his. "That's two questions."

Gently, she took the dress from his grip. He released it easily and watched as she stepped into it and covered herself, straightening and smoothing out the material. She pushed wet hair from her face before lifting her eyes to him again.

"Okay, I'll answer for you. You were protecting me, just like I'd thought. You didn't want me to go to jail. You were afraid for me and pretended to believe Marissa's claims. And you lied about marrying Hayden to get me to leave. You *lied* to save me. It's all right to tell me the truth now."

"W-why…is it all r-right?" Her voice shook as she gazed deeply into his eyes.

"Because Marissa finally owned up to the truth and revealed the true father of her child. She's come clean about it and now everyone knows I'm innocent. Alistair is furious with her, but he's not a threat to me anymore."

"Oh, thank heaven." She shuddered visibly with relief then confessed, "I never stopped trusting in you, Chance. It's plagued me all this time, letting you believe that I did. I never, for one instant, thought you were the father of Marissa's baby."

"I know that now. Believe it or not, Marissa helped me understand why you sent me away."

"It was the hardest thing I've done in my life," she admitted.

He took her hand in his, entwining their fingers. "I love you, Elizabeth. With all my heart."

Tears welled in her eyes. He waited for her response, hoping he wasn't too late, hoping for a second chance with her. He'd do whatever it would take to get her back. "Marissa said you love me. That's why you sent me away. Is that true?"

She nodded and whispered on a rush of emotion, "I love you, Chance. More than you know."

"I know that now, darlin'. I know." He took her face in his palms and brought her mouth to his in an eager, long-awaited kiss. She was all he would ever need in life. She made him whole and happy and as long as he could do the same for her, he would never want for anything else.

"I missed you, Chance," she said between kisses.

"I'll never leave you again."

"Promise?" she asked, searching his eyes.

"I promise. Now, close those pretty eyes and keep them closed."

"You're not going to dunk me in the lake," she asked with a little giggle.

"Not today, darlin'. Go on, close your eyes."

And once she did, he stepped behind her and carefully fastened the ruby necklace around her slender throat. It graced her with brilliance, looking altogether perfect. He set his hands on her shoulders and turned her around to face him. She opened her eyes and fingered the ruby necklace with a delicate touch.

"Oh, Chance," she breathed out, her voice incredibly humbled.

Swamped with overpowering emotion, Chance cleared his throat. "Only a true lady deserves this necklace. My mother wore it before you and no other woman shall ever wear it as long as we're both alive. I hope you will accept it, and the love I have for you. Marry me, Elizabeth, and have my children."

Lizzie's heart burst with joy. She'd known heartache and pain in her life. She'd lost so many people, but now, all she saw was a bright future with the man she adored. She couldn't possibly love anyone from the deepest part of her soul the way she loved Chance Worth.

She'd staked her claim on him from the moment he'd rescued her from this ever-loving lake. "Yes, yes. I'll marry you, Chance. I'll be your wife and we'll have babies together."

"We'll build the ranch to what it was. One day, you'll have your dream again. I promise." Chance kissed her and folded her into his embrace. Together they turned to the lake that had nearly swallowed her up—the lake that had brought them together, so many months ago.

With reverence, Chance said quietly, "From now on, we'll call these waters, Elizabeth Lake…in your honor, sweetheart."

She beamed and thought it proper and fitting somehow. "Yes, I'd like that. It's a place where all things are possible."

"And all things are beautiful…just like you."

Elizabeth "Lizzie" Mitchell looked out onto the glistening waters.

Life in Red Ridge was going to be good again.

Of that, she had no doubt.

* * * * *

HISTORICAL

Where Love is Timeless™

HARLEQUIN® HISTORICAL

COMING NEXT MONTH
AVAILABLE APRIL 24, 2012

A TEXAN'S HONOR
Kate Welsh
(Western)

RAKE WITH A FROZEN HEART
Marguerite Kaye
(Regency)

LADY PRISCILLA'S SHAMEFUL SECRET
Ladies in Disgrace
Christine Merrill
Three delectably disgraceful ladies, who break
the rules of social etiquette, each in need of a
rake to tame them!
(Regency)

THE TAMING OF THE ROGUE
Amanda McCabe
(Elizabethan)

REQUEST YOUR FREE BOOKS!

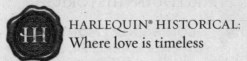

HARLEQUIN® HISTORICAL:
Where love is timeless

2 FREE NOVELS PLUS 2 **FREE GIFTS!**

YES! Please send me 2 FREE Harlequin® Historical novels and my 2 FREE gifts (gifts are worth about $10). After receiving them, if I don't wish to receive any more books, I can return the shipping statement marked "cancel." If I don't cancel, I will receive 6 brand-new novels every month and be billed just $5.19 per book in the U.S. or $5.74 per book in Canada. That's a savings of at least 17% off the cover price! It's quite a bargain! Shipping and handling is just 50¢ per book in the U.S. and 75¢ per book in Canada.* I understand that accepting the 2 free books and gifts places me under no obligation to buy anything. I can always return a shipment and cancel at any time. Even if I never buy another book, the two free books and gifts are mine to keep forever.

246/349 HDN FEQQ

Name   (PLEASE PRINT)

Address   Apt. #

City   State/Prov.   Zip/Postal Code

Signature (if under 18, a parent or guardian must sign)

Mail to the **Reader Service:**
IN U.S.A.: P.O. Box 1867, Buffalo, NY 14240-1867
IN CANADA: P.O. Box 609, Fort Erie, Ontario L2A 5X3
Not valid for current subscribers to Harlequin Historical books.

Want to try two free books from another line?
Call 1-800-873-8635 or visit www.ReaderService.com.

* Terms and prices subject to change without notice. Prices do not include applicable taxes. Sales tax applicable in N.Y. Canadian residents will be charged applicable taxes. Offer not valid in Quebec. This offer is limited to one order per household. All orders subject to credit approval. Credit or debit balances in a customer's account(s) may be offset by any other outstanding balance owed by or to the customer. Please allow 4 to 6 weeks for delivery. Offer available while quantities last.

Your Privacy—The Reader Service is committed to protecting your privacy. Our Privacy Policy is available online at www.ReaderService.com or upon request from the Reader Service.

We make a portion of our mailing list available to reputable third parties that offer products we believe may interest you. If you prefer that we not exchange your name with third parties, or if you wish to clarify or modify your communication preferences, please visit us at www.ReaderService.com/consumerschoice or write to us at Reader Service Preference Service, P.O. Box 9062, Buffalo, NY 14269. Include your complete name and address.

HHI1B

HARLEQUIN® HISTORICAL:
Where love is timeless

SCANDAL NEVER LOOKED SO GOOD
WITH FAN-FAVORITE AUTHOR
MARGUERITE KAYE

Waking up in a stranger's bed, Henrietta Markham
encounters the most darkly sensual man she has ever met.
The last thing she remembers is being attacked—yet being
rescued by Rafe St. Alban, the notorious Earl of Pentland,
feels much more dangerous! And when she's accused of theft,
Rafe finds himself offering to clear her name. Can Henrietta's
innocence bring this hardened rake to his knees…?

Rake with a
Frozen Heart

Sparks ignite this May!

*Lady Priscilla and the Duke of Reighland play
a deliciously sexy game of cat and mouse in
LADY PRISCILLA'S SHAMEFUL SECRET,
the third and final installment of the Ladies in Disgrace
trilogy, a playful and provocative Regency series
by award-winning author Christine Merrill.*

He was staring at her again, thoughtfully. "Considering your pedigree, it should be advantageous to the man involved, as well. You are young, beautiful and well born. Why are you not married already, I wonder? For how could any man resist such a sweet and amenable nature?"

"Perhaps I was waiting for you, Your Grace." She dropped her smile, making no effort to hide her contempt.

"Or perhaps the rumors I hear are true and you have dishonored yourself."

"Who…" The word had escaped before she could marshal a denial. But she had experienced a moment's uncontrollable fear that, somewhere Dru had been that she had not, the ugly truth of it all had escaped. And that now, her happily married sister was laughing at her expense.

"Who told me? Why, you did, just now." He was smiling in triumph. "It is commonly known that the younger daughter of the Earl of Benbridge no longer goes about in society because of the presence of the elder. But I assumed there would be more to it than that. And I was correct."

Success at last, though it came with a sick feeling in her stomach, and the wish that it had come any way but this. She had finally managed to ruin everything. Father would be furious if this opportunity slipped through her fingers. It would serve him right, for pushing this upon her. "You have guessed correctly, Your Grace. And now, I assume that this interview is at an end." She gestured toward the door.

"On the contrary," he replied. "You have much more to tell me, before I depart from here...."

If you like your Regencies fun,
sexy and full of scandal then you'll love
LADY PRISCILLA'S SHAMEFUL SECRET
Available May 2012

Don't miss the other two titles in this outrageous trilogy:
LADY FOLBROKE'S DELICIOUS DECEPTION
LADY DRUSILLA'S ROAD TO RUIN